Readers lc

In the Weeds

"Another solid, feel-good story that is perfect for coffee-time or to wind down at the end of the day."
—Love Bytes

"This story really has it all. If you like a great second chance, small town romance, cute kids, a touch of mystery and lots of feels, this is for you."
—TTC Books and More

Second Go-Round

"A beautiful story about two men each convinced they are doing what they were meant to do and neither ready to sit down and face some hard truths about their relationship. A story about reconnecting, a story about how communication is so important."
—Paranormal Romance Guild

Past His Defenses

"This whole group really embraces the holiday spirit. Definitely a great holiday read with a lot of those wonderful holiday feels!"
—The Geekery Book Review

By Andrew Grey

Accompanied by a Waltz
All for You
Between Loathing and Love
Borrowed Heart
Buried Passions
Catch of a Lifetime
Chasing the Dream
Crossing Divides
Dominant Chord
Dutch Treat
Eastern Cowboy
Hard Road Back
Half a Cowboy
Heartward
In Search of a Story
Lost and Found
New Tricks
Noble Intentions
North to the Future
One Good Deed
On Shaky Ground
Paint By Number
Past His Defenses
The Playmaker
Pulling Strings
Rebound
Rescue Me
Reunited
Running to You
Saving Faithless Creek
Second Go-Round
Shared Revelations
Survive and Conquer
Three Fates
To Have, Hold, and Let Go

Turning the Page
Twice Baked
Unfamiliar Waters
Whipped Cream

ART
Legal Artistry • Artistic Appeal
Artistic Pursuits
Legal Tender

BAD TO BE GOOD
Bad to Be Good
Bad to Be Merry
Bad to Be Noble
Bad to Be Worthy

BOTTLED UP
The Best Revenge
Bottled Up • Uncorked
An Unexpected Vintage

BRONCO'S BOYS
Inside Out • Upside Down
Backward • Round and Round
Over and Back
Above and Beyond

THE BULLRIDERS
A Wild Ride • A Daring Ride
A Courageous Ride

BY FIRE
Redemption by Fire
Strengthened by Fire
Burnished by Fire
Heat Under Fire

Published by DREAMSPINNER PRESS
www.dreamspinnerpress.com

By ANDREW GREY (CONT)

CARLISLE COPS
Fire and Water • Fire and Ice
Fire and Rain • Fire and Snow
Fire and Hail • Fire and Fog

CARLISLE DEPUTIES
Fire and Flint
Fire and Granite
Fire and Agate
Fire and Obsidian
Fire and Onyx
Fire and Diamond

CARLISLE TROOPERS
Fire and Sand • Fire and Glass

CHEMISTRY
Organic Chemistry
Biochemistry
Electrochemistry
Chemistry Anthology

DREAMSPUN DESIRES
The Lone Rancher
Poppy's Secret
The Best Worst Honeymoon Ever

EYES OF LOVE
Eyes Only for Me
Eyes Only for You

FOREVER YOURS
Can't Live Without You
Never Let You Go

GOOD FIGHT
The Good Fight
The Fight Within
The Fight for Identity
Takoda and Horse

HEARTS ENTWINED
Heart Unseen • Heart Unheard
Heart Untouched
Heart Unbroken

HOLIDAY STORIES
Copping a Sweetest Day Feel
Cruise for Christmas
A Lion in Tails
Mariah the Christmas Moose
A Present in Swaddling Clothes
Simple Gifts
Snowbound in Nowhere
Stardust • Sweet Anticipation

LAS VEGAS ESCORTS
The Price • The Gift

LOVE MEANS...
Love Means... No Shame
Love Means... Courage
Love Means... No Boundaries
Love Means... Freedom
Love Means ... No Fear
Love Means... Healing
Love Means... Family
Love Means... Renewal
Love Means... No Limits
Love Means... Patience
Love Means... Endurance

Published by DREAMSPINNER PRESS
www.dreamspinnerpress.com

By Andrew Grey (cont)

LOVE'S CHARTER
Setting the Hook
Ebb and Flow

NEW LEAF ROMANCES
New Leaf • In the Weeds

PLANTING DREAMS
Planting His Dream
Growing His Dream

REKINDLED FLAME
Rekindled Flame
Cleansing Flame
Smoldering Flame

SENSES
Love Comes Silently
Love Comes in Darkness
Love Comes Home
Love Comes Around
Love Comes Unheard
Love Comes to Light

SEVEN DAYS
Seven Days
Unconditional Love

STORIES FROM THE
RANGE
A Shared Range
A Troubled Range
An Unsettled Range

A Foreign Range
An Isolated Range
A Volatile Range
A Chaotic Range

STRANDED
Stranded • Taken

TALES FROM KANSAS
Dumped in Oz • Stuck in Oz
Trapped in Oz

TALES FROM ST. GILES
Taming the Beast
Redeeming the Stepbrother

TASTE OF LOVE
A Taste of Love
A Serving of Love
A Helping of Love
A Slice of Love

WITHOUT BORDERS
A Heart Without Borders
A Spirit Without Borders

WORK OUT
Spot Me • Pump Me Up
Core Training • Crunch Time
Positive Resistance
Personal Training
Cardio Conditioning
Work Me Out Anthology

Published by DREAMSPINNER PRESS
www.dreamspinnerpress.com

LOST
AND
FOUND

ANDREW GREY

Published by
DREAMSPINNER PRESS

5032 Capital Circle SW, Suite 2, PMB# 279,
Tallahassee, FL 32305-7886 USA
www.dreamspinnerpress.com

This is a work of fiction. Names, characters, places, and incidents either are the product of author imagination or are used fictitiously, and any resemblance to actual persons, living or dead, business establishments, events, or locales is entirely coincidental.

Lost and Found
© 2022 Andrew Grey

Cover Art
© 2022 L.C. Chase
http://www.lcchase.com
Cover content is for illustrative purposes only and any person depicted on the cover is a model.

Mass Market Paperback ISBN: 978-1-64108-443-7
Trade Paperback ISBN: 978-1-64108-441-3
Digital ISBN: 978-1-64108-442-0
Mass Market Paperback published March 2023
v. 1.0

Printed in the United States of America

To Dominic, my biggest fan.

Chapter 1

RAFAEL CARRERA stood on the top of the chute, looking down at the rankest bull on the circuit. He'd drawn the only bull that hadn't yet been successfully ridden that season... for very good reasons. Henny Penny had to be the worst-named bull Rafe had ever seen. This bull was as mean as they came. Henny was known to throw riders, then do his best to stomp on them, and sometimes gore them, as if to make the rider pay for daring to get on his back. So yeah, this was one nasty fucking bull—and Rafe had drawn him.

He was currently in second place. The leader was already out with an injury, standing at the rails, the man's big brown eyes targeting his back. Rafe could feel the heated glare of Duane Mendeltom boring into him, sending all the ill will and buck-off vibes he could.

Fifty points. That was all that stood between a championship buckle and everything that came with it... or second place. And it had to be Henny Penny that stood in the damned way.

"Okay, kid," the chute master said. "You ready?"

Rafe didn't answer, already in the zone. He just climbed up and got into position. Henny bounced under him, a thousand pounds of muscle and power ready to lay into him with everything he had. Eight of the longest seconds in sports… hell, it was the world's longest eight seconds, as far as he was concerned. His bull ropes were in place, just where he wanted them. The vest he wore would help protect him, but not against Henny's hooves. His lucky hat was on his head, and all it took was a nod for the game to begin.

The gate swung open, and Henny jumped up and out. He landed with a bone-jarring thud that usually did in most riders. Rafe was ready for it, though, letting his body ride with the movement, rolling his hips as Henny jumped, legs going out, body twisting under him in midair. Rafe let out a yell, thinking like the fucking bull, ready when the son of a bitch pivoted to try to sink him in the well. He leaned the other way just a little, countering the move, and damned if Henny didn't stop on a dime and twist the other damn way.

Rafe couldn't counter fast enough, but he held on with everything he had, his shoulder pulling, muscles straining. But Henny was not going to get the better of him. Rafe had been riding bulls for too damned long. Hell, he was the old man on the circuit, and this was it, his last chance. Even if this fucking bull ripped his arm out of the socket, he was not damn letting go. Another jump and Rafe felt his legs come up. His luck was about to run out.

Then the buzzer sounded, and Henny took one more jump. Rafe bailed and let the bull throw him in the air. He flipped and saw the roof of the arena for a second before somehow righting his legs and landing on his feet. As soon as he felt sand, he raced for the side and jumped as high as he could. He damn near ended up in the lap of a pretty lady who was grinning like she won the lottery. "Hi, darlin'," he said with a smile before turning around in time to see the clowns rounding up Henny and getting him out of the arena. Only then did he jump back down to the arena floor and hurry over to pick up what was left of his hat. It seemed Henny had stomped and gored it in his place. He held it over his head anyway, to deafening cheers from the crowd.

"Eighty-eight point three," the announcer practically sang. "That means our winner of the day, the go-round, and the championship buckle is none other than Rafael Carrera!"

He waved to the crowd once again, accepted the trophy and the buckle from the judges, and held both over his head as what seemed like a million flashes all went off at once. He turned slowly to let everyone see and to soak up the moment he'd thought would never come.

Half the circuit had written him off, including himself. He was almost thirty-three, an old man by this sport's standards, and yet here he was: PBR World Champion. After taking another bow, he walked off the arena floor and nearly bumped into Duane, who still glared at him. "You are one lucky fucker," he said with a sneer.

"I just rode the rankest bull on the circuit. I don't think luck had anything to do with it," he said as he turned to head away.

"Fucking queer asshole," Duane muttered under his breath. At least that was what he intended, Rafe was sure, but it came out louder, and one of the officials pulled Duane aside. Rafe continued back to the locker area, set his trophy and buckle on the bench, and shook hands with all the other guys, accepting their congratulations and praising the others who'd had great rides.

"Ladies and gentlemen…." The announcer's voice filled the arena, and the locker room went quiet. "Duane Mendeltom has been disqualified for ungentlemanly and unsportsmanlike conduct." Then he went ahead and listed the adjusted rankings. Rafe kept his head down, trying to stop a smile. That little remark had cost Duane a big payday, as well as his place in the standings for next year.

"Jesus, I would not want to be him," Hank Matise said as he handed Rafe his gear. "But you should go ahead and get packed up and out of here before he gets back. Duane is going to want to take it out on someone, and he doesn't have much to lose right now."

"Thanks, Hank." Rafe packed everything away, including the buckle and trophy, and headed out into the heat of the Las Vegas night. He climbed into his truck and was about to pull away when a man rapped on his window. Shit. His first thought was that Duane had already found him, but Duane never wore a polo shirt. Rafe lowered the window. "Can I help you?"

"Are you Rafael Carrera?" the man asked.

Rafe wondered what the hell he'd done. "That's me. I need to get back to the hotel." His arm ached like hell, and he wanted to ice it, get himself a huge meal, and maybe go down to the spa and take a deep soak in a hot tub before falling into bed. Tomorrow was soon enough for him to figure out what the hell he was going to do with the rest of his life.

"My name is Luther Gillian. I'm an attorney, and I have been looking for you for three months. I need to talk to you. And it's an important enough conversation that I don't want to have it out here in the parking lot."

"Fair enough. I'm staying down at the Mandalay Bay. If you want to follow me, we can talk there." After getting a nod, he waited while Luther hurried to his car and brought his BMW up behind him. Then Rafe pulled out of the lot and headed to his hotel. Once there, he parked, making sure there was a space for Luther next to him.

The whole time, he tried to think what the hell he could have done to have a lawyer after him. He hadn't done anything wrong, and lawyers didn't usually look for soon-to-be-retired bull riders with no future prospects other than trying to find a ranch that would take him on.

Rafe got out and grabbed his gear bags, then hauled them toward the hotel until a bellhop took mercy on him. His arm hurt like hell, but he knew what to do about it. The muscles had been pulled, and the arm needed rest and ice. Luther held the door, and the bellhop and lawyer followed him to the elevator and up to his floor. Rafe tipped the guy at the room and unlocked it, thanking him when he set the bags down.

"Mr. Gillis…."

"Please call me Luther," he said as Rafe pulled off his boots and sat down with a sigh. The adrenaline was wearing off… which meant the pain was setting in. "I'm here because of your uncle. I believe he was your mother's brother. MacDonald Greene."

"Uncle Mack?" God, he could barely remember him. "I used to go to his place when I was a kid. That was where I first learned to ride and saw the cowboys riding broncs and bulls. I knew what I wanted to do after one of those visits." Then, when he'd been about twelve, something happened. Rafe had no idea what it was, but those summer visits ended. All his dad would ever say was that things were not good with Uncle Mack, that he was ill and they all needed to pray for him come Sunday.

"It seems he remembered you. Your uncle passed away three months ago, and he left a will naming you as the sole beneficiary—you've inherited everything he had."

"And what is that?" Rafe asked, completely bowled over. "I mean, did he still have the ranch?"

Luther nodded. "That I've been able to trace. He does still have the ranch. Well, technically you own the ranch now. Once I found you, I was to give you this envelope. When your uncle asked me to draw up the will three years ago, he was very specific that you were to get everything." He opened a case and pulled out a sheaf of papers, which he flipped through. "I leave everything to my nephew Rafael Carrera. My sister Rachel and my brother Forrest are to get just what they gave me in life—nothing. The rest of my family is to get nothing either. I wish them all well, but they can continue living their lives on their own, with no help from me." Luther closed the papers.

"Well, I guess Uncle Mack told everyone how he felt. But why me?" Rafe asked. It had been twenty years since he'd seen his uncle. Though Rafe had sent a few letters and cards when his mama wasn't looking. He always wondered why he never got anything back.

"I can't answer that. All I have for you, other than the address of the ranch, is this envelope he left for you." The small manila envelope had been sealed, and Luther handed it to him. "I have no idea what's in it. He sealed it in my presence and gave me the instructions. After he died, I made arrangements with a friend of mine in the area to look after the three horses and the fifty or so head of cattle at the ranch." Luther smiled. "He's an old cattleman from way back… and he's also my dad."

"Thank you." Rafe didn't know what else to say. Hell, he could barely get his head around what was going on.

"That's about all I can tell you. Oh, the ranch is outside Telluride, Colorado. I can tell you that if you decide you want to sell, there are plenty of buyers who will be more than happy to scoop up the land. It's in a prime location."

Rafe shook his head. "I remember it. My memories aren't as sharp as they were when I was a kid, but I do remember." He yawned and apologized, setting the envelope in one of his bags. He figured he'd read it once he was alone. "Would you like to get something to eat?"

"I was going to go get myself a steak, so if you'd like to join me, I'd be happy for the company," Luther offered.

Rafe excused himself for a few minutes to shower and dress. Then he left with Luther to get something for dinner.

LUTHER LOVED his food, that was for sure. And Rafe wasn't about to complain—they had an amazing steak and seafood dinner at one of the casino restaurants. Luther agreed to meet him at the ranch in a few days, giving Rafe time to finish up PBR promotion and drive up to Colorado. After saying good night, Rafe returned to his room.

Rafe iced his arm for a while, took some anti-inflammatories, then lay on the bed, watching television. Then again, maybe "watching" was an exaggeration. He dug around in his mind for those old memories of summers he'd spent with his Uncle Mack. Rafe had learned to ride during those visits, first on a pony and then on a real horse. Hell, if he remembered correctly, Uncle Mack might have given him his own horse to ride. That had been pretty special, as had camping out under the stars while Uncle Mack played the guitar around the fire. He covered his eyes with his arm, plunging himself into darkness as the details began to emerge. Those had been fun times—the best times he'd ever had. And then they had ended with almost no explanation.

It had been so long ago, and yet memories of his time there returned easily. The ranch had left an impression on him, as had his uncle. Uncle Mack had actually *listened* to him. Rafe's mom and dad had constantly been absorbed in whatever they wanted or what they thought. Listening to either one of their kids was not high on their priority list. But Rafe and Uncle Mack used to talk for a long time, lying on the ground, looking up at the stars. He wiped his eyes and let his arm settle at his side once again. Sitting up, he blinked and then rummaged in the bag for the envelope. He opened it and tipped the contents out.

A few pieces of paper and a key fell onto the bed. Rafe checked over the key and set it aside before picking up the first piece of paper. It was the receipt for a safe-deposit box. At least that explained what the key was for. He slid that and the key back in the envelope before unfolding the last page.

Rafe,

I know you have to be wondering what's going on. You haven't seen me in a long time, but you are the only family I have who cared enough to remember me. I'm leaving you everything I own, and I hope it brings you some kind of happiness.

I hope you always draw the money bull,
Uncle Mack

Rafe read the sheet of paper a second time. It told him very little, other than the fact that his uncle had known he rode bulls. It made him wonder just how closely his uncle had followed his career. He'd already decided to head to Telluride, so he put the letter back in the envelope and stowed it with the other important things. And now that the painkillers had started to kick in, he cleaned up and slipped into bed.

FOR THE next three nights, his dreams took him back to his uncle's ranch. He wasn't sure how much of those dreams was real or simply what his mind was filling in. Maybe it was all some kind of wishful thinking, his mind conjuring up things the way that Rafe wanted to remember them.

But he was here now. He pulled his truck into town and stopped at one of the restaurants on the main street for something to eat, then continued on out to the address Luther had given him, trusting his little portable GPS unit. A few minutes later, he turned into the ranch drive and drove up to a small, low ranch house with paint faded by the sun and weather. Everything seemed to be intact, but it looked tired, as though the buildings—and even the land itself—had been ground down and laid low by life. Although Luther had told him it had been cared for, it lacked… life. Even the horses in their paddocks barely swished their tails as they looked up slowly from the grass they were eating.

"I see you made it," Luther said, coming out of the barn with an older man behind him. "This is my dad, Arthur. He's been looking after things."

"Good to meet you, and thank you for everything, sir," Rafe said, shaking his hand.

"Glad to do it. It got me out of the house and away from this one's mother for a few hours a day." He winked to show he was teasing. "Your uncle has had all of the horses for a while. I know they used to get ridden, but I have a feeling it's been a long time. But you got yourself fifty head out in the north pasture. They're in good shape and have water and plenty to graze on. I haven't moved them, but you might want to soon enough."

"Thank you. How is everything else?"

"Just about on its last legs, I'm afraid. I'd say there's lots of fence work to be done, and the paddocks need to be rebuilt. The barn is okay, but it needs repairs. Mack did what he could do, I suspect, but I figure things just got old and sort of reached the end of their life." Arthur handed him a key. "This is to the house. Every now and then, I'd go inside and check that it was okay. My wife cleared out the freezers and refrigerator, stuff like that. The place is clean enough, but you might want to check on the roof. It probably needs to be replaced before winter sets in."

Rafe should have figured that there would be plenty of work to do. But he wasn't afraid of any of that. "All right." He was already figuring how far the money he had saved up was going to go. He had never lived high on the hog. For the past decade or so, he'd basically been alone, and he had lived simply, so he had some savings. "What can you tell me about the folks in the area?

"You know Telluride. There are small ranches and then there are huge landholdings. They don't call the area out along the river Billionaire's Row for nothing. Your neighbor to the south is one of the huge holdings here. I'd check those fences first. Those guys have a ton of money, and yet they're often the biggest dicks on the face of the earth. Then, to the west is Grant Mendeltom's ranch."

Rafe groaned. "Let me guess. He happens to have a son named Duane." That would be just his luck.

"How did you know?" Arthur asked.

"Dad, Rafe just beat Duane in the finals. He took the championship away from him, and…." Luther grinned. "Duane got himself disqualified for bad conduct." Luther seemed a little tickled. Rafe guessed that Duane Mendeltom wasn't any more liked here than he was out on the circuit.

"Okay. Duane is an ass, and he comes by it honestly. Don't be surprised if Connor pays you a visit. He's wanted this land forever, and with Mack gone, he's going to see your inheritance as a golden opportunity." He shrugged. "To the north are the hills, and to the east, there's state land, which you let your cattle graze on if you have a permit. I'm sure your uncle probably had one, but I don't know where you'd find it. People are pretty nice here, I suppose. It just depends on who you run across. Locals are usually fine. But then there are those who like to think they own not only their land, but the rest of the valley as well."

"Good to know," Rafe said. "Are there any dogs?" He remembered Uncle Mack having dogs.

"They're on the back porch right now. The pups are really friendly." Arthur nodded slowly. "I guess the place is all yours now. I can tell you that it's a good thing you're young, because it's going to take some energy to whip this place into shape. Unless you decide to sell." He seemed kind of sad at that idea.

"I don't have anywhere else to land right now, so I don't think selling is in the cards. I'll probably stay here, see what needs to be done, and set to work." He also had a ton of questions about his uncle that he hoped he'd eventually find answers to. Maybe once he was able to look around inside, he'd find something.

"Don't hesitate to call if you need anything," Luther said. They shook hands, and then he and his dad took off, leaving Rafe alone with his inheritance. He unlocked the front door and let himself inside. The house was musty, so Rafe opened windows as he went, airing the place out.

"Well, look at all of you," he said with a smile when he reached the back porch. Three dogs bounded over one another. They were all German shepherds. He opened the door, and they hurried forward for pets and scratches, their tails wagging. Thankfully they each had a tag with their name: Riker, May, and Lola. They were obviously good dogs and all settled around him. Rafe found bowls and water dishes on the porch, fed each of them, and set out fresh water. Once they'd eaten, he let them outside to run in the yard.

Once the dogs were looked after, Rafe wandered through the rest of the house. One room had been set up as an office, and Rafe figured he would start in there. Maybe he'd figure out how the ranch was doing without much digging. The walls of the living room, office, and dining area were decorated with horse pictures—some recent and others faded with age. Rafe guessed they were animals his uncle had had over the years. The furniture was old and well worn but still comfortable. He checked out the bedrooms and found one set up as a guest room with an empty closet and dresser drawers. God, Rafe hoped his uncle hadn't spent his entire life all alone.

Everything was neat as a pin in his uncle's room. The bedside tables held a book and lamps. The dresser top was spotless. When Rafe lifted his gaze, it fell on an old, faded framed picture, and he found himself looking at his twelve-year-old self. In the image, he wore a huge smile, his uncle standing next to him.

The dogs suddenly began barking out front, so Rafe pulled himself out of his thoughts, then strode through the house and stepped out into the cooling November air.

He whistled, and the dogs all hurried over as a horse and rider drew nearer. The horse had to be one of the most beautiful animals he had ever seen, and it moved with a grace few horses ever achieved. Rafe's gaze shifted upward to the man on horseback, and he swallowed. He had seen stunning men in his time. He'd worked around cowboys all his life, men who built their bodies through hard work and hard living. But none of them held a candle to this man, with eyes the color of the clear Colorado sky and blond hair that fell to his shoulders from under a cowboy hat that was the same reddish chestnut of the horse he rode.

The man pulled to a stop and dismounted. He seemed to glide over toward Rafe as he moved.

"Can I help you?" Rafe asked.

"Rumor has it that they found Mack's long-lost relative."

The tone set Rafe's teeth on edge. "And you are?" The guy might have been stunning enough to stop traffic, but his manners left a lot to be desired. Still, it was difficult to take his gaze off him. And there was something familiar about him that he couldn't quite put his finger on.

The man's eyes grew wider for a second, as though he expected Rafe to know who he was.

His hesitation told Rafe there was something he'd missed. "Russell Banion," he answered.

Russell? Of course. Rafe extended his hand. "It's good to see you again. It's been a real long time." He shook Russell's hand, remembering them pony riding together as kids when he'd come to visit Uncle Mack. The Banions always had a big summer cookout, and Rafe had gone with Uncle Mack a few times. There had always been plenty of kids, but Russell had been the only boy his own age. They had spent a lot of time together back then, the way boys did when they were thrust together. But those memories had long been dulled by time and distance. "I just found out about this a few days ago."

Russell let his hand fall back to his side.

"I used to ride with your uncle every couple of weeks. Our places abut one another. My ranch is to the south, if you remember." Rafe turned in that direction, remembering what Arthur had told him about one of the mega ranches being in that direction. He figured Russell's family must own it or something.

"I see." He blinked as those intense blue eyes bored into him. He tried to remember details about Russell, but the memories were faded, and he couldn't recall a great deal. Still, the image of a swimming hole with a rope swing and Uncle Mack looking on as they played came to mind, and he felt his wariness subsiding.

"You could say that your uncle and I were friends." Rafe and Russell had been friends of a sort as kids, but that felt like a lifetime ago. Those blue eyes remained skeptical. "He never spoke about his family much other than to say that he hadn't talked to them in years. And yet, now here you are."

This guy's jeans were snug, and his white shirt and jacket stretched over his chest, but maybe he had taken to wearing a hat one size too small, because he was wound way too tight.

"He left me the ranch. I'm not here to try to steal it," Rafe snapped, feeling defensive. He let out a long breath. Arthur's words, as well as his own guilt about how his parents had treated his uncle, had obviously gotten to him. Russell wasn't his enemy. And from the sounds of it, he had been Uncle Mack's friend. "Look, I have no idea why he did that. I'm still trying to figure it out myself."

He turned back to the house. It looked so sad. "One thing I do remember—the place used to be a light tan with white trim, and Uncle Mack always had these huge rose bushes in front that climbed up the house and bloomed in late June." Why he was sharing any of this with Russell was beyond him. "Did Uncle Mack have a lot of friends?"

Russell paused. "I don't really know, but I doubt it. Oh, your uncle knew everyone around this area and they all knew him, but I don't know if your uncle would call any of them friends. He was well acquainted with them, though." The horse nuzzled Russell's shoulder, and he stroked his nose and down his neck.

Rafe wasn't sure what exactly was going on, but anyone who was so loved by his horse couldn't be too bad. And the dogs had all settled on the grass, stretched out in the sun, so they obviously weren't bothered by Russell either.

Rafe felt himself smiling slightly. "I see…," he said to fill the void.

"Somehow, I doubt you do," Russell said as he turned away. He stretched his legs and mounted the horse as though it was the most natural thing in the world. "But I'm sure you will soon enough." He paused and reached into a jacket pocket, then handed Rafe a business card. Then he smiled, and it was like the sun had just parted from behind storm clouds. "Just in case." He turned the horse and they rode off, heading south.

Rafe told himself that he wasn't going to watch him go, but he did it anyway.

Chapter 2

"DID YOU meet our new neighbor?" Russell's father asked when he strode into the entrance hall of the log mansion. "Is he going to sell?"

Russell could almost see his father breaking out the checkbook.

"I don't know," Russell told him as he hung up his hat and took off his boots. He placed them in the holder near the door. "The guy... I don't know. I knew Rafe as a kid, but the man he is now is a mystery."

His father's eyes widened. "You mean there's a man somewhere that you can't figure out? As I live and breathe, I never expected to see the day. You made a fortune anticipating what folks want and out-maneuvering your competition, but this man stumps you?" He grinned. Sometimes he could be a real smartass. At least he wasn't a huge prick. By and large, Russell considered himself lucky in the parent department.

"Dad, that's enough." He went into the living room and made a couple of martinis from the cart, then handed a glass to his father before sitting on the leather sofa positioned so it had an amazing view of the mountain peaks, already white with snow. Every day, it got closer to the valley floor. They had already had snow, but it had melted. Russell figured the next snowfall would stick, and then it would be a blanket of white as far as the eye could see until spring. "It turns out he's Mack's nephew. Remember him? He used to visit when he was a kid and seems to have good memories of his uncle."

His father's gaze hardened. "Then why did he leave Mack all alone? Mack didn't deserve to be treated that way." He sipped the drink and took his own seat, putting his feet up on the plush matching leather ottoman. The room had been decorated by his mother a little over five years ago, and neither of them had had the heart to change anything after she passed. Everything from the leather sofas and rustic tables and lamps to the original Charles Russell painting of a cowboy on horseback hanging above the fireplace was exactly as she had placed it.

"I don't know. But I get the idea that he isn't as big a dick as we'd thought. And Rafe's a real cowboy. I checked him out on my phone on the way back. He won the World Bull Riding championship a few days ago. He wasn't money grubbing either. He didn't know about the ranch and seems genuinely perplexed about his inheritance. And Mack's dogs seem to like him…." Russell cut himself off. There was no need to go into his personal observations about the man… like how Rafe's dark eyes and sun-kissed skin made Russell wonder what was below the V in his shirt. The man had obviously worked hard for a lot of years, judging by his arms and the pull of his shirt over his chest.

"How long did you talk to him?"

"Not long. I gave him our card. Hopefully he'll call when the vultures start circling. I don't think things between us got off to the best start." He sipped his drink and sighed softly. This was his favorite spot in the house.

"And why not?" his father asked.

Russell groaned. "I may have made some assumptions that turned out to be a little off the mark. Mack lived alone all these years, and his family never contacted him. The bastards found out he was gay and they cut him off as though he had some contagious disease." Russell set his glass aside, calming himself before his anger took over. "But I remember Rafe as a kid. We used to play together sometimes at the cookouts and such. He always loved it here."

"If you remember, I didn't necessarily take the news of your announcement with smiles and a coming-out party." He grinned.

Russell rolled his eyes dramatically. "That was bad."

"I thought it clever. But seriously, no parent wants their child to be gay. We can accept and support them, but we know life is easier for them if they aren't. I'll admit, it took me some time to get my head around it, but I never dreamed of cutting you off or kicking you out of the family."

Russell snickered nervously. "I'm really glad of that." He picked up his glass and drank the last of his martini. "Now, if you'll excuse me. I have some work to do in my office. There's a call with a conglomerate in Japan about to come in. What about you?"

"I should check on the men before the end of the day. Will I see you at dinner, or should I have something brought in for you?" his father asked.

"I'll be in. The call will only take about an hour or so. One of their divisions wants some of our beef, and another is interested in talking about having us adapt our software for their specific use." It was an interesting proposition and one his gut said could be beneficial for both sides. He took one last look out the large windows before heading to the other room and closing the door.

The Banion family had been ranching in this valley for generations, and over the years, they had amassed a sizable landholding with a large cattle operation. It wasn't as big as the ones in Texas or Florida, but it was healthy and provided the family with an excellent living. Everything changed after Russell went to college, though. His parents had fought him the entire way when he majored in computer science and engineering. They wanted him to study animal husbandry. But Russell had grown up on the ranch and on horseback and knew all about breeding and managing animals already. After college, he'd combined the two areas and developed a software system that not only tracked animals and their breeding, but also worked as a complete ranch and farm management system, adaptable for small, medium, and large operations. It was now in use in many countries, including Japan, South Africa, and throughout Europe. The Chinese government had expressed an interest, but Russell was checking with special security experts before he entertained their offer. Needless to say, the cattle operation was the heart of the family and his father's domain, but it had been Russell's tech abilities that had made them wealthy beyond belief.

He sat in his desk chair just as the call came through. "Konnichiwa," Russell said, bowing his head slightly, and the meeting began.

"I'M SORRY I'm late," Russell said as he took his seat at the large table off the kitchen. "Thank you, Violet," he added as she placed a plate with a small steak in front of him.

"You're welcome, Mr. Russell," she said softly, then returned to the kitchen. Violet had been with them for almost as long as he could remember. Russell had been trying to get her to eat with them, but she always took her meals in the kitchen.

He helped himself to the potatoes and vegetables as they were passed to him.

"How did it go today?" he asked one of the ranch hands who'd joined them for dinner. It had always been that way. Everyone who worked the ranch was treated the same, and that included taking their meals in the house. Neither he nor his father thought that should change just because the house had become fancier and they had more money. The ranch was a family, as far as his father was concerned, even if it was now a much larger operation than it had been.

"We need to check out the boundary we share with Mack's place," Dustin, one of the more seasoned cowboys, said. "We think some of it will need to be replaced." All the men seemed to have liked Mack, and the table grew quiet for a few seconds at the mention of his name.

"Did you meet the new owner?" Clyde asked, looking up from his plate. One of the other men bumped his shoulder, indicating that he shouldn't have asked anything. But Russell didn't take offense. Clyde was young, but a hard worker.

"I did."

"Should we go ahead and patch what's essentially his border?" Dustin asked.

Russell was about to answer but decided to hold back and allow his dad to take care of the question. The ranching operation was his father's, but Russell was slowly taking over some of it as his dad got older.

"We need to protect ourselves, so yes. And Clyde, Russell did meet the new owner, and we know nothing more than we have for months, other than he's Mack's nephew and that he used to come here as a kid."

"Is he going to sell?" Clyde asked. That was the topic on everyone's mind. "Are you going to buy it?" Clyde got another nudge, which made him lower his gaze to his plate.

"I don't have any idea. The man just arrived, and I paid him a short visit," Russell said. Which hadn't gone well because Russell had let his personal feelings for Mack get in the damned way. He should have

known better and put on a friendly face for his child-
hood playmate, regardless of his feelings for Mack.
Russell couldn't count the hours he'd spent sitting at
Mack's kitchen table, just talking. The time and attention Mack had given him had meant the world to him,
especially back before he'd come out, when he'd still
been trying to figure out who he was.

"I heard the new owner is a bull rider," Dustin
said. "Probably some hotshot wannabe."

"He's about as big a wannabe as you are a rancher," Russell teased Dustin. "He won the world championship a few days ago, and we used to go riding together around here when he and I were kids. So what
we have is the top bull rider in the world right now
living next door to us. Definitely not a wannabe." An
image of Rafe flashed in his mind, and damned if he
didn't force himself not to squirm as his jeans grew
tight. Now that he knew what the man looked like
in person, his imagination conjured up an image of
Rafe riding a bull, naked, those legs gripping, hips
rolling, and…. He swallowed and forced his mind
back to the present.

"So you think he'll want to stay? The ranch
could use a little muscle and someone who can keep
it up. But it was always a nice place."

"Let's hope so." Russell would be happy to add that
parcel of land to his dad's holdings, though it wasn't
necessary. Rafe's inheritance was sure to be coveted by
others. But Russell couldn't help but think it would be
the best of all worlds if Rafe was to hold on to it. Keeping things status quo might be the best situation of all.
It was likely to create less disruption.

Russell finished his dinner, excused himself, then returned to his office. He still had work to do documenting what had come out of his earlier call, then scheduling a design meeting with the guys.

His software company was largely virtual, and he ran it out of his home office. Most of the people who worked for him were people he'd gone to college with—people he knew he could trust. They were spread out over the country and even internationally, with Tamsyn in London. So work got done almost round the clock. It did make scheduling meetings a challenge, but they had worked that problem out some time ago. The real beauty was that his people could work from home during hours that fit with their families and, in some cases, their health challenges. Productivity was through the roof because people were happy.

Once he had the details down and his meeting scheduled, he got up from his chair and checked the clock. Then he followed the sound of a television and the scent of a fire to where his dad sat in the family room, watching television with his feet up. "Dad, I'm going into town with the guys. Do you want to join us?"

He shook his head. "I'm in for the night. Have fun, and be quiet when you come in. I need to be up in the morning to make the rounds of the ranch, and I don't want to feel like an old man when I'm done."

Not that his father was that old, but the cold got to him more than it used to, and he didn't have the energy Russell remembered him having. He said nothing, though. His dad was the backbone of the ranch, and Russell was in no hurry for him to retire.

"Besides, you young people don't need an old guy like me hanging around," his dad added.

Russell shook his head. "Dad, you know you're always welcome to come have a beer with us. Besides, I have to be up early too."

But his dad just shook his head and smiled.

A few minutes later, Russell was pulling on his boots and slipping on a coat and hat and heading out to his four-wheel-drive, because one thing was certain in the valley: the weather could change on a dime.

Marshall's was a bar outside the center of town where tourists flocked in the summer and skiers in the winter. He pulled into a parking spot and went inside. For a Thursday night, the place was full. Maybe it was the weather, but there wasn't a table or a chair free anywhere. Still, he unzipped his coat and headed to the bar, where Jackson was working as usual.

"Busy as hell," Russell commented. "Put a round of drinks on my tab for Dusty, Clyde, and the other men from the ranch." He smiled as they joined him at the bar. "You guys did good today," he said to them. They nodded and thanked him, then went to get a table. Russell turned back to the bar.

"Some guys stopped in to watch a game and it turned into a real party." Jackson slid him a beer and added it to his tab. "I needed this after the crappy summer we had." Then he continued down the bar to quench the thirst of other happy drinkers.

Russell turned to see if he could find a place to sit a minute. He wandered over to what looked like an empty table, but ended up standing across from Rafe. "Didn't mean to disturb you," he said, backing away.

Rafe motioned to the other chair. "Go ahead and have a seat. They're at a premium tonight. I came in here for a spot of dinner and a beer. I got the beer, but I'm still waiting for the dinner. The server says it will be right up. Do you want anything?" he asked, practically shouting to be heard over the din.

Russell shook his head. "I ate before I left the house."

"The cupboards were bare at home. Tomorrow after I see to the horses, I need to go to the store." Rafe sipped his beer, and Carly brought him a burger and fries. He took a bite and sighed.

Russell liked the fact that the horses came first with Rafe. That said a lot about the man. "Are you getting settled in?"

Rafe shrugged. "It's going to take a while. I got the house aired out and all the critters fed and bedded down. I gotta get some supplies so I can repair the paddocks for winter. In the spring, I'll do some of the heavier work, but for now the priority is getting the barn and paddocks through what's to come in the next few months."

"Sounds like you intend to stay awhile." Russell wasn't yet sure if that was good news, but at least Rafe didn't seem to want to sell. "Do you need help? I can loan you some men for a few days to help you get things done. Once winter sets in, it can be harsh."

Rafe set down his burger. "Are you kidding? After earlier today I figured...." He looked at him quizzically.

"Let's just say that first meeting didn't show us off at our best. We were friends as kids, and maybe I needed to remember that." That was certainly true for him. In business, he always told his people not to assume things—it only led to miscommunications that often spawned other problems. The issue was that he himself had made assumptions about Rafe that might not be true.

"I can't argue with you there. I didn't recognize you when I saw you," Rafe said with a smile. "And I appreciate your offer. I can see that there's a lot to do, and I'm not sure where to start. I figured the animals were a priority, so the first thing I should do is make sure they are safe. Which means fixing the barn and paddocks."

"That's as good a place as any. Maybe Saturday afternoon, a few of us can come over and repair a few things. We used to help Mack out from time to time. He never liked to ask, so sometimes a few of us would just show up to visit and end up getting things done." He caught the server's attention and ordered another beer and a water. Then he turned to Rafe and asked if he needed anything.

"One is my limit. I'm taking some pain meds right now. That last ride pulled a muscle in my right arm, so I'm taking stuff to keep the pain at bay."

Russell nodded. "That was some ride."

"You saw it?" Rafe asked, his smile growing wider, expression peppered with excitement. "The ride of a lifetime, one of the other guys called it, and I suppose it was. It isn't often you get to be the one to ride a bull for the eight seconds the very first time, and it wins you the championship." Rafe lifted his glass, and Russell did the same. "It'll probably never happen again. I won my championship, and now I'm trying to figure out what to do with the rest of my life. I'm too old to keep bull riding, even though I love it. So I have two choices. I can continue and beat my body up until I can't move… or worse. Or I can settle somewhere. And it seems like Uncle Mack has given me the chance to find my way."

Russell drank the last of his beer and leaned over the table. "I have to ask. Why did none of you ever talk to him? Was it because he was gay?" Russell's father always told him he needed to learn when to keep his mouth shut, but Russell had to know. Rafe didn't seem like a guy who would abandon a beloved relative.

Rafe thunked his mug on the table. "I didn't know he was." His expression grew rock hard. "All I know is that when I was about twelve, I was told that we had to pray for Uncle Mack because he was ill. I thought he had cancer or something. Every time I asked to visit, I was told that he wasn't well." He shook his head. "But now I guess it makes sense. To my messed-up family, being gay would equate to having something contagious." He shrugged, hurt suddenly filling those eyes. "There's a reason why I don't have much to do with them."

That was an interesting answer, and it had Russell wondering if what his gut was telling him was correct—that Rafe rode the same side of the fence that he did. "I'm sorry about that." He was at a loss for words. "It must have been a shock when you found out about the ranch."

"Yeah. And who knows how my parents will react when they find out. Not that I intend to tell them. We pretty much have an agreement—I don't talk to them, and they don't lecture me about the way I live my life."

Damn, there *was* more than a little bitterness there. Though Russell couldn't blame Rafe a bit. If Russell's folks had turned their backs on him, it would have hurt like hell.

"What I need to do is let that shit go and figure out a way forward. You know?" Rafe said.

"The ranch is a great place to do that. Being close to nature has a way of showing us what's really important." Russell took a drink of his beer. "So, what have you been doing besides riding rodeo?" he asked to change the subject.

"I worked on a number of ranches in the off season. Uncle Mack taught me how to ride and take care of horses when I was a kid, and I stayed pretty close to them when I could afterwards. When I graduated high school, I took off and joined the rodeo. I started out riding the bulls and taking care of the stock. It was a way to pay the bills and earn the entrance fees. Eventually I started to win, which really helped with the finances. The last five years or so, I've been in the top ten on the tour. But this is the first year everything came together and I took the championship."

"What you did was get fucking lucky," a voice slurred from behind him. Russell turned and groaned. "If I hadn't gotten bucked, you—"

Rafe shook his head. "That's the way it goes. You got bucked, I didn't, and I won. It was that simple." He stood. "I also rode a bull that bucked you twice during the season. So give it up."

"Fuck you," Duane snapped.

"Do you kiss your mama with that mouth?" Rafe asked. "No wait, you open it and get yourself disqualified." Duane must have been just drunk enough to be stupid, because he brought his hand back to take a swing at Rafe. But Russell caught him first, knocking him off balance, and Duane ended up on the floor.

"That's enough, Mendeltom," Russell said loudly as the Ralston brothers lifted Duane off the floor and hauled his sorry ass toward the door.

"They won't let him drive, will they?" Rafe asked. He picked up his chair and sat back down.

Russell shook his head. "No. What they will do is call out to the ranch and have his father come pick him up. That will go over like a lead balloon." He rolled his eyes. "If you think Duane is a piece of work, wait till you meet his father. If you look up asshole in the dictionary, there's a picture of Grant Mendeltom. Grant's meanness comes largely from being stingy, while Duane is full of himself and mean as hell." He snickered. "As you can guess, I've never liked either of them, but Duane…." He shook his head.

"No one on tour liked Duane much either. He had a few guys who hung around him, but I always thought they did it because Duane comes from money."

Rafe seemed to have a pretty good head on his shoulders. Russell watched as he finished his burger. "I saw you ride up from the south, and your horse was no stable animal, so I'm assuming it's your family that owns the adjoining ranch."

"My father does, yes," Russell answered. He was always leery of giving away too much about his family connections. It had gotten him in trouble more than once.

Rafe set down his mug. "I was told it was a pretty big operation."

"Is that your way of asking if we're rich?" Russell asked.

Rafe rolled his eyes. "Prickly much?" he countered. "And no, I certainly was not. I've worked on a number of small-to-medium-sized spreads, but I've never managed to see one of the real big operations. I do have more manners that that." He glared for a second, and Russell put up a hand in surrender.

"I didn't mean to call your integrity into question. Yes, we have a large operation, and like Duane, I had people who hung around me because of what they thought I could do for them. It got worse after I started Banion Software, but by then I was better equipped to handle it." He hated this part of his history because he always felt like such a complete fool. His dad had warned him to be cautious and to make friends carefully.

Rafe shrugged. "That's a problem I never had. After I left home, I spent a lot of my time just figuring out how to feed myself and keep a roof over my head. No one was lining up to hang around me other than the true friends I'd made."

Russell had to give Rafe credit—he seemed honest and straightforward. Russell liked that, and he lowered some of his guard. "Our ranch was built over decades. Dad has good instincts when it comes to the land and cattle. He saved the family more than once during some really hard years. But now it's doing very well." That was an understatement, but there was no need to brag. "When I was in college, there were a few times when people realized what my family had and cozied up to me in the hope that the friendship would get them something."

Rafe leaned closer. "From your expression, I'd guess that someone got under your defenses."

"Yeah, one of the guys did." He picked up his water glass, because if he told this story while he was drinking, he'd be tempted to continue and not stop. "He was one of those smooth guys that everyone liked. You know?" Russell said, and Rafe nodded slowly.

"We had one of those on the circuit," he said.

"I met him at a party of a friend I trusted. He and I talked a lot that night and on the phone afterwards. Normal dating kind of stuff. Jase seemed nice and he was attentive and all. He listened when I bitched about my parents. Not that they were so bad, but what college student doesn't gripe about their mom and dad every now and then? Anyway, I fell for him, and the two of us got an apartment together. Things were looking serious." He sighed, finding it hard to believe he was telling a near stranger this story.

Rafe half stood and moved his chair around so he sat closer. "You're as pale as a ghost. If you don't want to tell me this, you don't have to."

And just like that, Russell felt worse for the way he'd treated Rafe earlier. The guy seemed nice, and when Russell lifted his gaze from the table, Rafe's huge, deep eyes drew him right in.

But Russell managed to control himself. Because damn, just like Jase, Rafe was a nice guy with a killer body. But Jase would never have told him to stop or been concerned that Russell might be uncomfortable. Instead, Jase would have encouraged him to talk so he could use the information against him later.

Rafe signaled the server and spoke to her quietly. She hurried away and returned with a plate of crackers and another glass of water. "Eat a few of those. They'll settle your nerves."

Russell opened the packages and ate a few, feeling better after a few minutes. "I was so stupid."

"In matters of the heart, everyone is stupid at one point or another," Rafe said. The gentleness in his eyes told him Rafe knew exactly what he was talking about.

"I suppose. See, I fell for Jase hard, and he and I had this place together. I was the one with the car, so I drove where we needed to go."

"And you saw Jase's friends and his family, but not yours. And suddenly your sense of self was gone and he was controlling everything."

Rafe really seemed to understand. Russell's mouth hung open. "How did you know?"

"Controlling asshole. I've seen it on the tour. Kid named Archie woke up one morning to find his life was gone and so was his lover, as well as all the money he'd earned, and everything else too. He had a lot of promise, but the situation broke him and that was it. His next ride nearly killed him because his head wasn't where it needed to be." Rafe passed him a few more crackers, and Russell ate absently.

"That nearly happened to me," Russell admitted. "See, I had this business idea. I thought it was something Jase and I could start and run together— something to build our lives on. God, was I stupid, and I was *this* close to giving him half of it." He held up his fingers. "But my dad figured something was wrong and drove all the way to Denver to see what was going on. He showed up and assessed the situation in about an hour. Then he sat me down and coaxed my plans out of me."

"Did you believe him?" Rafe asked.

"Not at first. But what Dad said opened my eyes, and when I looked again, I saw what a shit show I'd made of things. Still, it took me another month for it all to sink in, and then I had to find a way to get the bastard out of my life. I could see what he was doing, but I didn't know how to stop it. I thought I was an adult and didn't want to ask my father for help." He shook his head slowly, trying to keep his thoughts from taking him right back there. "In the end, I kicked him out of the apartment, which was in my name because I was paying for it. I thought he was gone. I went back to my friends, who thankfully didn't give me too much shit. They never liked Jase anyway, and they were glad he was gone."

Rafe nodded slowly. "I get the idea that the story isn't over."

"Are you sure I haven't told you this story before?" He was teasing, but Rafe really seemed to know what was coming. "You're right. I kicked him out, but he kept talking smack about me. Once I graduated and started my company, he tried to say that I had told him it was ours. That I'd *promised*. He didn't have a leg to stand on, thank God. He was just after money. Dad handled that part for me, and I haven't seen him again."

"Shit." Rafe drew in a long breath. "That guy isn't worth getting yourself upset—and eating crackers—over." He smiled, then called the server over and paid his bill. "If I were you, I'd do my best to never think about him again. He ain't worth it. Just chalk it up to experience." He looked Russell in the eye. "And another thing…. I know you're embarrassed about it, but you don't need to be. We've all done stupid stuff when we were young." Rafe stood and placed his hand on Russell's shoulder. "It shows that you have a heart, and there ain't nothing wrong with that." He patted once and then his hand slipped away. "I need to get back. But I'll see you around. And thanks for the offer of help. I'm not too proud to accept."

Russell instantly missed the touch as he watched Rafe head for the door. Maybe heading home wasn't such a bad idea. They said letting go of the past was cathartic. He didn't know about that, but holding on to it was definitely tiring. And he had work to do in the morning.

Chapter 3

RAFE SLEPT in the guest room because the thought of sleeping in his uncle's bed didn't sit right with him. He figured that in the morning, he'd make the rounds with a list of chores to complete and get them started. There wasn't a lot of time until winter set in, so he'd have to patch what he could. But for now, he needed to figure out a way to sleep in a strange house. At least the dogs didn't try to sleep with him. He had left the door to his uncle's room open and found all three dogs on the bed, blinking at him in confusion before lowering their heads again.

He found clean sheets and blankets in the linen closet and made up the guest bed. Then he showered and climbed under the covers, clean and tired, crisp sheets sliding against his skin. He should have fallen asleep easily. After all, he was in a comfortable bed that wasn't in a hotel, and the bed was his. But sleep eluded him, and Rafe stared up at the ceiling for a while, then reached for the envelope his uncle had left him. He pulled out the key and let it dangle from his fingers. He'd have to clean out the house eventually, and hopefully he'd unravel some of who his uncle was.

Rafe rolled over and closed his eyes, setting the key on the nightstand. He was half asleep when the bed bounced and a heavy weight settled near his legs. He sighed and sat up, glaring at the dog, who jumped down and found a spot on the floor. He looked around. The others had moved into his room as well and were scattered around the bed. "Dogs," he muttered. Then he rolled back over, closing his eyes, and finally let sleep take him.

RAFE BOLTED upright the next morning at the sound of all three dogs barking. He hurried out of the bedroom. "Jesus, who the hell is outside at this hour?" he said to himself as he pulled on pants and a shirt and wandered into the living room. Using his phone, he checked the time and was surprised to find it after nine. Even more shocking was the sight of a large, shiny red truck parked in front of the house. The dogs continued barking, and Rafe shooed them out of the way, then opened the door as a heavyset man in a suit and tie stepped onto the front porch. "Can I help you?" Rafe asked.

The man extended his hand. "Grant Mendeltom."

"Rafe Carrera. Good to meet you. I understand we're neighbors." He blinked and wished he'd had the chance to down some coffee before this encounter.

"We rightly are." He pushed his hat back on his head. "I won't beat around the bush or blow smoke up your ass. This ranch is worn down, and if you want to sell, I'm interested in buying." Rafe wouldn't have been surprised if he'd pulled out a checkbook. "I'll give you a good price, and you can move on with your life." Grant looked around, curling his lips slightly as if he didn't like that he saw. "This land would make a nice addition to my spread, so it's more valuable to me than anyone else." He shook his head and sighed as though making his offer was doing Rafe some sort of favor.

"Would you like some coffee?" Rafe offered. "I could make some." He was going to be polite, though this man reminded him of a fat, slippery eel. Even if Russell hadn't said anything about him at the bar, Rafe would have known there was something off about him. His smile and the look in his eyes didn't match. The man's smile attempted to be warm and engaging, but his eyes were like those of a wolf, a predator ready to pounce at any second. Rafe couldn't wait for him to leave.

The dogs had all gathered around Rafe, not growling, but sitting together, watching, protecting, looking up at him every so often, as if they were just waiting for the sign to run this man off.

"No, thank you. But that's very kind," he said. He reached inside his jacket pocket. "Here's my card. Call me when you have a chance to look at this place and see all the work that will be needed. Save yourself the time and effort." That smile was back, and Rafe nodded, but stayed where he was. He refused to look away, even as Grant held his gaze. When Grant finally turned back to his truck, Rafe watched him go before returning inside the house.

He set Grant's card with Russell's, wondering what sort of collection he was going to end up with. Russell had told him his card was "just in case," whatever the hell that meant, but looking at the name made him remember the vulnerability Russell had shown him.

That sort of boggled his mind. It could have been some sort of play to get Rafe to trust him, but to what end? From what he'd said and the look of him, Russell had all the money he could want. And if he wanted to buy the ranch as well, he didn't really act like it. And since their stiff first meeting, he'd seemed to change. Although it was obvious he had money, when Russell looked at all the work to be done at the ranch, he had offered to help. When Grant Mendeltom looked at the ranch, his gaze had been predatory and filled with avarice. Grant wanted this ranch badly, for whatever reason.

Rafe had no intention of selling the ranch, though. It was his, and it could be a home. Granted, he wasn't looking forward to living next to Duane and Grant Mendeltom, but what the hell could he do about that? At least out here there was enough space between them.

"Come on, guys," he told the dogs, then took them in the house and got them fed. He was coming to the end of their food, so he really needed to drive into town for supplies. But before anything else, he had to check on the horses and cattle. They came first.

SWEAT BEADED on his forehead even though it wasn't that warm, but the sun shone as he made the final repair to one of the paddocks. At least with that done, he could put the horses outside when the weather was good. The dogs either played or lay in the sun while he finished the last of the repairs, thankful that there had been supplies in the barn. Once he put the tools away, he checked the gates and then let one of the horses outside for a while. The animal ran and explored his space happily while Rafe eyed the rest of the paddocks, assessing the work. Then he heard a car pull up.

"Lots to do," Luther called as he got out of his car with his dad, both men heading over. "I see you got right to work."

"No time to waste," Rafe said, shaking both their hands. "Arthur, I was out checking the herd, and some of them look like they'd be ready for market."

"You have a good eye. Yes, about half of them are, and you'll get a good price for them too. The others will either be for the spring or they are raising calves. I can help you out, if you'd like. Your uncle always sold to Banion's. I can call their man and help you separate the herd. The Banions stay close for the winter, so I'm sure someone will be around."

"They do more than ranch?" Rafe asked.

"Yeah, they own a beef processing facility. They only accept very high quality, and largely sell to the high-end markets or ship it overseas. They pay top dollar for good head, and your uncle always kept up to their standards." Arthur pulled off his hat and smoothed back his hair. "It used to be that Mack ran five, six hundred head here. It was a good-sized operation for a ranch this acreage. But as he got older, he kept downsizing. Not that I really blame him."

"Sounds good. I met Russell already."

"Young Banion? He's an interesting one. Some kind of ranching and farming computer system genius. Don't know all that much about it, but a lot of the big operations use his computers. Makes all the tracking and animal breeding and control information super easy for them, or so I'm told." He plopped his hat back on his head. "The family is well off, but I hear the son is worth more than the rest of them put together. He's supposed to be a real genius at business."

"Dad…," Luther said warningly.

"I ain't said anything that people in town wouldn't share if asked." Arthur smiled. "Luther does work for them sometimes." Luther cleared his throat, clearly a little uncomfortable. "Don't worry, son, I don't know nothing about nothing." He rolled his eyes, but it was pretty clear that Arthur was proud of his son.

"If you'd give them a call, I'd appreciate it. Russell Banion offered to send some of his hands over Saturday afternoon to help out around here too." Rafe pulled his jacket closed around him. Now that he wasn't working so hard, the cold seeped in.

Arthur and Luther shared a look that Rafe couldn't quite figure out.

"That's right neighborly of him," Arthur said.

"And I had another visitor today. Grant Mendeltom made me an offer on the ranch. Or at least, he said he wanted to buy it and that he'd give me a good price."

Concern flashed in Arthur's eyes for just a second. He glanced at Luther and then began looking around. "Son, I'll give you my opinion, and you can take it for what it's worth. This land, what you got here, is a real good place. And Mack left it to you. Why, none of us know. But this is your place, and God ain't making any more land. And once it's sold, then Mendeltom will do whatever he wants with it, and you'll be standing over there, looking in, wishing you still had a place like this to call home. There ain't many of us small ranchers left. Every year, the big guys get bigger, and the smaller places sell, either for homes or to guys like Mendeltom who want to get as big as they can."

Rafe smiled. "Thank you. I appreciate your honesty." And it only helped confirm his initial opinion.

Arthur grinned. "Son, I ain't being honest. If I were, I'd say that I'd give my eyeteeth to have this place. It's got amazing pastureland and all the fresh water you want, coming right down out of those mountains. If the cattle don't pan out, you can feed yourself from the trout in the stream."

Rafe didn't quite know what to say. "You make this place seem like an Eden."

"It ain't that, but son, let me tell you, it's as close as you're going to get in the state of Colorado. Especially for men like us." Rafe liked that Arthur included him in that category.

"Well, thank you. And I don't want to sell. I have memories here. They're faded and kind of misty, but they're there." This place could be where he made a home. Besides, there were things here that he felt he had to do. And one of them was to head down to the bank to see what was in the box his uncle had left him the key to.

"Can I offer you some coffee?" Rafe asked, motioning toward the house.

"No, thank you," Luther said. "We just wanted to check in. Dad will call Banion's and arrange for the cattle transport. He can also give you the names of some breeders who will sell you some calves, though Banion might be able to do that too. They often have some to sell."

"Good. I'd like to increase the herd come spring."

"We'll get you fixed up, don't worry," Arthur told him. "I was a friend of your uncle's for a lot of years." He patted Rafe on the shoulder.

"Thank you." He was starting to feel a little overwhelmed. "I'm going to go to the bank on Monday," he said to Luther. "I was wondering if you'd mind going with me, just in case there's something in there of a legal nature." He had no idea what he was going to find in his uncle's safe-deposit box.

"Sure. I can meet you there at ten," Luther said. Then he looked back to their truck. "Dad and I should go and let you finish up your work."

"I'll have the Banion rep call you to settle the details for getting the cattle to market," Arthur told him.

Rafe thanked both men, then watched them drive away before he returned to his work. If he wanted to get this ranch back on its feet, then he had a lot of work to do in a very short time. At least he'd finished one paddock. Once everything was put away, he let the dogs out with the herd, then got in his truck and headed into town.

Groceries were the first item on his list, followed by building supplies, and then a huge bag of food for the dogs. By the time he was ready to head back, the truck was loaded to the gills.

Twenty minutes later, he was home again. But when he turned into the drive, he found yet another visitor standing in his yard. "Is this fucking Grand Central Station?" he asked out loud. He got out of the truck as the man strode over.

"What are you doing here?" Rafe asked as his father approached. He hadn't seen his dad in five years or so, and the man had put on a lot of weight.

"I heard that you had inherited the ranch from Mack." He shook his head as he looked around. "The wages of sin."

"Oh, knock it off," Rafe said, actually smiling at his father's reaction. "I spent years listening to you spout that crap. I don't want to hear it anymore."

"Don't give me any lip," he snapped.

Rafe put his hands on his hips. "Or what? You'll beat me with the belt like you did when I was a kid? This is my ranch now, so you can knock off the whole dad routine. I don't care what you think, and you don't get to tell me what to do here. Now, I'll ask again. What do you want? I know you well enough to know you didn't come here because you've missed me. You want something. So, what is it?" He glared at the man who had raised him with one hand on the Bible and the other on the belt.

"Your mother believes that Mack squirreled away a fair amount of money over the years. And as his sister, she's entitled to some of it."

Rafe should have known. "Nope," he said calmly. "The will is explicit. Uncle Mack identified Mom by name and stated that she, as well as the rest of his family, would get nothing. He was very specific. And I intend to honor Uncle Mack's wishes."

He stepped closer. His father was a tall man who used his size to intimidate. "His wishes.... That man was a...."

"What, Dad? Gay? Like me?" He looked his father in the eye. "And you did the same thing to me that you did to Uncle Mack—threw me aside. I was no longer your son, remember? Hell, we haven't seen each other in five years, and now suddenly here you are. But it's only because you think you can get something." There was nothing redeemable about this man.

"We thought we were doing the best for you. Your mother and I figured you'd see the kind of life you'd have and you'd change your ways, leaving this whole gay thing behind you. That you could realize your mistake and be welcomed back into the fold. After all, we are told to turn the other cheek," his dad told him. "Your mother and I are prepared to forgive you and—"

Rafe was stunned. "I'm not the one who needs to be forgiven. I'm not the one who did anything wrong. You and Mom did." He glared at his father. "You turned your back on your only son the minute he didn't meet your expectations. Parents are supposed to love their children unconditionally, but you couldn't do that." He sucked in a deep breath. "It took me a long time to figure out who I am, and I'm not afraid of you any longer. You lost your authority and any respect I might have had for you long ago. So please, just go away." He kept his voice level. It was time he let go of the anger. His parents hadn't had any power over him in years, and he refused to give them any now.

"Your mother and I were only doing what we thought was right, what we thought would be best for you." His father's eyes blazed the same way they'd done when Rafe was a kid. Back then, Rafe had thought it was the fire of God. Now he knew it came from a very different place. "We'll fight you," his father threatened.

"On what grounds? The will is bulletproof." He whistled, and the dogs raced across the open range and headed over to him. He greeted each of them. "Now I suggest you go home. There's nothing here for you."

"You'll change your mind."

Rafe shook his head. "No, I won't. When you turned your backs on me, you told me I was nothing, that I would never make it without you and Mom. Well, I've proven that I don't need you and probably never did. I'm a world champion bull rider, and now I have this ranch to call home. I haven't had you or Mom in my life for years, and I don't want you in it now. So please just go." By this point, Rafe knew that words weren't going to change his father's mind. Saying anything more was a waste of effort.

His dad turned away and stalked toward his car. Rafe petted the dogs and watched until his father had driven out of sight, wondering why it was that every time something good happened, everyone came out of the woodwork determined to take it away from him. He wished he could have someone who gave a damn about him for once… just once.

He let the dogs inside, thinking of what the day had brought so far. He was tired and disgusted at how blatantly greedy his father was. And Grant Mendeltom? Well, at least he could understand the man. He was just another grasping rancher who thought he could take whatever he wanted. But his own father coming around to see what he could get? That was just shitty.

Rafe made himself and the dogs some dinner and ate in front of the old television set before going to bed, hoping that the following day would be better. Because it sure as hell couldn't get much worse. The dogs settled on the sofa and the floor around him. At least the only thing they wanted from him was love.

Chapter 4

"ALL RIGHT, guys. Is everything under control here?" Russell asked. "Are you ready to head out to Rafe's place?"

"Yeah, it's all good here. All of the ranch chores are done," Clyde reported. "What I don't get is why we're doing this."

Russell pushed the lift gate of his truck closed. "Because it's the neighborly thing to do. It was Mack's ranch, and he was good to me." He didn't tell the men that *he* would be paying them for the time they put in at Rafe's ranch, not his dad. That wasn't something they needed to be concerned about. "So let's go." He climbed into his truck, and the men got into the others, all of them heading out and around to the road that led to Rafe's.

When he pulled into the yard, Russell was surprised to see the amount of progress Rafe had already made. "Hey, Rafe," Russell said as he climbed out of the truck. "I brought some help and some supplies. What do we need to get done?"

Rafe looked surprised as hell. "There are still some paddock repairs, and…."

"Dustin, unload the supplies and take Brad with you to get the paddocks finished. Then check out the barn to make sure it's solid and cleaned out." Dustin was an amazing leader. Taking charge was in his nature, and Russell stepped back and stayed out of the way. "You two check out the roof. I saw some patches that are going to need to be repaired. Scope out what you're going to need and then go back and get the shingles from our place. We need to get the roof ready for winter."

Rafe shook his head. "You said you'd be here to help—I wasn't expecting a whole construction crew." The guys were already getting to work. One had set up a portable saw and tool station, while others put a ladder up and headed to the roof.

"What do you need me to do?" Russell asked. "These men know what they're doing. They've been building and repairing things on the ranch for a long time."

"Well, the stalls in the barn need fixing. Some of them are unusable right now. I'd like to get them rebuilt and eventually breed some horses. The barn is too big for the three horses I have, and there's no way they'll stay warm in the winter without the benefit of body heat. I was going to try adding some supplemental heat, but I don't know if the electrical system can handle it."

"Then let's get on it," Russell said. "I'll get the tools and meet you inside."

"You can do electrical work?" Rafe asked.

Russell grinned. "You better believe it." He grabbed the box and followed Rafe out, trying to keep his gaze from traveling to that tight cowboy jeans–covered rear end in front of him.

Inside the barn, Russell checked the electrical wiring and breakers. "This looks okay. The box was replaced not too long ago. One less thing to worry about, right?" he said, happy that Mack had been careful about things like electricity. Rewiring the barn would have been a big job. "But you're right, these stalls are done. We should clear them out and rebuild the walls and doors. I wasn't sure exactly what we were going to need, but I brought lumber and supplies with us. The paddocks and stalls needed work, even when Mack was still here."

"Then let's unload what we need," Rafe said softly, seeming a little overwhelmed. "And in case I forget later, I want to thank you and your men for doing this."

Russell nodded slowly, the appreciation in Rafe's eyes getting to him. Russell had always helped his neighbors when he could, but none of them had ever seemed as overwhelmed as Rafe was at this moment. He simply blinked and stood still, as if he couldn't quite believe this was actually happening.

"Come on, let's get started," Russell said. As he headed out, he heard the whine of the portable saw. The guys weren't wasting any time, and he was glad of it. It was already after noon, which meant they only had five hours or so of daylight. So they all moved quickly, including him and Rafe, to get the supplies unloaded. Once that was done, he and Rafe took down the stall walls and dismantled them. They reused what was good and replaced what wasn't. The process was tedious, but not as slow as rebuilding everything.

Russell took the lead, with Rafe cutting and helping place the new pieces. It didn't take long before Russell just concentrated on his work. Usually he kept an eye on his men, but Rafe seemed to understand what he wanted. Not that Russell had an easy time of it. Every time Rafe returned with a board, his musky rich scent would surround Russell, and he'd end up pausing just to take it in. And as the day wore on, sweat and work only increased it. Russell knew that he needed to keep his mind clear, but he kept failing.

By the time they got the pieces of the first stall together, his head spun a little and he'd nearly nailed his foot to the base, instead of the board. "It looks really good," Rafe said as he opened and closed the door.

"Let's finish the next ones. Now that this one is solid, we can build on it." Russell stood and turned to find Rafe watching him. He smiled and began laying out the next sections to be worked on. "Is something wrong?"

Rafe shook his head. "Sorry. I was woolgathering a second."

"What about?" Russell asked. Rafe blushed and muttered *nothing*, but Russell had a pretty good idea. Still, he kept his thoughts to himself. He didn't need a bunch of complications in his life right now, and Russell had no idea if Rafe was even going to stay...

though he hoped that this show of neighborliness would make a good impression.

"I had a visitor a few days ago," Rafe said as they took the side wall apart to make the repairs. Russell noticed the change of subject but let it slide. He was already hyperaware of Rafe, and he didn't need them talking about anything personal. "Mendeltom came by. He said he'd make me an offer on the ranch."

Russell tensed for a second and damn near banged his hand with the hammer. "What did you tell him?" Fuck, he had known the biggest vulture of them all would circle—he just hadn't realized how quickly. "Because if you want to sell, I'll beat any offer anyone makes." He finished getting the bad boards out.

"Is that why you're here?" Rafe asked, a touch of what might have been hurt and suspicion in his voice.

Russell set the hammer down. "No. I'm here because it's the neighborly thing to do. Period. But are you even thinking of selling?"

"Arthur Gillian told me that this land is special, that I'd be a fool to sell," Rafe said, watching him like a hawk.

"And Arthur, as usual, is right." Russell liked that Rafe seemed shocked. It was good to know that he could surprise people every once in a while. "You would be a fool to let this place go. It's an amazing spread, with fresh, clean water right down out of the mountains." He sighed. "But if you want to sell, I will beat anyone's price, period." He lowered his gaze because the thought of Mack's place going to a man like Grant Mendeltom made his blood run cold. And knowing it would eventually end up in Duane's hands was even worse.

"Why?" Rafe asked as he measured one of the boards for replacement. "What am I missing?"

Russell paused for a second. "There are reasons why Grant wants this land, and then there are reasons I would. Grant wants this place badly because of the water. The stream that you have running through the property is clean and clear and perfect. Mendeltom would take all that water and use it to grow his operation as big as he could make it." Russell swallowed.

"And you?" Rafe asked, cautiously.

"If you decided to sell, I'd want it because Mack and I used to fish for trout in that stream." Damn it all. Why did Rafe bring out the emotional shit in him? "Mack and I were friends. Things between me and my parents weren't always rosy because I was a surly teenager. My parents didn't know why, but when we'd fight, I'd come over here and Mack would take me fishing or we'd ride out to the stream and sit. Your uncle didn't talk much, and he rarely spoke about his family. But I knew who he was, and he knew me. And when I was growing up, that was enough." He'd said plenty. "So the thought of the Mendeltoms getting their hands on this place makes me see red."

Rafe leaned the board to be cut against the completed stall wall. "I have no interest in selling and even less in letting Duane's father get his hands on this land. But I won't be selling it to you either, I'm afraid. I want to build a home here, something I haven't had in a long time."

Russell smiled and nodded. "Cool. Then let's get back to work."

Rafe went to grab another board from the truck, and Russell took a deep breath and tried not to watch Rafe walk away. He failed. There was something about Mack's nephew that pulled Russell's attention.

"Boss," Dustin said as he strode inside, "put your eyes back in your head."

Russell had always been one of the guys. Growing up on the ranch, he had worked alongside most of the hands, and he liked that they treated him as one of them, rather than the boss. That title was reserved for his father, and Russell hoped things stayed that way for a long time yet.

"Ass," Russell muttered as he went back to shoring up what was left of the stall wall. "What do you need?"

"We got the roof repairs underway, and they seem to be going well. The paddocks are done, so I have some of the men repairing a few places on this barn to tighten it for winter. There's the equipment shed, which needs work too, so I'll be sending the men over there next." He knelt down close to him. "You really like this guy, don't you?"

Russell didn't answer. "I brought you here to help with what needs to be done, not to stick your nose in my business." He tried to put some snap in his voice, but Dustin had known him way too long and simply ignored his remark, the way he usually did.

"Fine, I'll go back to work, and you two can go back to whatever it was you were doing." He smiled and hurried out of the barn before Russell could throw something at him.

Once Rafe returned with the trimmed boards, he slotted them into place, and they put the wall together, raised it, and shimmed it before finishing the front panel with the door.

RUSSELL'S HEAD swam by the time he and Rafe were finished. Spending hours so close to Rafe, listening to his deep voice, smelling him, knowing Russell could just reach out and touch him any time… it was driving him crazy. There were times when they were right next to one another, Rafe's hand so close to his. Russell had been so tempted to take it, just to feel what Rafe's hand on his skin would be like. And the thought of leaning over and tasting Rafe's full lips was making him breathless.

He stood back, looking at the bay of stalls, and smiled. They looked solid and would last a good number of years. "I should check on the others," Russell said.

"I'll put the tools away," Rafe offered, and started out of the barn. Russell followed him, watching every movement, each clench of an ass straight from heaven. God, he was tempted to see if Rafe might be interested in hanging out with him. It had been a long time since he'd spent time with people who didn't work for him or he wasn't related to. And both of those were off romantic limits for a number of reasons. But he'd never been tempted the way he was now. Hell, Rafe was hot enough to tempt the devil himself.

As soon as he left the barn, he inhaled the fresh air. He found Dustin just as the sun began to set. "How is it?"

"The paddocks are done, the stalls are fixed. We repaired the barn and equipment shed as well as the roof." He smiled. "The guys did amazing work, and I'd say this place should make it through the winter."

Russell turned to all the guys. "Good work."

"Yes, thank you all," Rafe said from near the barn. "I can't believe you'd all do this for a guy you barely know, but I owe you a great deal." Rafe shook hands with each of the guys before they climbed into the trucks and took off. That left Russell alone with Rafe.

"I've heard of people being neighborly, but you and your men went overboard today. I don't know how to thank you." Rafe licked his lips, and damn it all if Russell wasn't tempted to kiss the spot where that tongue had just touched.

"You're welcome," Russell said. "And if you can't understand what neighbors are for, then you haven't had the right neighbors." He managed to control himself and patted Rafe on the shoulder before heading to his truck. He'd better get out before he did something he regretted.

"HOW DID it go at Mack's?" His dad handed him a martini and sat on the sofa. "You look beat."

"We got a lot done, and Rafe was overwhelmed, I think. He thanked each of the men individually." He sipped his drink slowly. "I think he was really touched." He leaned forward, holding the glass by the stem, looking into it but not really seeing the liquid. "It was as if we handed him the moon when all we did was help out. For us, it was no big deal. But for him...."

His dad nodded. "I think I see."

Russell rolled his eyes. "No, you don't. Rafe couldn't believe anyone would do something like that for him... and I think it's because no one ever has." He was beginning to see just how lucky he was. And he couldn't help wondering about Rafe's home life. Russell had been so lucky in that regard. But he was starting to understand why Mack had left his ranch to Rafe.

"You always had a good heart," his dad said.

Russell laughed and then coughed, setting the glass down. "Since when do you talk like that?" Russel's dad wasn't a touchy-feely kind of guy. He was more of the strong, silent type. Russell had become quite good at reading him over the years, but this was something new.

"Don't get smart with me. I'm still big enough to whoop you if I have to." But there was no heat in his admonition. Russell cocked his eyebrows, waiting for an explanation. Finally, his dad relented. "I, uh, I went to the doctor while you were out. He asked me to come in when I told him I haven't been feeling like my usual self. He's running some tests but isn't sure what's wrong...." His dad's glass shook slightly in his hand. Russell could never remember his father showing any weakness before. "I don't know, son. Maybe I'm just feeling a little... mortal."

"Dad...." He swallowed. "You should have told me."

The man had the audacity to shrug. "At first I didn't think it was anything other than old age. And my stomach has always been a little dodgy. But when I talked to the doctor at my last checkup—you know, the one that you made me go to—he wanted to see me again. And so I went. And now he's going to run some tests, just to be sure." The fear behind his father's eyes was something completely new to Russell. "I know I'm not going to live forever, and I want to see you happy."

Russell shook his head. "Dad, I am happy. The ranch and my work, they make me happy. I have a life most people would be jealous of."

"So...?" His dad leaned forward, his drink in hand. Russell bit his lip to keep from asking his dad if he should be drinking at a time like this. But that would only piss him off, so he kept his mouth shut. "Your mother and I were happy together for over thirty years. You need to find someone who will make you as happy as she made me." Then his dad sat back and finished the cocktail, watching him.

Suddenly Russell felt like an exhibit in a museum... or a specimen under a microscope. "What are you doing?"

"Wondering about our new neighbor." He got up to get a glass of water, then sat back down.

"I was just being neighborly," Russell said way too quickly. The room felt warmer to him when he thought about Rafe.

"If you say so. But taking two truckloads of supplies and a number of the hands from the ranch seems to me to be a bit more than 'neighborly.' I can't help but wonder just how neighborly you want to get with this guy." His dad looked smug as hell. "Maybe I'll have to pay him a visit and see just what kind of neighbor he is."

Russell rolled his eyes, but his dad only grinned.

"It's Mack's place. I don't want to see it go all to hell." The last thing he wanted was for his father to get involved. The man could be such a yenta. "And before you get yourself all worked up, no, I am not intending to ask him out… or anyone else, for that matter. Thanks to my experience with Jase, I know better than that. I still haven't gotten over the hell he put both of us through."

"Bullshit," his dad snapped. "Yeah, I never liked him, but not everyone is like him. You know that. So he was a shit—do you think our neighbor is one too?"

"I don't know. That's the problem. I thought Jase was a good guy, and look what happened." In so many areas of his life, Russell was in charge. He knew the ranch like the back of his hand. He built and ran a noncentralized business that was the best at what it did, and he had clients all over the planet. But the thought of venturing into a relationship with any-one—even a guy as hot as Rafe—scared him. And yet, there was something about Rafe that got past his defenses. And that frightened him too, because he couldn't control it.

"Well, if you want my advice, build a bridge and get over it."

Sometimes his father really got to the heart of things, and maybe he was right. Russell was smart enough to know the root cause of his issue—he wanted control over every aspect of his life. He didn't need a shrink to tell him that. After the fiasco with Jase, it had just been easier to stick to the things he knew. And relationships? Well, he was definitely at a loss when it came to them.

The front bell rang through the house, and Russell got up, eager to put an end to this conversation. When he opened the door, he barely managed to stifle a groan. "Grant. Duane. What can I do for you?" These two were the last people he wanted to see.

"I came to speak with your father," Grant huffed.

Russell stepped back. "He's in the great room." He motioned toward where his father was still sitting, then closed the door and went to his office. He'd find something to do. Anything was better than having to spend time with that man.

Grant had always given him the creeps, but Duane had this air of darkness around him that got Russell's Spidey senses tingling. When he was a kid, Russell had believed Grant to be the bogeyman. Now he knew the man was just an asshole, and Russell valued his time too much to spend any of it with him. Still, he was curious about what they wanted, so after a few minutes, he wandered in.

"We need to keep that land in the hands of people who belong in this valley," Grant was saying.

"What sort of people are those? And what right do *we* have to say who gets to own what?" his dad asked in that way he had that let Russell know he was only playing along with Grant.

Duane stood behind his father, arms over his chest, as if he was trying to be intimidating.

"I want the valley to prosper and be sustainable," Russell's dad continued. "I also want our community to be healthy. Are you saying it isn't?"

"With people like *him*?" he asked. "My son tells me that Rafe is just like his uncle. I figured that with him gone, we could get someone upstanding to take over the ranch." He glanced at Duane, who nodded and sneered.

But they were no match for his dad. Russell watched his father letting Grant wear himself out on the line like some trophy fish.

"What we need to do is get him out of the valley," Grant said.

His dad drew slightly closer. "And what is it exactly that you object to? Is it the fact that the man is gay—or the fact that he beat the shit out of your son here in the world championships?" There was more than a hint of glee in his dad's voice, especially when Grant's expression fell like a bad cake. Duane, on the other hand, had gone red and seemed ready to blow.

"My son is gay as well," Russell's father said. "The way I see it, if a person wants to spend their time with someone else—straight or gay—it's no business of mine... or yours. And as for the community...

when did you ever give a crap?" Grant's face grew redder by the second. "You talk about what's best for it, even as you try to force your neighbor out. How neighborly is that?" His father was in rare form, and Russell was glad *he* wasn't on the receiving end of his bite.

"Then I guess you aren't angling to get your hands on it either, right?" Grant snarled. "The whole town is already talking about how Russell and your new neighbor were seen together acting all chummy in the bar."

Grant Mendeltom was a real piece of work. But then, Russell shouldn't have expected anything different. "I think that's enough," Russell said, striding into the room. "I don't need to justify myself to either of you. My business is exactly that—mine." He pointed toward the door. "I suggest you go... now. You have worn out your welcome." Russell kept his voice even but let a hint of menace enter it.

Grant stood. "I should have known coming here would be a waste of time. You're all in league with one another, standing against good God-fearing folks. But you aren't going to get away with it."

"Yeah," Duane echoed.

"With what?" Russell asked, drawing nearer. "I suggest you watch your threats, or I might be forced to do something about them. We defend our own out here." He drew even closer and lowered his voice. "And you know... I have enough resources to buy you out many times over. God knows why you think you have the right on your side, but I'd tread carefully if I were you. So I suggest you crawl back into whatever bigoted hole you dragged yourself out of and stay there." He met Grant's eyes, his own gaze fierce and determined. "I'll be sure to let the men here know that neither of you are welcome on our property."

The hatred that glared from Mendeltom's eyes almost made Russell step back. "Like I said, I should have known," he growled.

"Then why did you bother coming?" Russell asked before quickly closing the front door behind Grant and Duane. He took a deep breath, willing his anger to subside. Then he returned to where his father waited in the great room. "Sanctimonious asshole." He really wanted another drink, but it was a bad idea right now. So instead, he poured himself some water.

"You know he's going to cause trouble," his dad said.

"I'm not so sure. Grant usually manages to get his own way. But not this time. I don't think he knows what to do when he's thwarted. At least, I hope that's the case," Russell muttered as he sat down. "Though it's Duane I'm worried about. I think Grant is mostly talk, but Duane? He's a loose cannon. And ever since Rafe beat him, Duane's ego, which is definitely bigger than his brain, has taken a hit."

The smile on his father's face caught him by surprise. "Isn't that the pot calling the kettle black? You usually get your own way as well, you know." He leaned forward slightly. "Just make sure that what you want this time is the right thing." He held Russell's gaze. "We have a lot of money, and that means we have a great deal of influence. Just make sure that whatever you do is the right thing, for the right reasons."

Instantly Russell thought of Rafe. And he knew, deep down, that helping him was what he was going to do. As for his reasons? Well, he'd figure them out... soon.

Chapter 5

Rafe wasn't sure why he was so anxious, but he could hardly sleep. After a full weekend working on the ranch to get it ready for winter, he should have been exhausted, but his mind refused to settle down. And so he just lay there, thinking about Russell and wondering what could be in his uncle's safe-deposit box. Why had Uncle Mack been so secretive about it?

Rafe rolled over again, the dogs huffing as he moved. Clearly they had no trouble sleeping. God, he hated this. He rode bulls for a living and had nerves of steel, and yet his mind whirred with thoughts of the damned box... and Russell.

He could almost smell him in the room, and that alone got him excited. Hell, on the circuit, the few times he'd dared to be with someone, the wham-bam would be long over by now and he'd have moved on to another city. But this was different—this ranch was now home, a place he intended to put down roots. But what should he do?

He'd never had a relationship that had worked. Hell, not even his family wanted him. And now he had a chance to make his mark here in the valley, and he sure as hell didn't want to mess that up... even if every cell in his body was wondering how things could be with Russell.

Lola shifted from the corner of the bed and came over to lie next to his back, pressing right against him. Rafe lightly stroked her head a few times. He was being ridiculous about all of this and he knew it. Whatever was in the box would still be there in the morning. And as for Russell, well, that would work itself out too. Most likely with Russell finding someone a fuck-ton more interesting than Rafe.

He must have finally fallen asleep, because the next thing he knew, Lola was nudging him awake as light streamed in the window. He got up, dressed, fed the dogs, and headed out to finish his chores, pretty much on autopilot. The life of a rancher was going to take some getting used to.

After finishing with the horses and checking on the cattle, he made some breakfast and set the dogs out with the herd, then headed into town. He drove to the bank, the key in his pocket and a copy of the legal papers on the seat next to him. Hopefully, if he needed anything else, Luther would be able to provide it.

The bank was one of those imposing buildings built to look like a classical stone temple, extremely out of place in this western community of mostly wooden and brick buildings. The image was meant to portray strength, even though like most banks, it was built on people's confidence in the institution and little more. He parked in front and went inside, the sound of his boots loud on the old stone floor. He checked around the lobby for Luther but didn't see him yet, so he sat down in one of the chairs off to the side, sliding the key through his fingers.

Waiting was something he didn't do very well. At the rodeo, there was always something to do, like watch the other riders for comparison, or gauge the performance of the various bulls, because chances were at some point, he'd draw one of them. There were fans to meet and then his own rides to get ready for.

"Can we help you?" a young lady in dark blue pants and a jacket asked him, smiling.

"I'm waiting for Luther Gilliam. He and I are supposed to review the contents of my uncle's safe-deposit box," he explained.

She smiled warmly. "You must be Rafael Carrera. Luther called a little while ago to make sure that we were aware of the situation and would have everything in order." The way she said Luther's name hinted that she might like him. Just the mention of his name brightened her smile and relaxed her features. "Just come over to that desk when you're ready, and I'll help you."

"Thank you, ma'am," he said, tipping his hat politely before going back to watching the door.

"Thanks, Mark," a familiar voice said from just out of his field of vision. Rafe tugged at his collar, instantly a little warm. Damn, Russell Banion did that to him in seconds. His heart already beat faster, and when he turned, he found Russell on his way over. "Rafe. Getting things set up for the ranch?"

He swallowed, ready to lose himself in those eyes. "Luther handled a lot of that for me already, so we're good there. No, this is some stuff for Uncle Mack." He shoved the key in his pocket. "It's probably nothing. But…."

Russell shook his head. "If it's something Mack set up, then it isn't nothing. Your uncle never did anything he didn't mean to." He sat down. "I know you hadn't seen him for a while, but he was a deliberate man, and he knew his mind and his own plans. He didn't do things by halves. And though he didn't say much to a lot of folks around here, when he did, he was honest and said what was on his mind."

"That's good to know." Rafe shrugged. "I've been living in his house for a few days and it tells me almost nothing about him. I haven't been using his room, though. Maybe there's something in there that might give me more of a clue about who he was." He found himself more and more curious about his uncle the longer he was at the ranch.

"Wish I knew what to tell you," Russell said softly, as though he were holding on to his own memories. The things Rafe had been told by his parents about his uncle had been blatant lies—he knew that now. And he felt a little ashamed that he'd listened to them all these years and not called them on it. Not that it would have mattered—they wouldn't have let him visit his uncle. In their eyes, Mack had been "unnatural."

And like they'd done with Mack, his parents had turned their backs on Rafe when he came out too. Maybe the clues had been there the whole time and he just hadn't seen them. After all, for almost six years, they'd told him that Uncle Mack was sick. He should have figured it out sooner. And now that he knew the truth, he was kicking himself for not going to see his long-lost uncle before he died. They might have had a lot in common.

"I wish I'd had a chance to really get to know him," Rafe said. Just then, Luther entered the bank. Rafe stood, and so did Russell, each of them shaking Luther's hand.

"I see you two know each other," Luther said as he looked between them.

"I was just meeting with the manager about some corporate matters and saw Rafe waiting. So I stopped to say hello. But I should be getting back to the ranch." Russell smiled at Rafe. "My father and I wanted to invite you over for dinner, maybe Wednesday, if you don't have plans. He'd like to meet you. I was going to drop by the ranch later to ask, but you saved me the trip."

"That would be very nice. What time?" Rafe asked.

"Five, if you'd like to join us for cocktails. Mom started the tradition a long time ago, and neither of us has had the heart to stop it, even though it's just the two of us now."

Rafe nodded. "I'll see you then."

Russell left the bank with a spring in his step, and Rafe couldn't help following the handsome cowboy with his gaze.

"I see," Luther said quietly. "You already have your eyes on the prize."

Rafe swallowed. "Excuse me?" he asked, a little irritated at the insinuation. He hadn't been that obvious, had he?

"The women in the valley and half the men have tried to capture his attention over the years, but Banion Junior isn't one to let his head be turned. Yet here you are with an invitation to the inner sanctum. And from what I hear, he and his men were helping you out this weekend. Word gets around pretty quickly, especially when it comes to our very own local internet celebrity… well, of a sort."

"Is that a problem?" Rafe asked.

Luther shrugged. "Maybe to some people in town, especially those who were hoping he'd show them some interest. But Russell is a good person who's seen more than his fair share of shit come his way."

Luther's expression suddenly grew less serious and his lips curled upward. "Stacey," he said, his smile turning radiant. Rafe couldn't help noticing her interest in Luther was most definitely returned. "Thank you for helping us out."

She returned Luther's smile with a slightly coy one of her own, and Rafe wanted to ask if they wanted to be left alone. He was definitely feeling like a third wheel.

"Anything I can do to help." She motioned them both to the office, where she guided them through the paperwork to gain access to the box. Once that was done, she led them to the vault, and Rafe inserted the key. He had expected a small box, but what Stacey pulled out was large and seemed quite heavy. She led him and Luther to a small side room just outside the vault and placed the box on the table. "Let me know when you're done." Stacey left the room, and Luther backed away.

"Do you want me to stay? What's in the box is yours. It's really none of my business."

"Stay. I'm a little worried about what I'll find in here, and I could use the support," Rafe said as he opened the lid. He slowly removed things. There seemed to be papers on top, and he looked at them before giving them to Luther.

"This is the original deed to the ranch." Luther seemed to read it over. "Interesting."

"What?" Rafe asked as he removed more papers and handed them over.

Luther went through them all. "The original deed is for forty acres, but the others are for the remaining four hundred acres. A lot of ranchers have had their land re-deeded to put the parcels together, but your uncle didn't. Maybe he planned to sell off some of the land, or just wanted to leave the option open, and thought this would be easier." He placed the papers in a neat pile on the table.

More followed, and Luther reviewed each of them, creating two more stacks on the table before he was done. Rafe checked in the box and found no more papers, just cloth bags and stacks of small items. "What's all that?" Rafe asked, pointing to one pile.

"I need to check on these, but this stack is stock certificates. Most of them are within the past ten years, but some are older. There are Microsoft shares and Oracle. I'm assuming that they haven't been sold because the certificates are still here. He had other stocks as well—I'll research those for you too. I've made notes, so I have all I need to check everything out. As for this other stack, these are bonds. I'll have to find out just what they're worth right now too." Once again, he started jotting down information. When he was done, Rafe gathered up both stacks of papers, put the rubber bands back over them the way Uncle Mack had had them, and tried not to let himself get too excited about any of it.

Then he pulled out the first of the cloth bags. It was heavy, like *really* heavy. Rafe peeked inside, and his eyes widened at the glint of silver from a lot of old coins. Rafe figured he could look them over later, and checked the other bags. The second one was even heavier and was filled with gold coins. "Damn, this is like a treasure hunt of some kind." The third and final bag was larger but lighter. At first he thought it was empty, but he pulled out a set of papers. No, not papers. They were letters—three of them. He glanced over them and saw that each one was addressed to Mack.

He opened the first one, read it over, then placed it aside. Then he smiled. Here, at last, was what Rafe had been looking for—a clue about his uncle's life. Thanks to these letters, he got the impression that his uncle hadn't always been alone, and that he had been loved, even if for a finite time. He glanced through the other two letters and found more of the same. They weren't outright love letters, but they were close, even if very carefully written. Once he was done, he folded the letters and put them back into the envelopes.

"More certificates?" Luther asked, but Rafe shook his head, happy with what he'd found. Somehow, his uncle wasn't so much of a stranger anymore. Then he tied the letters back up in the string and placed them aside to take with him.

The last thing inside the box was an envelope, pressed to the side. It had his name written on it in a slightly shaky hand. He pulled it out, then set everything back inside.

When he opened the envelope, Rafe was hoping for some sort of message from his uncle, but the papers inside just seemed to be an inventory of the items they had found in the box. The three letters were not listed. He showed Luther the note and then returned it to the box and went through the contents once again. "I guess I was hoping for more."

"More?" Luther asked incredulously. "You're kidding, right?"

"Not more wealth. But I was hoping to find something that would tell me more about my uncle. I mean, he was a saver and managed his money well, it seems, but there's very little here that tells me about who he was as a person." Well, except for those letters, of course. But overall, his uncle had left behind a house and a box with things in it—all the trappings of a life—but so far Rafe had found out very little about the man himself. And that was what Rafe wanted most. "I guess I was just looking for some reason why he left everything to me."

Luther smiled. "I'm sorry I don't have any answers for you." Rafe closed the lid on the box and stood, resting his hand on it. Maybe if he stayed there long enough, some vibrations would come through and give him what he wanted. "If you've been through the whole house, then…."

Rafe winced. "I haven't been through Uncle Mack's room. It sort of feels like I'm intruding." But that was likely the only place he'd find the answers he looked for. His uncle was a bit of a mystery, that was for damned sure.

"He's gone, and the house is yours." Luther got up and stood across the table from him. "You don't need to eradicate Mack from the house, but it's okay for you to change things so that it feels like your home now. That is, if you intend to stay."

"I do," Rafe said. "I want put down roots. But it's like I just stepped into someone else's life, and I can't figure shit out. Uncle Mack was a rancher, and yet he had stocks, bonds, and bags of silver and gold. God only knows how much all that is worth. And then there's the ranch itself, without a mortgage as far as we can tell. I mean, it's a huge amount of money. There was no way he'd have put all that together by simply raising a few hundred head of cattle over the years." What he'd found raised more questions than answers.

Luther shrugged. "Your uncle didn't go into detail about what he had. He kept his business private, at least from me." He packed his notes in his case and locked it, then called for Stacey. A few minutes later, Rafe had slid the box back into its place, the door closed and locked once more.

"Thank you for coming," Rafe told Luther.

"I'll be in touch just as soon as I find anything out," Luther said. "It won't take long."

Rafe headed back toward his truck, his mind racing. He had more questions rattling around in his head now than he'd had when he came in. The box had told him little about the man his uncle was. But those letters *had* told him something. And now, Rafe just had to find out what.

"I'M GOING out, so don't rub against me, okay?" Rafe told the dogs, who promptly ignored him. He had finished his chores and taken a shower, then put on his best jeans and shirt. He had thought of dressing up, but Russell seemed like a cowboy—even if he was a posh one. So he figured it was better to just be himself. Still, he didn't want to arrive covered in dog hair.

Over the past few days, he'd made some progress in going through the house, but he still hadn't had the heart to tackle his uncle's room. He'd found a few notes and a stack of comics in one of the desk drawers that made him laugh. It seemed Uncle Mack was a fan of *The Far Side*, just as he was. There had been hundreds of comics clipped out and piled in the drawer. Just the sight of them had made Rafe smile, so he'd left them there… for now. He knew he'd eventually have to clear out his uncle's things, but there was no rush. Rafe wasn't ready to remove all his uncle's belongings from the house. After all, he wanted to somehow find his uncle, not wipe him away.

Rafe checked the time and made sure the dogs had water before heading out to Russell's.

Rafe wasn't sure what he had been expecting when he first set eyes on the Banion place, but it sure as hell hadn't been this. The house was huge. On one level, it was impressive as hell, but it also fit into the landscape, as if the builder had wanted it to blend in rather than be ostentatious. Rafe had never seen anything like it.

He rang the bell and was surprised when Russell answered the door himself. With a place so big, he'd have expected Russell and his dad to have people who did that sort of thing.

"Come on in. Dad is just mixing up martinis. But if you'd rather have beer or something else, we have it." Russell shut the door behind him, and Rafe couldn't help noticing that Russell seemed a bit nervous. That was surprising—Russell didn't seem the type.

"A martini sounds good," Rafe said.

They walked into a great room, where Russell's dad was seated. Feeling a little ill at ease himself, Rafe was grateful when he was handed a glass. The drink might calm his nerves.

"Dad, this is Rafe, our new neighbor."

The older man held out his hand. "Elliott Banion. It's good to meet you, Rafe. Russell has told me some about you." He gestured for Rafe to take a seat, and Rafe made sure he didn't spill his drink as he took it. "Are you getting settled in?"

"As much as I can, I guess. The house isn't mine. Well, I suppose it is, but it's still Uncle Mack's, really." He sipped the drink, the gin going down smooth. "Did you know him well?"

Elliott nodded. "Going back almost forty years, I guess. That was when he came to this valley and put together that ranch of his. I met him shortly after. Your uncle kept to himself a lot of the time, but if someone needed help, he was always there. We had a fire here maybe ten years ago. It took out one of the barns. Your uncle was here the next day to help clear away the mess so we could rebuild. He and Russell were close. They used to fish together a lot of the time."

"Did it bother you that Mack was gay? Once my folks figured it out, I never saw him again."

Elliott narrowed his eyes. "What a man does in his own home is up to him. I never judged him, and when Russell told us that he liked bulls instead of cows, Mack was there to help him."

Russell nodded. "We all knew. At least I did. And when I got old enough to realize that I was gay too, Mack and I went fishing, and he told me the facts of gay cowboy life." Rafe leaned closer. "He said that you don't rub your business in other people's noses, and you don't talk about it or go marching in parades. But he also said that when I met the right person, that I needed to hold on to them. And if push came to shove, I had to be prepared to fight for the life I wanted. He told me that people will respect you if you did that, no matter what side of your bread you buttered." Russell smiled.

Rafe nodded. "Do you know if Mack ever found someone?" Those letters had gotten him thinking.

They were kind, gentle, but filled with heart if you read between the lines—love letters written by someone who was afraid of being caught.

Russell only shrugged, but Elliott nodded. "I think he did, some time ago. He started going into Denver every few weeks for a couple days. But then he just stopped." He shook his head. "The only reason I know this is because he'd asked if we'd look after things while he was gone." Elliott's eyes glazed over, and he seemed to lose himself in memories. "That was about twenty years ago. Why do you ask?"

The timing matched the letters. "My God," Rafe said as the pieces finally came together. "Twenty years ago. That was when everything changed for my family—the year I was twelve." He sighed as a clearer picture of what had happened—a broader one than he had known—came into focus. "Did either of you ever meet any of his friends?"

Russell leaned forward. "You found something," he probed.

Rafe found himself nodding before he could really think about it. "Maybe. But I think you're right," he said to Elliott, "and it's very possible it didn't end well." He shook his head. "I'm sorry. In trying to dig up parts of my uncle's life, I seem to have gotten a little buried myself."

He sipped the drink and hoped they let the subject drop. He wasn't really ready to talk about it yet—not until he'd learned more. "I really appreciate the invitation to dinner," Rafe said. "But more than that, I want to thank you both for all the help you gave me. You have no idea how much I appreciate it.

If there's ever something I can do to help you, just let me know."

Elliott leaned forward. "There is," he said plainly. "Don't fucking sell your place."

Rafe met his gaze. "To anyone other than you?" he asked. There had been too many people inquiring about his land, and it was time he found out where people stood.

"If you want to sell, I'd hope you'd come to us." Elliott smiled. "But you should keep it. Land remembers. I know it sounds dumb to you kids, but it has a memory, and your uncle put his blood and sweat into that place. It was his life, and he built it out of nothing at all. The entire ranch was nearly bone-dry when your uncle bought it. There was only a fork in a stream for water, and that Mack had to haul up every last drop."

"What happened?" Rafe asked, because that certainly wasn't the way things were now.

"Freak of nature," Russell said. "I remember that winter because Dad made me play inside the whole time—at least, it seemed that way. Avalanches happen up in the mountains, and that winter we had a ton of snow. I loved being outside. The snow was piled up everywhere, and I used to sneak out whenever I could, building forts and pummeling the ranch hands with snowballs." For a second Russell looked just like that naughty kid again. It was a shame Rafe had never visited his uncle's ranch in the winter. He and Russell could have been hellions together.

"An avalanche started high up, bringing down snow, then rock and debris. It was a real mess.

Nearly took out Mendeltom's house. It stopped maybe a hundred feet away." There was a little delight in Elliott's eyes. Rafe could understand; he was not a fan of either the guy either.

"At least it didn't take out his home," Rafe said.

"True, but it did something worse. It dammed up the water flow and created a small lake in the spring. When the water broke through, it created a new channel that left the old one high and dry. So the water now ran on Mack's property the way it does now. Mendeltom accused Mack of stealing his water and actually sued to try and get it back." Elliott rolled his eyes. "Didn't work. The courts laughed at the old jackass and sent him on his way. After that, Mendeltom did everything he could to convince your uncle to sell. For a while there I thought he was actually trying to drive him out. Mack got the police involved, and the harassment stopped."

"So Uncle Mack's place went from being small and hardscrabble to prosperous and having a lot of potential almost overnight."

Elliott nodded. "Mendeltom even went as far as to say that your uncle started the avalanche." Elliott finished the martini and set his glass aside. "That's the dumbest thing I ever heard. No fool would do that. An avalanche could take out half the valley if it happened just right." As if to punctuate his point, flakes of snow began to fall, fluttering down to the ground. "It's about fucking time."

"Dad…."

"We need snow, and the weatherman said we were going to get some. It's not too cold, and the wind is staying away, so a good snow will do us good. And it will help us come next summer." Elliott leaned forward. "Mendeltom and his kid don't get it, but everything is related. The snow we complain about in the winter feeds the streams and small lakes that sustain us all summer. A good snowfall also allows everything and everyone to rest for a while before spring arrives... and all the chores with it."

He shook his head in disgust. "What Mendeltom doesn't understand is that what he does on his ranch affects not only him, but the rest of us. The Banion cattle operation is run in a way that will sustain the land and the community around us. We have berms to keep field run-off out of the water supply. And we don't use chemicals that could possibly end up in the water or seep into the ground. Everything we do protects the land and this ranch so it can be passed to the next generation—and the one after that—better and more prosperous than we found it." Elliott sat back, and Rafe grinned.

"You should do commercials, because you sold me," Rafe teased. Elliott laughed, and Russell pointed at his dad.

"See, you missed your calling. Maybe you should think about it. You would do great as a spokesman for hemorrhoid cream, or maybe you could convince people to buy old-age insurance." He winked.

"Bullshit. I think I should be the face of Stetson or something like that." Elliott smiled and sat a little straighter. "Let's go eat before we have to swim through the bullshit you two are flinging to get there."

He left the room, and Russell was about to follow, but Rafe hung back.

"I like your dad," Rafe said. "He's something."

"That he is. Dad has always had the cowboy 'tell the truth even if it hurts' thing down pat." He motioned toward the other room, but Rafe stood still, a little lost in Russell's eyes. "Is there something wrong?"

Rafe shook his head. "Just that sometimes I'm a little slow to pick up on things." He stepped closer. "I really appreciate the way you and your men helped me out. It was way beyond neighborly, and I've been trying to think of a way to thank you." The heat around him grew more intense by the second.

"And what did you come up with?" Russell asked, his tongue darting along the edge of his lips.

Rafe swallowed hard. "I wanted to do something personal." He reached out and slid a hand along Russell's neck. When he didn't pull away, Rafe drew him closer before tilting his head slightly. Russell came nearer, and Rafe closed the distance between them, just touching his lips. Fuck, he really didn't know how to do something like this. Fucking he could do; sucking, yes; everything else sexual—that was in his wheelhouse. But just kissing another guy? That was something he didn't have much experience with.

Russell ran his hand over Rafe's, holding his arm, and deepened the kiss, pressing more firmly, his tongue slipping lightly along Rafe's lips. The heat continued building, and Rafe so badly wanted to crush himself against Russell, to hold him, hell, to take him to a quiet room and touch and taste firsthand what he felt through his jeans. But they were in Russell's home, so Rafe pulled back. The last thing he wanted was to lose control.

"That was the best thank-you I've had in a long time," Russell whispered.

"Cool. Because I had thought about sending a card or writing you a note, but I don't think either would have had the same impact," Rafe said, smiling. Russell rolled his eyes but remained standing close. So close it took all of Rafe's willpower not to kiss him again.

"Are you two going to come on in for dinner, or just stand there ogling each other until the food gets cold?"

"Dad…." Russell sounded like a teenager. Then he turned to Rafe. "Come on. Let's go eat before Violet gets upset. She's the best cook in the state, and she hates it if her food gets cold. Believe me, we don't want to upset her."

"But she's the cook," Rafe said. Clearly there was something he was missing.

"She's also one of the most amazing ladies I've ever met. I used to hide out in her kitchen when I was in trouble. She'd give me milk and cookies and listen to me. By the time I left, she'd told me why I was wrong and helped me figure out how to make it right. My mother always knew where to find me at times like that, and yet she left me alone because she knew that somehow Violet would straighten me out."

"Sounds like you're lucky to have her," Rafe said, following Russell into the eat-in area of the large kitchen. He had passed a huge dining area with enough room for twenty people, and yet he somehow knew that this table, big enough for six, was the true heart of this home.

"I know you men like your steaks," Violet said as she set a platter on the table. "I also found some fresh vegetables at the market. So don't just eat meat." She glared at Elliott for a few seconds. "And I made a salad."

Elliott rolled his eyes but tried to pass the salad on without taking any.

"Dad, you know what the doctor said." Russell handed him back the bowl, and he added some salad to his plate, as well as a huge steak.

"Mr. Elliott," Violet said, her hands on her ample hips, a twinkle in her eyes. "How am I supposed to keep you around until I'm old enough to retire if all you eat is red meat?"

"We're both plenty old enough to retire and you know it," Elliott countered before pointing at the empty chair. "Now, sit on down and have some dinner with us. You made plenty. Always do." But she stepped away.

"She always eats on her own. She says she shouldn't be eating at the table with the family," Russell said quietly. "Even after all this time, she still stands on formality."

"Please join us," Rafe said to her. "You can tell me stories about Russell when he was a child."

She looked like she was going to turn away, but then grinned. "That boy never stopped moving, let me tell you." Finally she pulled out the empty chair, and Russell practically jumped up to get her a plate and silverware. "He would run all day long, from dawn until nightfall. You could always find him either in the stables or the kitchen."

"Me too," Rafe said, meeting Russell's gaze and his soft smile. "Mom said I had hollow legs."

"You were growing boys. Of course you did." She took a steak and then some of the potatoes, as if she really wasn't thinking about it, then ate a few bites. "Has he told you about the time he decided to make his mother cookies for Mother's Day?" She grinned.

"Those were good cookies. Mama loved them," Russell protested.

She smiled indulgently. "He was nine and wanted to make cookies for her. He got the recipe and mixed everything together. Then he made the cookies and put them on the pan. The only thing he let me do was put them in the oven for him. Then the little stinker shooed me out of the kitchen. The thing was, he misread the recipe and put the cookies in the oven for an hour. Then he left the kitchen, and I came back to smoke pouring out of the oven."

Russell was aghast. "That didn't happen."

"It surely did. But he was so proud of making something for his mama that I whipped up a batch from his recipe, threw out the burned ones, and…."

"Violet," Elliott said, trying not to laugh. "You let him think your cookies were his."

She shrugged. "They were for his mama. What was I supposed to do, let him serve her burned crumbs? No, sir. But I didn't let him cook in my kitchen again until he was old enough to know better."

Russell sat still, his mouth hanging open. "No way."

"You were nine. And it all worked out. You were happy, your mom was happy, and the entire kitchen didn't burn down."

Rafe turned away, trying to hide his laughter. Russell still looked skeptical, and Elliott just smiled. "Russell was lucky to have someone who cared so much," Rafe said once he pulled himself together, tapping Russell's foot under the table. "I didn't have that."

"Didn't your mom bake?" Violet asked.

"If it was for a church bake sale or to raise money for missionaries, then Mom would give it a try, though usually she just bought something to donate. She was never very domestic when it came to cooking." His mother had been more of a menace than a master in the kitchen. "She was always busy doing other things. When the church needed her to lead a prayer circle or to stand in during Bible study, she was there before the minister even knew he needed her. But when I fell and broke my arm at school, it took hours for the school nurse to track her down." Rafe didn't have happy memories of cookies and baking. "What else did Russell do?"

"I think we've heard enough embarrassing stories about me as a kid," Russell pronounced.

Elliott set down his fork and turned to Rafe. "Did you always want to be a rodeo cowboy? I watched you win the world championships. That was one amazing ride."

"I used to watch rodeo all the time when I was a kid. Mom hated it, but Dad liked it, and he used to let me watch on the sly when Mom wasn't home. I'd been around horses at Uncle Mack's, of course, but I never dreamed I'd be able to compete. All that changed when, well... my life changed." He took a few bites and wondered why everything seemed to come back to that one point in time. Even a conversation about his big toe could somehow wind its way around to the moment his parents had turned their backs on him when they found out who he was. It had been years ago. In a few years, it would be half his life ago, and yet everything still seemed to revolve around it. "Anyway.... Dinner is amazing, Violet."

"Thank you," she said quietly, almost drawing into herself, as if she had just become aware of what she'd done in joining them for dinner. Rafe watched the others as they continued eating, but Violet seemed to grow more uncomfortable.

"You know you've always been part of this family," Elliott said, seeming to sense her discomfort.

"I know you think so, and I'm grateful for it, I really am." She set down her fork. "But you know my niece, the one who went back east? Well, she's asked me to come live with her because she needs help."

"I know that Coreen was having difficulty getting around. Is her leg giving her problems?"

"Yes, and she's afraid she won't be able to manage alone in her apartment. I really don't want to leave, but she's the only family I have. Her firm is going through some issues right now as well, so, she's worried about almost everything. It's a lot for someone to handle on her own."

Russell set down his fork. "She's a CPA, right?"

Violet nodded. "Top of her class in business school."

"Then ask her to call me. The person who heads up my accounting department is leaving, and I was about to advertise for someone to replace her. Coreen sounds like she might just be the answer to my problem. If she's interested, she can either telecommute or move out here to be closer to you." He drank from his glass of water, then went back to eating. Rafe, on the other hand, simply took in what had just happened and stored it away.

Once dinner was done, Violet cleared the table, and Elliott headed outside, probably to the barn. Rafe joined Russell in the great room in front of the fireplace. "Just wondering…. Did you offer Coreen a job just to keep Violet?"

"No. Violet is a member of the family, and she would be hard to replace. But if that was what she wanted to do, I'd hug her and wish her well. Coreen is exactly the type of person I need, and if I can help both of them as well as myself…." He shrugged. "I try to run my company the way we run the ranch. I pay well, but I try to make sure that anyone who works with me fits into the company and that we fit into their lives too. I employ people all over the country. And I have a small office in town that you'd pass by a dozen times before you realized it was even there. Some folks work all night and sleep during the day. One woman's husband is an ER doctor, so she works the same schedules he does so they can be together. If we can help Coreen and she can help us, then that's what we'll do." He put his feet up on the ottoman to get comfortable. "Violet is family, and that's what family does."

Not my family. Rafe kept his feelings to himself. He didn't need to go back there again. Still, it was nice to see a family who actually cared about each other. "You have a strong sense of what's right and wrong."

"Don't you?" Russell asked.

Rafe got the impression that this question was a test of sorts, and he wondered how he should answer. If he was honest, then it was possible that Russell wouldn't want to have anything to do with him. But he'd never been any other way.

"I believe in honesty, in doing the right thing. But the kind of ideals that you have? I've never been able to afford those." He set his glass on the table and stared into the flames. "You know that I was turned away by my family. I had nothing other than what I had in a bag I could carry and the few dollars that I had saved so I could afford to put gas in my car. That was it. Everything else was taken away."

"And you found the rodeo," Russell supplied in his easygoing way, as though he had the answers and was content in them.

Rafe swallowed and nodded. "After about six months. Up until then, I worked a few odd jobs. When you're hungry and cold, you'll work hard to survive." And Rafe had done just that. He'd made it through and eventually found the rodeo, which had saved his life in many ways, including giving him a job.

"Your parents left you that desperate? How could they?" Russell asked. "What kind of fucking people were they?"

When Rafe turned back to look at Russell, he saw fire in those usually calm blue eyes. "Ones who wanted me to bend to their will. I hadn't guessed before then that their love was conditional on me being exactly what they expected. Anything different wasn't tolerated. And like everyone else I ran into before joining the rodeo, they had a price for their affections."

"My God... I...," Russell stammered. "I know that a lot of gay kids have family issues, and I was lucky—I know that. But I never dreamed that anyone would have to do... what you did to survive."

"And I was luckier than most. I worked the jobs that I could and found the rodeo before I got in too deep and it cost me my health and what little self-respect I had left. I got even luckier in that I was good at riding and soon started to win. Then there was money coming in, and I was able to build a life that didn't include back rooms and the stuff that came with it." He couldn't believe he'd told Russell all of this. Rafe had spent more than the past decade trying to forget all about it. But he was proud of the fact that he'd not only survived, but thrived. He had built a new life for himself, one that didn't require his parents' approval or support. In fact, they were the ones coming to *him* now.

"I don't know if I'd call that luck. But you were resourceful and damned strong. I don't know if I could have done what you did. My life has been damn near perfect compared to yours. I had everything I could ever want. Hell, Dad even bought me my first pony when I was five years old."

"My mother bought me puzzles based on Bible stories."

"I had my own boots and hat, and Dad taught me to ride almost as soon as I could walk," Russell said.

Rafe nodded. "I was lucky to have Uncle Mack. I first learned to ride when I visited him. But when Mom learned that he was gay, those visits stopped. After that, I only got to hang around horses when I hung out with my friend Archie. His mom and mine were friends of a sort. I'd go over there when Mom was busy. She wasn't a church lady like my mother, but they got along… even if Mom thought she was a heathen." He smiled. "All I can say is, thank God for heathens."

"Yeah, I guess." Russell raised his glass, and Rafe did the same, clinking them.

"Here's to the worst toast in history."

Russell sipped his drink and then set the glass aside. He stood and walked in front of Rafe's chair, placing his hands on the arms before leaning closer. "Maybe. But there are other ways to toast the important things in life. One of them just happens to be the fact that you survived and are here now, in one piece."

"More or less," Rafe deadpanned.

"Considerably more," Russell told him. "Our pasts only make us what we are today. The baggage we take along with us is our choice." He held Rafe's gaze. "It's like a damned suitcase, and all we need to do is let go. Leave it behind and let airport security dispose of it."

"That's easy for you to say…."

Russell stiffened. "Don't think for a minute that you're alone in having pain in your past. It comes with being alive." He leaned forward and kissed Rafe hard enough to press him back in the chair. Rafe wound his arms around Russell's neck and deepened the kiss. Damn, the man tasted like heaven, and Rafe wanted to get as much as he could. Before Rafe was ready, Russell pulled back, his gaze warm, breath lingering over Rafe's still damp lips. "And so does that. Pleasure and happiness are part of life too, and maybe you have to let go of one so you can have a chance at the other."

Russell held his gaze, and Rafe blinked, wondering if Russell was talking about Rafe or himself. Maybe the sentiment had been meant for both of them.

Chapter 6

STILL HOLDING Rafe's gaze, Russell smiled. Then, slowly, he sat back down.

Russell's heart pounded in his ears. He needed a few minutes to get ahold of himself.

Kissing Rafe had been incredible, and he wanted to do it again. But he wasn't sure he was ready. His experience with Jase was never far from his mind. Still, as his father had said, Rafe wasn't Jase. And if Russell was ever going to open up to someone, he had a feeling it would be Rafe. Still, he didn't want to jump into anything. "How did it go at the bank earlier? Did you take care of everything?"

"Yes. Luther and I went through Uncle Mack's safe-deposit box. It was interesting…. Another thing I found interesting? It seems my lawyer and one of the bankers have eyes only for each other."

"Luther and Stacey?" Russell said. "Yeah, those two have been dancing around each other for the past few years. From what I hear, Luther just won't start the engine… or something."

"It seems neither one of them is ready. Either that, or they don't have the courage to take the leap." The way Rafe said that made Russell wonder if Rafe was talking about him. But that was stupid—they had just met each other.

"Anyway," Rafe continued, "I found some surprises in Uncle Mack's box today." He leaned forward. "Uncle Mack had gold and silver—a lot of it—as well as a large number of stocks—important ones, it seems—as well as bonds. Luther is checking them out for me. If all of them are still good, there's a great deal of money there."

"Makes sense. Your uncle saved and invested." Russell wasn't sure why Rafe seemed jittery.

"But where did it come from? Yeah, he had the ranch and he probably lived simply, but still, that's a lot of money—possibly too much money—for someone to have just... saved." He lowered his voice. "I mean, the bag of gold coins weighed at least twenty pounds. That alone is a shit ton of money. I looked it up, and a pound of gold is worth a small fortune. I guess what's bothering me is... where did Uncle Mack get it all?"

Russell was surprised, to say the least. Mack never acted like he had anywhere near that kind of money behind him. Maybe that was why Russell had liked him so much.

"There were also letters in the box," Rafe continued. "And it looks like your dad was right about Mack having someone in his life." Rafe left the room and went back to the foyer, where he'd left his coat. A few minutes later, he returned with a sheaf of papers.

"I brought these with me on the off chance that you'd want to see them. I know you and Uncle Mack were close." He placed them in Russell's hands as if they were precious.

Russell opened each letter and read the contents carefully. The letters were long—the first one included several paragraphs about the writer's life in Denver. But near the end, Russell's eye stopped. He read the final paragraph again.

I'm looking forward to your visit on Friday, and I have some special things planned for us to do. The house will be all aglow as I wait for your return. Drive carefully. I'll be watching for you.

The letter was signed Dale.

"There's nothing overt here. It was as if this Dale was expecting someone to be reading this," Russell said as he went through the next letter. The tone in this one was more urgent, the sentences clipped and anxious, with little of the description he'd included in the first missive.

I need you to come and soon. Please. You're the only one who can help me. Your visits mean so much to me. As always, I'll be watching for you. Come as soon as you can.

Russell blinked a few times. He could almost feel the anxiety behind the words. Shaking his head, he picked up the final note. This one was short, but the words in it tore at his heart.

It's sometimes hard to put words on paper, but I'm going to try. Thank you for your last visit. Our time together is precious, especially because I know that it will have to end soon. Neither of our families will allow it. And when they find out, there will be trouble. Being honest is the best course of action, but honesty about this comes at a price that I don't think either one of us is willing, or able, to pay. I will look forward to your one last visit, and once it is over, I will hold it close to me forever.

This note, like the others, was simply signed Dale.

"Look at the dates," Rafe said. "Each one was written about a month apart, fourteen years ago—the same year I turned twelve."

Russell folded the letters and handed them back to Rafe. "I don't know what to say, but I have to agree with you. I think there's something to this."

"Do you have any idea who this Dale might be?" Rafe asked. "I've thought back to the men Uncle Mack had working at the ranch when I was a kid, but I don't remember anyone named Dale."

"I don't remember a Dale either. But I think that by the time I got to know Mack really well, Dale would have already been in Denver." He thought back to the talks he used to have with Mack. Never once did Mack mention someone named Dale. Of course, those talks had been more about Russell than Mack.

"Well, I guess the only thing to do is to go through Uncle Mack's things and see if there are any answers there." Rafe held the arm of the chair. "I was wondering…. Would you like to do it with me? You were close to him too. And if we come across anything that's important to you, you could let me know."

Russell nodded. There were a few things he'd
love to have, things that would remind him of Mack
and the hours they'd spent together. "In the living
room, there's a horse statue on one of the shelves.
I gave it to him for his sixty-fifth birthday. He and
I had it commissioned from an artist in town. It's of
Chaucer, one of his horses, and...."

"Of course," Rafe said gently. "Come over tomorrow and we can sort things out. You can take the
statue home with you."

"Tomorrow I'm heading out to Los Angeles. I'll
only be there a few days. I should be back by this
weekend."

Rafe nodded. "Sure. That will work. Let me
know, and I can make us some dinner. It won't be
as good as Violet's, but I'm a passable cook when I
have to be."

Elliott strode into the room, lit the fire that had
been laid, and lowered himself into one of the other
chairs. The kindling took hold and started to crack-
le, filling the room with warmth. "What are you two
talking about?" he asked gruffly.

"Mack. Just sharing stories," Russell said. He
didn't want to mention the contents of the letters.
Rafe had only shown them to him, so he figured it
was privileged information. "Do you have any?"

Elliott got back up and walked over to the bar
cart, where he poured three glasses of whiskey and
handed them around. Then he added more wood to
the fire and sat back down. "I got plenty. But first,
you need to know that Mack was a cowboy. Period. Nothing else matters. Mack went out with his

boots on—that matters too. The rest is just gossip for people who have nothing better to do." Elliott raised his glass and then belted this drink back. Russell and Rafe did the same. Elliot turned to Rafe. "Your uncle lived by the cowboy code, and I suspect that was what drove him to tell the family the truth about himself."

Russell had a pretty good idea now that there was more to it, but he'd let his father think what he wanted. He certainly couldn't argue with his father's sentiment.

"Not that it mattered in the end. Mack wanted to live an honest life and was willing to pay the consequences. I admired him for that. There were times when we sat together at the kitchen table, talking. One time he told me that he questioned whether it had been worth it. That was after he'd had more than a few of these." Elliott held up his glass, and Russell took the opportunity to refill it, remembering that real cowboys drank whiskey, and usually more than one.

"What did he decide, do you think?" Rafe asked.

Russell's dad turned back to Rafe, his expression serious. "He told me that his only regret was you. The rest of the family wasn't worth the powder it would take to blow them up, but you were the one he missed. So maybe it's fitting that he left it all to you. Maybe it was his way of trying to reconnect."

"Rafe, I've been wondering. Why didn't you try to get in touch with him after you left home?" Russell was more than a little curious. But he covered his expression by getting up and adding more wood to the fire.

"I tried, but I never got an answer back," Rafe said softly.

Russell let the topic go. It was pretty clear that Rafe was as confused as he was. He'd been lied to so much over the years and probably had no idea what was true and what wasn't. But he believed Rafe was telling the truth. Everything about Rafe told him that he'd cared for his uncle. Russell just wished that things had been different… for both Rafe and Mack. Maybe their lives would have been less lonely.

"Shit happens," Elliott added.

"Real poetic, Dad. Maybe you should take up writing bumper stickers. Oh wait, someone already did." He smiled.

"Don't be a little shit," his dad replied with a smile, the way he always did. "Things happen. I remember when I was dating this one's mother." He motioned in Russell's direction. "She was something else. I'd been after her for two months to go out with me, but I couldn't get her to give me the time of day. Finally I wrote her a letter telling her how I felt. But somehow she never got it. I don't know why, but she never did. And that cost me months because I thought she was embarrassed and not interested. And it was all because of a mix-up with the mail. It happens all the time. So if you sent Mack something and he never responded, then maybe he didn't get it, or maybe you never got his response. But something must have happened. Why else would Mack have left you everything?"

"I'm still trying to figure that out," Rafe said.

"Maybe we'll find something on Saturday once I get back."

Rafe just nodded, obviously lost in thought.

THE THREE of them talked for an hour or more, sharing stories about Mack. Even Rafe was able to add a few tales about the times he'd spent with his uncle. Rafe stopped drinking after two, while Elliott continued with the whiskey until Russell had to help him off to bed.

When he returned a few minutes later, he walked over to the wall of windows and looked out into the darkness, seeing the mountains jet black against the starry sky. "I love this view, day or night," Russell admitted, then strode over to the sofa and sat down. Rafe joined him.

"Have you ever thought of leaving?" Rafe asked. "I know the ranch is here, but you could move your business anywhere. Wouldn't it be easier if you were in a city somewhere?"

Russell nodded. "At one point, I considered it. I wanted to see the world. But then I'd come back here and look out that window at the mountains—my mountains. I used to wonder what the world looked like from up there, so I went to see." He smiled and turned to Rafe.

"What did you find?" Rafe whispered.

"I hiked up to the very top and saw the valley sprawled out below me. And my gaze went right to this ranch, this land. What I saw was home." He leaned slightly against Rafe. As one of the logs popped, Russell slipped his arm around Rafe's shoulder and drew him closer.

"I think I'm starting to understand how that feels," Rafe said. "I've been on the move with the rodeo for years and never gave much thought to settling down." Russell turned and found Rafe looking back at him, his gaze searching. "Then out of the blue…." Rafe drew Russell closer, and the heat level in the room intensified. Russell's eyes closed as Rafe's lips touched his.

For a second, Russell wondered if Mack had ever had this kind of moment. He felt so alive, so overwhelmed by Rafe—his taste, his scent. He pressed forward, pushing Rafe back against the cushions, and instinct took over.

But then, as if realizing what he was doing, Russell pulled back slightly. As much as he wanted Rafe right now, this wasn't a good idea. He'd rushed into things before, and if he wanted a different result this time, maybe he needed to look at his own behavior. Besides, Rafe was just finding his feet. Taking things too quickly might unbalance him, and that was the last thing Russell wanted.

Slowly he backed away and let Rafe sit back up. "You make me forget myself," Russell whispered. Then he stood and walked over to stoke the fire, taking a second to get his racing pulse under control. A few minutes later, he sat back down and put his feet up, pulling Rafe close once more.

"I know how you feel," Rafe said, his voice rough. Neither of them moved, the fire casting light that danced through the room. "I hate to leave, but I should probably get home." Rafe didn't, though, and Russell was reluctant to break the moment.

The fire had burned down to embers before Rafe shifted. Russell stood up and got Rafe's coat before showing him to the door.

"Thank you for dinner." He smiled slightly. "I'm glad Uncle Mack had good people who cared about him." Rafe leaned down to kiss him and then stepped out into the snowy night.

Russell watched him through the windows and then turned out the lights before heading to bed himself. He had to get up early if he was going to make his planned flight—the helicopter was picking him up just before eight in the morning. Still, once in bed, Russell didn't sleep very much. Thoughts of Rafe filled his mind.

The man sure as hell could get his motor running. And when Rafe kissed him, Russell never wanted to let go. But then his insecurities got the better of him, and he realized he wasn't quite ready to hold on either.

"YOU NEED to get your butt out of bed," his dad grumbled from the doorway to his suite. The space had started as his room when he'd been a kid, but Russell had taken over the room next door as well and had opened up the wall between them.

"I didn't get in until almost midnight," he groaned, pushing back the covers. "We had to wait for the weather to clear in Denver." He pushed back the covers but didn't move. He was completely worn out. All he wanted to do was sleep.

"Violet has coffee and pecan rolls in the kitchen," his dad said. He knew from experience how to entice Russell out of bed. "Was the trip at least productive?"

"Yes. I got a national beef producer on board and spoke to the rep for one of the largest ranches in the nation. And while I was there, I secured another contract for our beef at amazing prices with that same producer. They will take all we can give them." He sat up, scratching his head lightly.

"So you've sold all we can produce," his dad said with a smile. "That's damned fine."

Russell sighed and stretched, trying to get a kink out of his back. Then he stood and pulled on his robe. "No, Dad. I've sold enough that we can expand and sell that as well. What I sold gives us room for guaranteed growth."

"But we're nearly at what the land can support already."

"I know. But I have a few feelers out. I was thinking of seeing if Rafe would lease us some of his land. A lot of it has been sitting fallow for a long time, so it should be very productive. We could graze on some of it and use the rest to grow feed. I also have my eye on the Brompton ranch. John and his wife have been talking about retiring." He pulled his robe tighter around him to keep the cold at bay. This room was always chilly, no matter what they did. "I was wondering if you'd talk to them, see if they're interested in selling. They could keep the house and be free to travel to their heart's content."

"And we'd get another five thousand acres." His dad smiled. "Okay. I'll stop by in the next few days. But is that kind of outlay going to stress us?"

Russell shook his head. "No, Dad. I already worked things out with the bank. Our line of credit is free and clear. Everything has been paid."

His dad gaped at him. "You mean there is no mortgage anymore?"

"That's right. We're solvent. The company has been doing really well and has been generating ex- cess cash. So I used it to take care of our debts. Now we can buy whatever we need without worrying about it." He was pretty pleased with himself. That mortgage had been hanging over his father's head for a long time.

"And now, since you got me up, I might as well get dressed. I think I have time for coffee before I have to head out to Rafe's."

Russell hated to admit to himself just how badly he wanted to see Rafe again. In fact, through hours of meetings, he'd often found himself drifting off, thinking about the way Rafe had looked at him. More than once, he'd needed a glass of water to cool himself down.

"Good. Go have some fun."

Russell rolled his eyes. "I'm helping him go through some of Mack's things. I don't expect this to be a party."

"No. But I'm not blind. The snow has finally stopped, and the sun is trying to come out. Go help him with Mack's things and then go for a ride or something. Get out, have fun." Sometimes his father was so transparent. "Whatever you're afraid of, just let it go."

Russell narrowed his gaze. "You found out something. What did the doctor say?" He should have known.

"I'm fine. I need to change my diet and eat more greens and shit like that. Less meat. But he said that I'm going to be okay. It wasn't cancer, and I didn't have a heart attack or a stroke. Just a bout of bad indigestion. So I need to eat better." He huffed. "I already told Violet, and she smirked at me."

"What about Coreen?" Russell asked, his mind already whirring with what he needed to do. "Does Violet want to leave?"

"Apparently Coreen is going to call you. So we'll see." With that, his dad left the room.

Russell got dressed, then went downstairs and had breakfast, with plenty of coffee to get him moving. Finally he hopped into his truck and made his way over to Rafe's.

The dogs greeted him like a long-lost friend, and he doled out pets and scratches before they raced off to the barn, where Rafe emerged.

"You made it back," he said with a smile.

"I would have called, but I got back so late," Russell told him. "I messaged you but didn't get an answer, so I took a chance and came over."

"I'm glad you did. My phone fell out of my pocket and one of the horses stepped on it." He motioned to the house, and Russell followed him, glad he had sunglasses on. Snow blindness was a real thing, and Russell knew he'd have to let his eyes adjust once they got inside.

"How are you managing otherwise?" Russell asked.

"Really well. I've finished up some more chores. And your people came to take the cattle I wanted to sell. They were very professional and efficient. Everybody really knew their jobs."

"I'm glad to hear it. We try to hire the best," Russell said. His father had a real knack for finding the right people. He was in charge of the ranch and cattle transportation. They had developed their own fleet of cattle transport years ago to cut costs, and since then it had turned into a profitable side business.

The light began to dim as more clouds moved in. Rafe led the way to the back door and they went inside. The dogs followed, shaking off the snow, then checked out their dishes before making themselves comfortable in a pile near the fireplace.

"I figured that was where Mack kept a bed for them."

"Yeah, he did, though they tended to sleep near him at night. He told me that sometimes there was barely room for him in bed." Russell snickered at Rafe's expression. Clearly he'd found that out himself.

"I brought out a box and some packing material," Rafe said, pointing to the sculpture. "If you want to pack it up now, it'll be ready when it's time for you to go." He half smiled as his shoulders drooped. "I keep thinking about what we're about to do. I want to find some answers, and yet it feels wrong to be going through my uncle's things."

"They are your things now. And the sooner we start, the sooner it'll be done. Then you can make decisions about what you want to do." He took off his coat and boots and left them near the door to dry, then followed Rafe down the hall. He paused outside Mack's closed door, as if preparing himself for what he'd find.

When Rafe finally opened the door, Russell inhaled the remnants of Mack's awful aftershave. Apparently he had used the stuff for years. And maybe it was time, or just his memories, but somehow it didn't smell as bad as he'd always thought it did. "We can start with the closet," Rafe said.

"Good idea." He held back, letting Rafe direct things.

"I bought some large plastic bags for the clothes and other things I'll want to donate to the thrift store in town. Uncle Mack seemed to be smaller than me. If there's something you want, let me know, okay?" Rafe seemed a little lost.

"I will. And we need to decide where to put the things you'll want to keep," Russell said. "Maybe on the bed?"

Rafe nodded and began pulling out clothes. Russell folded them and placed them in a bag. It turned out to be an effective system—Russell folding dozens of shirts and jeans and adding them in the donation bag while Rafe pulled out everything Mack had kept in his closet. The underwear and socks from his dresser went into a bag they'd set out for trash, as did some shirts that had seen better days.

Finally they got through everything Mack had had hanging up. Russell carried the donation bags out of the room and set them by the back door, along with a full bag of trash. He put on his boots and ran the bags out to this truck. It had started to snow, so once he was back inside he kicked off his boots before returning to the room, where Rafe sat on the edge of the bed.

"What is it?" Russell asked.

"I was going through the boxes on the top of the closet. Most were shoes, but I found this...." He opened an old Buster Brown box, probably from the eighties or nineties. It had clearly been around for a while.

"What is it?"

"These are the cards and things I sent my uncle." He pulled out some Christmas and Easter ones from their envelopes. "He did get them. My mom and dad didn't know I'd sent them. They'd told me he was sick, so I sent get-well cards too." He lowered his gaze, shaking his head. "They're all here, and so are the return letters he sent me." Rafe held up envelope after envelope, all with Return to Sender.

"You didn't forget him," Russell said, placing his hand on Rafe's shoulder. "He knew that. You kept sending cards even though you didn't get a response. If you ask me, that's probably why he left his estate to you."

Rafe opened one of the earliest cards. A pair of twenty-dollar bills fluttered to the floor. Rafe left them there and read the card. Then he scooped up the bills, put them back inside the card, and placed it in the envelope before setting the entire box aside. "At least that answers one question. He did get the cards I sent him, and he tried to answer me."

"You never saw anything from him?" Russell asked.

Just then, a bang sounded on one of the doors. It repeated, and Rafe set the box aside and left the room. Russell finished up folding the last of the clothes to donate.

"What do you want now?" Rafe's voice traveled through the house. The edge to it sparked Russell's curiosity, so he followed the voices into the kitchen, where an older version of Rafe stood next to a woman who had to be Rafe's mother.

"We're your parents—you owe us. It's only fair," she said, her lips pinched as though it pained her to say anything. "Do you have any idea how hard it is for us to come here to ask… someone like you… for this?" she added, sending Russell's blood pressure soaring. He stepped into the room, and Rafe turned to look at him. It took every ounce of willpower Russell had to keep silent. But it wasn't his place to get between them.

"Then leave," Rafe said. "You gave up any right to ask for anything—or to even come here—when you kicked me out of your lives."

"We just wanted you to get some help. But you refused. We had no other choice," Rafe's mother said, seeming close to tears.

"Yeah, right. I was supposed to go somewhere to make myself acceptable to you. To be the son you wanted. But you know what? That's bullshit. I knew it then and I know it now. You're both just too small-minded to even consider you might not be right about everything. But that isn't my problem— it's yours. I'm gay, and I'm also the world champion bull rider. I made something of myself, no thanks to either of you. I did it all on my own."

"You didn't get any of this on your own," Rafe's father snapped.

"Actually, I think I might have. I kept writing to Uncle Mack, sending cards and letters to him, even after you ostracized him. And I just discovered that he sent some to me too. Only you sent them back. Well, I have them now, and in a weird way, I'm getting to know my uncle, even if it's late. I'm also learning even more about what pieces of crap my parents are."

The slap reverberated through the room like a clap of thunder. "I will not tolerate that," Rafe's mother said, pulling her hand back to strike him again. But Rafe caught it this time.

"Don't try it, old lady. Hit me again and I'll break your wrist." He tossed away her arm like it was something that stunk. "Now, I need you to get the hell out of here. You are not welcome here. And if you show up again, I'll have the sheriff escort you away." The anger in the room welled like a black mass as Rafe opened the door. "Leave. You walked away from Mack and did the same to me. You have no place here."

"Your father and I did what was right."

"And so am I," Rafe said, pushing his father out the door.

His mother crossed her arms over her chest. "I'm not leaving." Her eyes burned with enough hatred to warm the outside. Russell felt it from where he stood.

Rafe shrugged. "Russell, call the sheriff and tell him we need him to take care of a few trespassers." He turned and winked. "Or better yet, go get Mack's gun."

At that, his mother blanched and finally backed away. "You aren't the son we raised," she snapped.

Rafe smiled. "Of course I am. I'm just like you—heartless, uncaring, and selfish. You two will get nothing from me. Uncle Mack called you out in his will and specifically said that you were to get nothing. Do you hear that? *Nothing.* And I intend to honor his wishes."

Rafe and his mother stood glaring at each other. When she still didn't move, Rafe turned to Russell again. "Russell, please get the gun." She flinched and finally turned and walked away. Rafe slammed the door behind her.

Once Rafe's parents were gone, the dogs wandered in, all nuzzling to get close to Rafe. "I'm glad you stayed away," he said, petting each of them. "It was safer for you not to be here. Besides, if any of you had bitten them, their bitterness would have left a bad taste in your mouth."

The dogs followed him as he headed back toward the bedroom. When Russell joined him, the dogs had all flopped on the bed, and they stayed there as he and Rafe went back to work.

A FEW hours later, Russell was almost finished putting the last load of bags in the truck. Most were things to be given away. It suddenly hit Russell just how much of a person's life ended up in the trash or a donation bin after they died. Still, there was a lot that remained.

"What are you going to do with the rest?" Russell asked. It seemed that Mack had kept a lot of things over the years. They'd found several shoeboxes filled with all kinds of things at the top of the closet, behind the clothes, and even under the bed. They set them aside for Rafe to go through later.

"I'm not sure. I'll know better when I see what's there."

Russell shooed the dogs off the bed and stripped it to the mattress, which seemed brand-new. He found fresh bedding and remade it, then brought in Rafe's pillows. "You might as well use this room. It has a bigger bed." Once he was finished, they put all the boxes in the extra bedroom. "The dresser is empty."

"But this is still Uncle Mack's room," Rafe said.

"No. This is your house now, and you need to make it yours." Russell approached Rafe, holding his gaze. "This is your life and your home. Mack left it for you, and he would want you to make yourself comfortable. So I suggest you do that." Russell hated that Rafe seemed so tentative. "You're a damned bull rider, and yet you're scared to make this place your own?"

"It feels like I'm erasing Uncle Mack," Rafe told him. "And I didn't get the chance to know him that well. The last thing I want is for him to disappear." He shook his head. "This doesn't have anything to do with being brave. I want to know where I come from. I know who my parents are…. Hell, you do too, now. You saw them today in all their glory."

"You aren't going to erase Mack by living in the house." Russell gently removed the picture of a very young Rafe from the wall. "Because he's still here. And a part of you has always been here too. See that smile and those eyes? I'd know them anywhere. And so did Mack, because he kept this picture close. And just like the picture, part of him will remain here too."

"I guess." Rafe took the picture and set it aside. "After I figured out why my parents had turned away from Mack, I couldn't help wondering if he ever found someone who accepted him, who loved him. And thanks to those letters, I'm pretty sure he had someone in his life. Maybe that was how the family found out about the two of them. Maybe that was why they rejected him. The timing adds up. But I can't help feeling there's more to the story."

Russell drew Rafe into an embrace. "Sometimes it takes time for all the pieces of a puzzle to come together. Rushing it isn't going to help."

"I see," Rafe whispered as Russell stroked his cheek. "But it seems that someone here is growing impatient… maybe even rushing a little bit." Rafe grinned that wicked smile of his. "Not that I'm complaining, but are you sure about this?"

Russell drew closer, sliding his arms around Rafe's waist. "I should be the one asking you. It isn't as though we spent the day doing the most romantic of activities."

"I know." Rafe wound his arms around Russell's neck, running a hand over his head. "For a long time, I didn't think I was worth much because of the things I'd had to do to survive, and that carried itself into other parts of my life. I didn't think I had anything to give... anyone. And I acted like it, taking risks and not really caring what happened to me."

"What are you saying?" Russell asked, his mind jumping to some pretty frightening conclusions.

"That I've learned some things. Yes, up until a little while ago, I rode bulls and took a lot of chances with my life, but that time is over. I'm through with being an adrenaline junkie. I need to slow down and take things one step at a time."

"I see. Well, my days weren't spent on the back of a bucking bull, but if you think starting a company from nothing and building it into a successful business isn't an adrenaline roller coaster, you'd be mistaken. I can pick the right people for almost any job, but...."

Rafe smiled. "In your love life, you always choose the worst fit?" he asked, and Russell nodded. "I see. So what does your intuition tell you about me?" he whispered, drawing closer.

Russell closed his eyes. He'd thrown his instincts out the window the moment he'd met Rafe.

"I don't know." Russell hated that answer, but it was all he had. "It is surprisingly silent right now, and I'm not sure if that's bad or good." His legs vibrated with excitement, while at the same time, he wondered if he was doing the right thing. Russell inhaled deeply, Rafe's intense scent filling his nose, sending his brain soaring. He closed the gap between them. This wasn't the time to be analyzing the situation the way he would a business proposition. Russell needed to use other parts of himself, and even though he had reservations, his heart and body had ideas of their own.

As soon as Russell's lips touched Rafe's, all he could think about was how to make it last. Their kisses a few days ago had only whetted his appetite. Russell pulled their bodies together, deepening the kiss as Rafe held him so tight, any space between them disappeared to nothing. Hell, Russell wanted to climb Rafe like a damned tree.

Rafe drew away first, and Russell blinked. "Not in here," Rafe said. He pulled Russell across the hall into his room, then closed the door. Rafe pushed right against him, the door panels pressing into his back, but Russell didn't care. Rafe was like a live wire, radiating energy in all directions, and Russell took it in, his own body sizzling with each of Rafe's touches.

"Damn…," Russell whispered. "I always knew cowboys were hot…."

Rafe flashed a quirky smile. "You don't know the half of it." He threaded his fingers through Russell's hair, tilting his head slightly upward before taking his lips in a kiss that left Russell breathless and his mind completely short-circuited. His knees grew weak, with only the door and Rafe's embrace keeping him upright.

Finally Rafe pulled him toward the bed, and Russell fell onto it with a slight bounce. He couldn't take his eyes off of Rafe as he tugged open his shirt and then shrugged it off. Holy hell, the man was stunning! He thought his imagination had done a pretty good job of filling in what was under Rafe's shirt, but damn, his mind had fallen far short. Just the sight of Rafe's warm skin, dusted with dark hair across his pecs, had Russell's mouth watering. He leaned forward, winding his arms around Rafe's waist, and latched his lips onto his skin, longing to taste him. Rafe was heat personified, and Russell stroked up his back, his lips blazing a trail across Rafe's skin.

Rafe pressed him back down onto the bed, tugged his shirt up over his head, and then tossed it to the floor. Their kiss completely took away Russell's ability to think, so he simply went with it, letting go of everything in favor of pure instinct. He had spent days thinking about Rafe, and now he had him in his arms. Whatever consequences there might be, they could come as they would. Russell could do nothing to stop this now.

"Holy Jesus…," Russell muttered when Rafe snapped the button on his pants and shucked them down his legs, then swallowed Russell's cock in one smooth movement. Russell refused to wonder where Rafe might have learned that and groaned hard, his eyes rolling to the back of his head as wet heat surrounded him. "Rafe...," he whimpered, winding his fingers through his soft hair, unable to move. Rafe had him completely under his spell, and Russell sincerely hoped the magic never ended.

Rafe backed away and kissed him hard, and Russell tasted hints of himself on Rafe's lips. Somehow Russell had expected Rafe to be more tentative. He wasn't sure why, but damn, he loved that Rafe wasn't shy. And for that matter, neither was Russell. He rolled Rafe on the bed, smiling down into his intense eyes, loving the fact that Rafe seemed to look at him with maybe a touch of wonder. Russell loved the look and loved that he'd been able to put it in Rafe's eyes.

Since neither of them had their boots on, the rest of their clothes came off relatively easily. They rocked against each other, flailing their legs until the last of their clothes fell to the floor and Russell found himself skin to skin with Rafe. The man was fine in every sense of the word, and Russell made time to look at him, running his fingers over the lines that crossed his chest and side.

"What happened?" Russell whispered.

"That one is courtesy of Whirlwind, and the one on my side was given to me by a bull named Bumblebee. That bastard had one hell of a sting." He shimmied slightly as Russell ran his finger along the old wound.

"Does it hurt?" Russell asked.

"No. It only feels funny when it's touched," he whispered.

Russell drew closer, locking their gazes together. "Then maybe it hasn't been touched the right way."

"I have lots of scars," Rafe said. "I hope they don't put you off."

Russell shrugged. "We all have them. Some are on the outside, there for all the world to see." He kissed Rafe and then slid his tongue around a nipple, eliciting a groan that echoed in the room. But Russell didn't stop there. He slid downward, running his tongue over Whirlwind's memento. Rafe shivered. "See what I mean? Sometimes all we have to do is own the scars that we carry and then they don't have as much power over us." Russell bore his own scars, though they weren't as apparent as some of Rafe's.

"I don't know about that," Rafe said.

"I do. The people we let into our heart are the only ones who have the power to break it. But...." He kissed one of the scars again. "Letting someone else in can heal it too."

Rafe sat up and cupped Russell's cheeks in his hands. "How do you know?"

Russell blinked. "Because I've had my heart shattered. And it almost cost me some things I truly love—the business I poured my soul into, as well as my family. He could have taken everything from me. And it's taken me a long time to learn to trust again, to let go. Hell, I'm not even sure I'm there yet. But I'm trying." He didn't continue. There was no need.

"So what do you suggest?" Rafe asked seriously.

"I don't know." He grinned. "More of this." He kissed Rafe again, holding him as tightly as he could. Life held no guarantees for anything except hurt and pain. That also meant that when the chance at happiness came his way, he'd be a fool to turn his back on it. "Lots more of this." He kissed him again, and this time their lips were busy for long enough that talking seemed like a waste of breath, energy, and time. Because while he had Rafe in his arms, no words were necessary.

RUSSELL LAY back on the mattress with Rafe, half asleep, his head resting on Russell's shoulder. He didn't want to move, but he could hear the dogs outside the door and he figured at any minute…. Sure enough, a single scratch followed another.

"I think the dogs are jealous," Rafe mumbled.

"Your uncle spoiled them rotten," Russell said. "He loved all three of them."

Rafe nodded and rolled over. "Maybe if we're quiet, they'll go lie down." He sighed and nuzzled closer. "I remember a black lab when I was a kid."

"Skipper," Russell said. "I remember him too. He died about ten years ago, I guess. Mack was so upset, and he swore that he'd never have another dog again." Russell put an arm around Rafe's shoulders.

"What changed his mind?"

Russell shrugged. "One of the dogs on our ranch had puppies, and we brought one of them over here. Mack took one look and the protestations died on his lips, especially when the little mutt crawled up onto his lap, licked his face, and then tore into the house, looking for food. Mack named her Lightning because of her coloring, and she was with him up until last year. When she passed, he had two of the other dogs, and I brought Lola over when we had another set of pups." The scratches came again, and Russell got up and opened the door. All three dogs pranced in, and he managed to make it back into bed before three heads peered up looking for room.

"Lie down," Rafe told them, and they huffed before sprawling out on the floor. "God, all three of them are such big babies."

Russell hummed his agreement as his belly rumbled. The dogs lifted their heads, peering up toward the bed to find out what the noise was. "Maybe it's time to make some dinner," Rafe said before he slipped out of bed and began pulling on his clothes.

"You know, there's no rush." Russell grinned as he sat up.

"I know," Rafe said, and Russell could almost see Rafe's walls started to rise once again.

Russell rolled over, his chin on his hands. "What is it that you're afraid of? Me getting to know you and rejecting you?"

Rafe shrugged. "I don't know." He sat on the edge of the bed. "Maybe if I keep everyone at bay, then they won't get the chance to reject me." He slumped forward. "All I figured when I came here was that I'd have the chance to build some sort of life after the rodeo." He turned around. "I didn't expect to find you and your family... or see the chance to have a normal life."

"You mean rodeo isn't normal?"

Rafe scoffed. "It's the anti normal. Constant travel. Hotels and quick meals and... hell, quick everything." He turned back to face Russell, smiling. "I loved that life for a lot of years. There were no commitments, and relationships, other than friendships, didn't seem too important. There was always the next rodeo and the next ride to look forward to. When I got hurt, I went to the hospital and got fixed up, then trained as soon as I dared and got back on the bulls most likely too soon. But if riding was paying for the food and the place to stay, then I had no choice. I had to ride in order to live. Working to live is normal; taking your life in your hands… is not."

"And yet you loved it. I can tell by the light in your eyes." A chill went through Russell, and he pulled the blankets over him, even though the chill had nothing to do with the temperature in the room. "You'd go on riding."

"Oh God, yes. It's in my blood." Rafe grabbed one of the bags from the chair next to the bed and began pulling things out. "These are my buckles— the prizes I received for my wins." He placed a huge one in Russell's hands, the weight of it considerable. "That's the world championship prize. I also have a trophy that's in one of the boxes in the corner. I rode to win each and every time." He shrugged. "As much as I would love to go back into rodeo, I'm getting old, and I don't heal the way I used to. My arm still aches from my last ride, and it will for a while. As much as I might want to go back, physically I can't do it anymore. I need to figure out a life away from there."

"And thanks to Mack, you have the chance for that life." He rubbed Rafe's arm. "But it doesn't have to be rodeo-free. You could raise bulls or horses for the rodeo. You know good stock because you've been around it for years. This is your ranch. All you need to do is figure out what you want to do with it."

Rafe half smiled. "That's the question, isn't it? I mean, Uncle Mack raised cattle, and I could continue to do that if I wanted."

"Yes. The herd is small right now, and if you wanted, you could raise more. I have contacts in all areas of livestock and could put you in touch with a lot of people. But I can tell you that starting out in any venture takes money, and I hate to say, but it takes a lot of it." From what Rafe had said, there was some in the estate. But building a good bucking program took years of work, expertise, and what could amount to millions of dollars just to get started.

Rafe smiled and leaned back until his head was right near Russell's. "I don't think I have to make any decisions right away."

"No, you don't. And before I forget, Dad wants to talk to you about a business proposition. He told me what it is, but I think it's best if it comes from him directly." Russell wanted to distance himself from that part of the business. This way there couldn't be any misunderstandings. The last thing he wanted was for Rafe to think Russell had had sex with him to get him to lease Russell's dad the land.

"I see." Rafe's expression darkened.

"It's not bad or anything. Just that it's Dad's idea and he should be the one to talk to you about it." Russell slipped off the bed and got dressed as the dogs all jumped up, taking the warm spots. Rafe finished dressing as well, and then they both headed to the kitchen.

"YOU HAVE to be kidding me," Rafe said, laughing.

"I wish I was. John's kids were playing in one of the puddles, and they had mud up to their ears and smiles as big as Texas. I stood next to him and said he was going to need a crowbar to get those kids to stop playing. I turned back to the kids, and the next thing I know, John was gone. I looked around for him and found him in one of the barns, looking for tools. The guy was actually trying to find a crowbar." Russell could barely talk, he was laughing so hard. "I'd always known that John was none too bright, but that takes the cake." Russell grinned.

"You're full of shit," Rafe said. He ate his last bite of salad before setting down his fork.

"I wish I was. John was amazing with the livestock, but a box of rocks had more common sense than he had. I felt sorry for his kids, but they seemed normal and healthy enough. That had to be his wife's doing."

Rafe collected the plates and carried them to the sink. "I wish I could offer you something for dessert. I think I might have some cookies or something. I can cook basic things, but baking is beyond me."

"I can't do that either, and Violet is pretty militant about her kitchen. Not that I want to step on her toes. She takes good care of Dad and me." Russell sat back in the chair, his belly full.

Rafe brought coffee refills and then sat down. "I appreciate all the help today and, well...." He grinned, and his cheeks reddened. "Let's just say it's been a while for me and I don't know how to behave. Do we talk about it? Or...?"

Russell shrugged. "Is there something to talk about?" He took Rafe's hand. "I thought that you did plenty of talking when we were together. It turns out that you're very expressive." He winked and leaned over the table. "It was really hot."

Rafe smiled. "I don't know. Like I said, most of my experience didn't involve talking, and it sure as hell didn't end with dinner afterwards." Russell squeezed his fingers. "I like it this way. I felt dirty most of the time back then." He lowered his gaze. "I always thought there was something wrong with me. It didn't matter that I'd stood up to my parents. They still rejected me. The people who were supposed to love me most turned away and didn't want me anymore. So there had to be something wrong with me. Then I met guys to help pay for food, and those encounters were furtive and quick because they didn't want to get caught." He shook his head as if trying to make the thoughts disappear.

"You know that sex isn't dirty. It isn't something that you need to be ashamed of any more than you need to hide your past. You did what you had to in order to survive." Russell tried to put himself in Rafe's position, though he found that nearly impossible to do because his experiences were so vastly different. But one thing was certain—Rafe still carried a lot of baggage about what had happened to him. He might have made it to the top of the rodeo world, but inside, he was still riding that bull, trying to hold on and figure out who he really was.

Russell had always known who he was. He'd figured out the gay thing pretty early, and his parents' support, especially his mother's, had gone a long way to helping build his self-esteem. Still, his experiences with that jackass Jase had managed to give that self-esteem a good thrashing. In many ways, he was no better than Rafe when it came to relationships.

Night had fallen some time ago, and Russell watched as snow floated down past the window. "It looks like I should be heading home." He checked his phone. "The snow is expected to continue well into the night. If I don't leave now, I'm not going to make back to the ranch." He stood and took his mug to the sink.

Rafe sat still and didn't say anything. Russell figured that Rafe had things he needed to work through. They had found some items that had obviously brought up difficult memories for Rafe. On top of that, the two of them had ended up in bed together. It had been hot and wonderful, but for Rafe, sex wasn't merely fun. Hell, it wasn't *just* fun for Russell either. Sex meant emotions, complications… and both of them had shadows in their pasts.

Russell liked the idea that Rafe took what they'd done seriously. It filled him with the hope that something might be possible between them. Then he might be able to put the ghost of Jase behind him for good.

Maybe it was best that he go home tonight. A little distance might allow him to think—something that was hard to do with Rafe so close. Even as he gazed out the window at the snow, he was still keenly aware of Rafe standing up and approaching him. He could almost feel Rafe's hands before they slipped around his waist.

He closed his eyes as Rafe's warmth pressed to his back. Russell soaked it up and didn't dare move in case the spell between them broke. Neither of them seemed inclined to move, but Russell took a chance and slowly turned in Rafe's arms.

"Do you really need to go?" Rafe asked.

Russell shook his head. "I just thought you might need some time alone, that maybe things had moved a little fast." He stroked Rafe's stubbled cheek. "I didn't want to push you." His heart raced at the warmth in Rafe's eyes, and Russell slowly closed the distance between them just as the dogs trooped into the room and pranced to the door.

"I'd better let them out before they flood the kitchen floor." Rafe stepped back and went to the door. When he opened it, a blast of cold air jetted into the room as the dogs raced outside, tails wagging. "They're good dogs."

"Yeah, they are," Russell agreed.

"If you want to go into the living room, I'll be there in a minute. I need to check on the horses for the night. When I get back, I'll make us some cocoa—the perfect thing on a winter night."

Rafe pulled on his boots and coat, then gave Russell a quick kiss before heading out into the snow. Russell hadn't been sure what to expect when he'd first met Rafe. They had seemed like oil and water, but maybe they were just two guys trying to figure shit out.

Russell went into the living room and watched through the window as Rafe trudged out to the barn, the dogs romping around him. Damn, he could watch that man for the rest of his life. That idea both thrilled and scared him. Rafe seemed to push all the right buttons, but Russell knew better than to rush into anything. That was where he'd gone wrong before.

Chapter 7

"I'LL BE there in about ten minutes," Luther told Rafe first thing Monday morning.

"No problem. Just be careful," Rafe said. He ended the call on the phone Russell had loaned him and put the tractor in gear to clear the last of the snow from the drive. He was just putting the equipment away when Russell pulled in, followed by Luther. Elliott and Russell got out of one truck while Luther parked his. He'd never had so many people around at the same time.

"Luther," Elliott said as they shook hands. Then he turned to Rafe. "We were on our way into town, and I thought we'd drop by on the way. I want to talk over some business with you."

"It seems everyone wants to do that this morning," Rafe said. "Y'all come on in where it's warm and we'll take care of things." He smiled and whistled for the dogs, who bounded out from inside the barn. Rafe was more than a little confused by all this activity, and he exchanged a look with Russell, who

seemed contrite. Rafe figured coming over was Elliott's doing.

"Let me put some coffee on," Rafe said once
they were inside. He started a pot, and they all took
a seat at the table.

Elliott cleared his throat. "I'll make this quick so
you can get on to other things. We're in a position to
expand our beef production, and you may be able to
help us with that."

Rafe swallowed. "You want to buy the ranch?"
He turned to Russell as a sense of betrayal welled up.
Why did everyone think that if they threw enough
money at him, he'd just go away? Maybe he should
have expected it, but after Saturday and spending
time with Russell—

"No. This is your family land," Elliott said. "I
meant what I said to you the other night. You need to
keep it. But there's quite a bit of it that is going un-
used, and it has been that way for a while. What I'd
like to do is lease some of that land from you. You're
using a few hundred acres at most right now. We'd
be willing to lease whatever you don't think you're
going to use."

"Oh, I see," Rafe said, relieved.

"It will take some time for you to build up your
herd. In the meantime, we will take good care of the
land, treating it like it was our own. You have a little
over a thousand acres of land that you haven't been
putting to use. So we'd like to do that for you." Elliott
met his gaze. "You don't need to give us an answer
immediately. Just think about it. If you have plans for
the land, then that's great and we'll understand."

"No, I've got no plans." He poured them each a mug of coffee. "I haven't had the chance to give it much thought, honestly. But I appreciate the offer. I'll definitely think about it." So much had been happening in the past few weeks that he had barely had time to sleep. The lease would give him the opportunity for the land to bring in some income. Then he turned to the lawyer. "Luther, what do you have for me?"

Luther glanced at Elliott and Russell, as if to ask if it was okay to speak about private matters in front of them. But Rafe had already told Russell about what was in the safe-deposit box, so he simply nodded.

Luther cleared his throat. "I verified this morning that the stocks are still valid. In some cases, they have even split, and dividends were used to buy more stock. I'm still getting final figures, but it looks like there's quite a bit of money there."

"I see." Rafe turned to the others. "I keep wondering why Uncle Mack didn't use any of that for himself," he said, biting his lower lip. "Luther, would you mind doing some additional digging for me?"

Then he turned back to Elliott and Russell. "Uncle Mack kept some letters—Russell knows about them. It seems that Uncle Mack had a friend." He looked at Luther. "And, well, I want you to try to find him."

Then Rafe hurried out of the room. He returned a few minutes later with the three envelopes. "His name is Dale from the signature on the letters."

"No last name?" Luther asked.

"No. But we have some clues. The envelopes have a return address on them, so that's probably where he is… or was. Could you look into it for me? Try to find him if you can." He passed over the envelopes. "Please be careful with these."

Luther nodded. "I'll make copies and return the originals." He put the letters in his case. "And… there's been a development you should know about. I got an email from an attorney representing your parents. As executor, he had to notify me that they intend to try to break the will on the grounds that your uncle was ill when he wrote it." Luther rolled his eyes.

"How was he ill?" Rafe snapped. "My parents didn't bother with him, so they wouldn't have known if he was sick or not. They're only saying he was ill because he was gay." He shook his head, swallowing hard. "Can they do that?"

"Well, it seems they are," Luther said. "They don't have a leg to stand on, though, and the bar for breaking a will is pretty high. They are going to have to prove that Mack wasn't in his right mind, and under the influence of someone else, which they can't do." He shook his head in obvious disbelief. "However, what this *does* do is to stop the distribution of the estate. You can live here, but we can't distribute any of the assets." He turned to Elliott and Russell. "You can lease the land if you like, but any proceeds will need to be held in trust until this is over."

"I see. So anything else I want to do for the ranch…."

"Needs to be approved by the executor, and that's me. Basically, it's my job to make sure the estate business is handled properly. So for now, no distributions can be made. And that also means that the things we found in the safe-deposit box need to stay there." He rolled his eyes. "I'll do my best to head off whatever comes. But I think this is your parents' attempt to wear you down so they can get what they want."

Rafe nodded. "I know that's what it is. They didn't care about Mack, and they don't care about me. But I know my parents need the money. Dad already came to me asking for it."

"If we have to, we could offer them something to settle."

"No," Rafe snapped. "They threw me away just like they disowned Uncle Mack. So they're not getting a penny from him. He was very specific in his will. Once the court sees that, they'll throw this whole thing out. I'm sure of it."

"Then I'll get back to their attorney and tell him that if he wants to pursue this, we're prepared to defend the will in court. This whole thing could simply be a ploy to get some quick money."

"If you need anything, let us know," Russell said. "Not that I want to step on your toes, but if you need any assistance, we can provide it. I have lawyers for the corporation who can help. Dad and I think the same thing you do—that Mack's will should be honored." He patted the table for emphasis. "I met Rafe's parents the other day, and let me tell you, they are pieces of work. Selfish doesn't begin to describe these people."

"Good to know. I can tell their lawyer that we are prepared to depose them and that we will force them to go to court to get any information at all. That will also rack up billable hours and ensure that this costs them a lot of money. Sending a letter or having a lawyer call is cheap. Bringing this kind of suit is not." He finished his coffee and then stood and shook everyone's hand, ending with Rafe's. "I'll call as soon as I know something else."

"Okay. What should I do about the house?"

"For now, nothing. Live your life. I know you have some of your own money, but repairs to the ranch and ongoing business expenses can be paid out of the estate. Just save the receipts. Once we clear this up, we can finish probate and get the estate settled." He said goodbye, then headed out into the nearly blinding sun glinting off the snow outside the house.

"I should have known they would try something." Rafe finished his coffee. "They live in a world of their own, believing everything runs the way they think it should. And if it doesn't fit, they discard it. The same way they did their son," he groused, wishing he could leave that hurt behind. It had been years ago and he was an adult now. He should be able to let that shit go.

Elliott slowly raised his mug to his lips. "Son, you don't get to choose your family—you get the one you get. Some of us hit the lottery while others get the booby prize. And I'm afraid you definitely got two of the biggest boobs around." He finished the coffee. "But now you get to decide what sort of life you're going to live and what you're going to do. You rode your way all the way to the world bull-riding championship. Your parents had nothing to do with that. *You* did that. So stick to your guns and make your own way. The rest is all bullshit." He turned to Russell. "The same thing goes for you and that asshole ex of yours. When you let shitty people's actions affect you, it gives them power over you. When you do that, they win." He got to his feet. "And no matter what, you should never let the ass-holes win."

"Is that a royal pronouncement?" Russell teased.

"You bet your ass," Elliott retorted. "Now come on and take me home. Rafe has work to do, and so do the rest of us." He put his mug in the sink. "It's Violet's day off, so we're eating in town. Come by Whisky Jack's about seven. They have amazing burgers, and their trout is spectacular."

He left first, then Russell quickly gathered Rafe in his arms and kissed him hard.

"Try to make it tonight if you can. Dad loves these night outs. The food is good, and you'll get a chance to meet some of the other people around town." Then Russell kissed him again and hurried out after his dad.

RAFE WAS tired and cold. He'd just finished cleaning the stalls and had brought in fresh bedding. The barn had been warm enough, but another line of snow was moving in. When the sun disappeared in the afternoon, it grew cold again. Still, the barn was clean, and he'd had a chance to exercise the horses before the sun went down.

The dogs met him when he came inside, and Rafe fed them before hitting the shower and changing his clothes. Then he checked to make sure the dogs were set and everything was turned off before he pulled on his winter gear and strode out to his truck to head toward town.

He drove slowly as flakes fell through the headlight beams. The country roads were a little rough and in need of a more thorough plowing, but the closer he got to town, the clearer the roads became. Still, he was grateful when he pulled into the parking lot and got out of the truck.

The bar was everything you'd expect from a cowboy hangout—beamed ceilings, rough walls with neon beer signs, scarred tables, and chairs that had seen better days. The room was packed with people all talking and laughing, a cacophony of overlapping voices that hit him like a two-by-four. After days of quiet, the sound was nearly overwhelming. Still, he looked around and found Elliott and Russell at a table on the side of the bar farthest away from the pool tables.

"This end of the bar is usually the quietest," Russell said as Rafe pulled out a chair. "Do you want a beer?" Russell waved, and a server hurried over. Rafe ordered a beer, and she gave him a menu before hurrying away. "If you like fish, the trout is fantastic."

"It seems like a strange thing to get at a place like this," Rafe said, setting the menu aside.

"The chef's family raises trout on their farm just outside of town, so it comes in fresh every day. And he knows exactly how to cook it," Elliott said.

When the server returned, they placed their orders, and Rafe looked around. "Is it always like this on a Monday?" The place was absolutely packed.

"Every night," Elliott said, raising his glass. "A few years ago, I asked the owner why he didn't expand the place. He told me he was afraid that if they got too big, the place would lose its character."

They drank their beers, and the server got them refills, then brought over their meals, which looked amazing. Rafe ate slowly, enjoying his dinner and the company. It was hard to talk over all the sound, so he stayed quiet and enjoyed every bite.

"The pool table is free," Elliott said, nudging Russell, who stood and rolled his eyes.

"Very subtle, Dad." Russell waited for Rafe, and together, they headed to the table. Rafe was about to put in his quarters when someone sneaked in front of him, dropped in their money, and pushed in the lever to release the balls.

"Hey, we were next," Rafe said. Then he turned and saw Duane. Shaking his head, he said, "I should have known."

"This is our place. It's not for the likes of you," Duane snarled.

Did Duane really intend to pick a fight here? In front of everyone? Rafe knew the guy was a jerk. And now, it seemed, Duane was about to show everyone just how big a dick he really was. Rafe studied his nemesis, looking for weaknesses. Just one punch in the right place….

Suddenly a whistle pierced the air, and the room instantly became silent. "Hey, y'all," Russell said into the quiet. "We have a celebrity in the house. Rafe Carrera, a new resident, and now one of our own, is here. He's the current world bull-riding champion!"

The place erupted in cheers, and Rafe took a step away from Duane, then took off his hat and gave the room a smile. He didn't need to look at Duane to know he would be seething. And obviously that was exactly why Russell had done it.

"Assholes," Duane snarled from behind them. "You couldn't do it again if you tried."

Rafe had had enough of this bullshit and was ready to leave. Russell, on the other hand, had other ideas. "Look who's talking—the sore loser of the century." He said it loudly enough for others to hear.

"Russell… just let it go."

"Yeah, walk away," Duane added. "This is my hangout. Find yourself another one. There's a ballet school down the way. Why don't you go there, Twinkletoes." Duane was full of clichés.

Rafe drew himself up to his full height. "I've had it with you."

"No fighting in the bar." One of the bouncers, dressed in black, stepped in front of Duane.

Rafe nodded. "Nope, no fighting. But I'll play you." He looked down at the table. "The loser goes on down to the ballet studio, as you put it." He stepped closer to Duane.

"You're on," Duane snarled. "I'm going to wipe the floor with you."

Russell racked up the balls as Duane went down to the end to break. Russell growled, but Rafe shook his head. "Most balls sunk," Duane said before snapping the cue to take the first shot. One ball fell. Then Duane took a second shot and failed to sink the seven.

"Are you sure about this?" Russell asked, taking Rafe's arm. "Half the damned town is watching."

"I know," Rafe told him. "I'm tired of this asshole. He dogged me the entire tour, and now he and his father are trying to run me out of town. I don't know what Duane's game is, but I didn't take his crap on the circuit, and I'm not going to now."

"But can you beat him?" Russell asked.

"Are you two going to do each other's nails or are we going to play pool?" Duane snapped.

A ring formed around the table as Rafe lined up his shot. He shot lightly and sank the one and then the fifteen before moving on to the eight and the eleven.

"Lucky shit," Duane groused, color rising in his cheeks.

"No luck involved." Rafe grinned, winking at Russell before sinking the next two balls with ease. They lined right up on the table, and he sank the seven before finishing off Duane with the nine. "That's it." He lifted his gaze from the green felt. "Do you want me to run the rest of the table, or do you give up?" He rested the cue on the floor as Duane stalked off. "You'll look good in a tutu," Rafe called after him. Folks laughed, which probably rankled Duane even more.

"Where did you learn to play like that?" Russell asked as the crowd around the table began to drift away.

"I'd hustle pool some nights after I was done with the rodeo. I learned to make money any way I could," he answered softly as some of the guys slapped him on the shoulder. He stepped back from the table and handed the cue to one of the other men starting a new game.

"What's his deal? What does he have against you?" Russell asked once they returned to their table. The dishes had been cleared, and Elliott sat with a smile and a half-eaten piece of cheesecake. Russell growled at his dad. "You know you're not supposed to have things like that."

"It's once a week," he said flatly before taking another bite. "I'm old, not dead." He set down his fork. "Nicely done, by the way. Mendeltom junior has always been a bullying pain in the ass. I'm glad someone put him in his place."

Rafe shrugged. "The guy already hated me for beating him in the championship." He wondered what he was going to do next. Duane Mendeltom was not someone to let things go, and tonight he'd been embarrassed in the place he called home. Rafe looked around the room and saw Duane as he headed for the door, expression downright murderous. Rafe wanted to smile and wave, but Duane Mendeltom wasn't even worth that amount of effort, so he turned away and grinned at Russell. "Who would have thought that pool hustling could be so rewarding? And there wasn't even any money involved."

"Damn, kid, is there anything you haven't done?" Elliott asked.

Rafe met his gaze. "Elliott, a guy will do just about anything in order to eat." Thank God those days were over now.

Music started and folks got up to dance. Rafe watched the couples move together and purposely didn't look at Russell. He loved to dance and was damned good at it, but he figured the town wasn't ready to see him and Russell cut a rug. Still, he caught Russell's gaze and moved closer to him. As they stood there, watching the dancing, Russell's hand rested lightly against his leg.

Elliott ordered another beer, but Rafe switched to soda. He still had to drive, and the weather would make that tricky enough. Russell seemed content just sitting and watching the others. "My ex and I used to go dancing sometimes," Russell commented.

"You can't let him stop you," Elliott commented, his words slightly slurred.

"You're as bad as a gossipy old lady," Russel teased his dad. "Stop trying to matchmake." Elliott rolled his eyes and smiled, sipped his beer, and ordered some more food. "Jesus…."

"I have a hollow leg," Elliott said. And when the server set another plate of food in front of him, he proceeded to down almost a whole order of wings. "And I'm going to enjoy things while I can."

"Dad…," Russell said warily.

"The doctor says I'm fine. But I'm not getting any younger, so…." He burped and drank the rest of his beer, then ordered another. Russell cautioned him again, but Elliott brushed him off and finished his wings, then started in on the fresh beer before heading to the bathroom.

"What's going on?" Rafe asked as Elliott weaved slightly through the crowd.

"I don't know. He doesn't usually drink this way." Russell shook his head. "I don't get it."

"What is today?" Rafe checked his watch. "November 14. Does the date mean anything to you?"

Russell swallowed hard and then nodded. "I didn't realize. Mom died five years ago." He sighed softly. "Maybe it's not so bad to let him tie one on tonight. Dad has done pretty well since she passed away, but I know he still misses her. We both do."

Elliott returned and slumped in the chair, raised his beer, and then downed a good part of it. "Come on, Dad," Russell said. "Let me take care of the tab and we'll go on home."

"I don't want to," he said softly.

"It's okay to miss her, Elliott," Rafe said. "You go ahead and drink all you want. Russell and I will get you home and pour you into bed."

Elliott patted Rafe's cheek a couple times. "You never knew my Isabelle. She was an amazing lady. Hell, she put up with me for thirty-five years." His eyes filled, but he blinked and took another swig of his beer. "Then the doctor said she had cancer, and she was gone in six months." He turned to Russell. "You don't know what it's like to go to bed alone after having someone like your mother beside you all that time."

Russell nodded, and Rafe signaled the server to ask her for three mugs of coffee. When they arrived, Rafe set one in front of each of them, and Elliott drank his without complaint.

"I hate beer," Elliott said. "You don't buy it; you rent it." He headed to the bathroom once more.

"Do you need me to help you get him home?" Rafe asked.

"No. It'll be fine." Russell paid the bill, and Rafe followed as Russell guided his weaving father to the truck. "I'm sorry about this. I should have paid closer attention to what day it was." He got into the truck, and Rafe stood out of the way as Russell backed out and waved before disappearing into the snowy night.

THE THREE dogs greeted him at the door, tails wagging. He petted each of them and made sure they had water and food. Then he flopped onto the old sofa, turned on the near-antique console television, and flipped through the channels to find something interesting.

Lights turning into the drive caught his attention, and he got up and went to the front door. The snow seemed to have let up, thank God. But then he sighed when he saw Grant Mendeltom get out of his car and charge across the snow-covered drive like a damned bull. "What the hell do you think you're doing?" He slid to a stop at the base of the steps. "You little shit!"

"What? All I did was beat Duane at a game of pool. He's the one who issued the challenge," Rafe told him as levelly as he could. "I think you and your son need to back off."

"Why? We don't need people like you in this town. It was bad enough living next to Mack with the shit he pulled." He stepped closer, trying to intimidate. "I know that damned uncle of yours caused that avalanche and took away most of my water. And come hell or high water, I'm going to get it back."

"Just get the hell away from here. I don't know what happened between you and Mack, but I'm staying. And let me tell you this. Even if I was to sell, it certainly wouldn't be to you. So get the hell off my land." He'd had all the bullshit he could take for one day.

Mendeltom grinned. "I don't know…. There are some holdups on the estate, from what I hear." Rafe ground his teeth. Mendeltom had been talking to his parents. Hell, maybe the asshole and his parents had been communicating for years. Rafe wouldn't put it past any of them. "When the will is broken, your parents and I have a deal. They'll sell the land to me, and that will be the end of it."

"Not going to happen. So get going—*now.*" Rafe raised his voice, and the dogs gathered behind him. "Hey, guys." The dogs growled, and Grant took a step back, then finally went back to his truck. Rafe got the dogs inside and closed the door, watching as Mendeltom left.

"Fucking hell," he muttered under his breath, suddenly realizing something else in this messed-up situation. Not only had his parents cut Uncle Mack off, but they'd kept tabs on him through the damned neighbor. This was really fucked all to hell. And it showed Rafe just how far his parents were willing to go to get what they wanted. He flopped back onto the sofa with a sigh, wondering what the hell he was going to find out next.

THE WINDOWS rattled as Rafe pried his eyes open. His back ached, and he blinked from under the old blanket he'd pulled over himself. Something had awakened him, but he couldn't figure out what. The dogs were curled together on the floor, and Rafe shivered as he straightened out. The house was stone cold and dark, with no light inside or out. He reached for a lamp and got nothing. "Looks like the power is out," he said softly. And that obviously meant the heat was out too.

He quickly built a fire and grabbed his phone to check the time—four in the morning. He groaned as the wood caught and some heat started to flow into the room. The dogs gathered close, and by the time he'd added a few logs, the cold room was starting to feel warmer. Rafe sat on the sofa once again, sprawling out under the blanket to try to get a little more sleep. He had to get up in a few hours to check on the horses and make sure the ranch was bedded down for what seemed like one hell of a snowstorm.

When he woke again, the dogs were fussing at the door. Lola barked once, and the others whimpered. Rafe pushed the covers back and got up, then threw another log onto the fire before going to the door. He peered out the window as a figure weaved down the drive. Rafe hurried through to the kitchen, pulled on his boots and coat, and headed outside.

The wind and snow whipped around him, the cold going right through his clothes. He pulled the coat closed, watching as a figure materialized out of the snow squall. "Russell?" Rafe asked as he reached him. "What are you doing out in this?"

"I was supposed to travel and got caught in this storm. The truck slid off the road and got stuck." They reached the back door and went inside, warmth settling around them once they got out of the wind.

"Go into the living room and sit in front of the fire. I'll get us something hot to drink." The wind continued whistling around the sides of the house, but they were safe and warm inside. "While you're at it, be sure to message Elliott. You know he'll be worried."

Coffee was the last thing they needed, so Rafe made hot chocolate and brought two cups into the living room. Then he sat next to Russell on the sofa.

"This storm came in so fast. Usually they pass right through here. And I didn't see anything on the weather about squalls." He sipped, and Rafe put more wood on the fire, building it up to try to warm at least this part of the house. Then he went to the linen closet and got some more blankets. He handed a few to Russell.

"Just get yourself warm. That's the most important thing," Rafe said, worried that Russell might be suffering from hypothermia after being caught out in that mess. "Where were you supposed to go?"

"Los Angeles again. I'm trying to finalize a deal on some software. We were close, but one of the men said something that raised a bunch of questions, and now I need to go press some flesh, answer questions, and put their mind at ease. I do that kind of thing a lot." He grinned and pulled up the blankets. "I should have just stayed home. But I didn't think it was this bad—usually squalls like these are localized. But this one is bigger than most."

"It looks like the storm whipped up close to here and it's still building." Rafe showed Russell the local radar on his phone, grateful that he had a signal. When he'd first arrived, he'd been pleasantly surprised to discover that the service was pretty decent, probably because there were so many people in the valley who had a lot of money and plenty of pull.

"Well, crap," Russell said. He sent a few more messages and then set his phone aside. "You don't mind if I crash here with you for a while?"

Rafe snuggled closer. "You can crash any time." He moved closer and kissed Russell. Heat built in an instant, and it had nothing to do with the fire. The wind, the snow, the fire—all of it seemed to conspire to bring Russell to him.

The dogs jumped down from their side of the sofa as Rafe pressed Russell back onto the cushions. They stretched out, a blanket draped over them as Rafe tugged at Russell's shirt. His hands roamed over heated skin as his lips found a cold peaked nub, tongue circling, warming Russell's skin. Moans filled the room, and Rafe heard the dogs humph and then the tinkle of their collars as they left the room. Obviously the dogs didn't appreciate the show.

"You know, you tend to be a little loud," Russell said, a twinkle from the fire in his eyes. "Maybe it's a good thing the dogs left."

"Me? I think you should have a name tag—'Hi, I'm Russell and I'm a screamer.'" Rafe grinned. "Though I will tell you that it's damned hot." He captured Russell's lips, determined to make Russell cry out as much as he wanted, loud enough to rival the wind outside. "Really hot."

"I see." Russell groaned as Rafe slipped his arms around his waist, sucking at the base of his neck. There was no rush, and Rafe did his best to take his time, even though he wanted to rip away Russell's clothes to get at the full glory of him.

"Dammit, you drive me fucking crazy," Rafe whispered.

Russell cupped his cheeks. "Then how about you fucking fuck me until I scream down the damned house?"

Rafe moaned as a surge of desire raced through him. Russell tugged off his shirt, bringing them back together, their chests pressing to each other as Rafe ground their hips together. Russell shimmied under him, and the tension around his waist eased as Russell unsnapped his jeans. Thank God—those pants had been getting tight. He sighed and kissed Russell harder.

Both of them quivered against each other. Somehow Rafe managed to get Russell's pants unhooked with his shaking fingers. Their shoes and jeans hit the floor, Rafe's desire rocketing upward by the second. There was no way he could get enough of this man. "Damn," Russell whispered.

"I know. I can't seem to get enough of you…." Rafe sucked at the base of his neck.

"Oh God," Russell whimpered softly. "Rafe, you gotta stop."

Instantly he stilled. "What's wrong?"

"Nothing. But if you keep this up, it's going to be over before we even get started." He rested his head on Rafe's shoulder, breathing deeply.

Rafe sighed and held him. "We should move to the bedroom, but it's cold as hell in there." He rolled Russell on the sofa, careful not to knock them both to the floor. Finally, he lay on the cushions with Russell on top of him, allowing him to take control. And damned if live-wire Russell didn't take over and blow Rafe's mind.

Never before had Rafe had this type of connection with anyone. Russell's intense taste burst in his mouth as Russell worked down his briefs, freeing Rafe's cock. As soon as Russell's were pushed aside as well, Rafe spread his legs, and Russell settled between them. Rafe pulled the blanket up over both of them and looked up into Russell's eyes as the fire glimmered in them.

"Your sofa is a little small," Russell teased. "But I don't want to move."

"Me neither." Rafe ran his hands down Russell's back and over the curve of his tight ass before cupping it and pressing the cheeks together. Rafe rocked slowly, and Russell groaned, their cocks sliding past each other. The friction was amazing, and Rafe held Russell tightly, not wanting the moment to end.

"This is strange," Russell said.

"I know. It's like we're in our own little cocoon of warmth."

"Yeah."

Rafe drew Russell's face down for a kiss. "I'd take things further, but I'd need to get supplies. And that would mean that we'd have to go out into this storm, which isn't a pleasant thought." He pulled the blanket up around Russell's shoulders, cradling them both in warmth as they rocked, passion and desire building slowly.

He loved that there was no rush. Taking his time with someone not only made this special—it was an incredible way for Rafe to show that Russell was more than just a lay. He was so used to being just a body and nothing more.

"Stop whatever it is you're thinking," Russell said.

"I'm sorry." He caught Russell's gaze. "It's just that…." Dammit, he didn't want to go into this at a moment like this. He had spent too much time buried in the past.

"You're here with me now," Russell whispered as a log in the fire popped. "So just let it go. It's just you and me, in a blizzard. There's nowhere to go, and no one will interrupt us." Russell lifted the blanket, and his head disappeared under it.

Rafe shivered for a second and then inhaled sharply as Russell's lips surrounded him with the wettest heat he could imagine. "Russell," he whispered, having no idea why he felt the need to be quiet. There was no one around to hear them. He could scream at the top of his lungs if he wanted to.

The only response he got was more suction and intensity. He gasped for breath as Russell sucked him harder. He grabbed the edge of the of the sofa cushion, holding it as his eyes rolled to the back of his head. Damn, this was incredible. And all he could do was hold still while Russell worked his magic with his mouth and hands.

"Jesus Christ!" Rafe cried as he half sat up when Russell took all of him, holding him deep. "What the hell are you doing to me?"

The only answer he got was a chuckle from under the blanket as Russell proceeded to push him higher. Closer and closer, Rafe gripped the last threads of his control while Russell drove him nearer to the point of no return.

He tried to hold out, giving Russell as much warning as he could before tumbling over the edge, his entire body thrumming with passion that spent itself in a wave of desire.

Rafe lay there, quiet and still, breathing deeply as Russell shuffled under the covers and finally joined him. Rafe drew him down, kissing and holding him as he floated on warm clouds that seemed to go on forever. "Give me a minute and…."

Russell kissed him again. "It's okay. I came when you did," he whispered, pulling the blanket around both of them. The fire popped a few times, and Rafe sighed softly, then got up and put another log on. He stirred it, then got the dogs settled on a blanket before joining Russell on the sofa. He climbed under the blanket and lay on his side, spooning Russell to him. As soon as he got comfortable, he closed his eyes. The last couple of nights, sleep had been elusive, but holding Russell relaxed him, and, letting out a long breath, he let sleep carry him.

When he woke again, the fire was nearly out, but the house was still warm, so the power must have come back on, even if the view out the living room window was nearly pure white. "It's nice in here," Russell whispered, kissing him as he stretched out. "I take it the snow is still falling?"

"Yes. How you thought you could travel in this…," he chastised gently. "Your father has got to be worried sick."

"I messaged him when you asked me to. So he should know I'm here." Russell searched for his phone and held up the screen. "He's seen it and is fine. Apparently the power was out at home too." He settled back on the sofa while Rafe climbed off and hurried to the bedroom.

He dressed and then fed the dogs their breakfast. "I need to check on the horses and livestock."

"I'll come with you," Russell offered.

"There's no need. I'll get the chores done quickly, and then we can have some breakfast and hunker down for the duration." Rafe pulled on all his cold-weather gear, bundling up as much as he could before heading out to the barn.

The horses were fine, but the barn was colder than Rafe expected. He got the warmers going while he filled the mangers with hay and a few oats. Rafe also made sure that all the doors and windows were closed tightly to keep in the heat. Once that was done, he watered the horses and put light blankets on each of them before heading back outside to check on the cattle. He found them clustered together in the shelter of an outcropping, waiting out the storm. Rafe dropped off bales of feed from the back of his four-wheeler, made sure they had available water, then headed back inside.

As soon as he stepped inside, he was over-whelmed by the scent of bacon and pancakes. His belly rumbled while he took off his gear. Then he joined Russell in the kitchen just as he was pouring pancake batter onto the griddle. "I found some blue-berries in the freezer, so I added them."

"Sounds wonderful." He sat down, and Russell put a heaping plate in front of him. "Where did you learn to cook like this?"

"Violet. She told me that a man should know how to cook basic things because not everyone was lucky enough to have someone like her cooking for them." Russell grinned. "She made sure that when I found myself on my own, I could feed myself with-out having to resort to eating that 'awful fast food' all the time. I managed to learn to make a few basic dishes, and pancakes was one of them. Of course I can grill, and I know how to make a few other things pretty well. Heck, I could even make a basic choco-late cake from Violet's recipe. But not much beyond that." He brought his own plate to the table and sat across from Rafe. It was almost domestic.

Rafe had been on the road for so many years that even something as simple as sharing breakfast with someone else seemed like a big deal, especially since it was in his own house as opposed to a diner somewhere. "Thank you. These are delicious."

"Violet gave me her recipe. She actually told me her secret, though she swore me to secrecy," Russell said with delight. "She also told me that cooking for someone is a way to show you care."

Rafe swallowed hard and felt himself smiling. That was certainly good to know. Not that Rafe intended to press. But if Russell wanted to make him pancakes, he'd eat them and be happily thankful.

"I'm grateful to her." Rafe loaded up another forkful, then paused. "I think I need your help."

Russell stopped eating. "What kind?"

"Old man Mendeltom. You heard my parents threatening to challenge Mack's will when they were here. Well, Mendeltom stopped over, angry as hell because I'd whooped Duane's ass at pool." He rolled his eyes. "I think he'd been drinking—he let his mouth run away with him."

"That sounds like him. If Grant Mendeltom spent as much time working as he does drinking and flapping his jaws, he'd be a lot better off." Russell took a bite of bacon. "What did he say?"

"That when my parents break the will, they've agreed to sell him the ranch. It seems that he's some sort of friend of theirs and has been in touch with my parents for years." The thought made Rafe ill. "Poor Mack had little privacy, even after the family threw him aside. I bet they hounded the hell out of him, one way or another."

"Jesus," Russell breathed.

Rafe set down his fork and got up, grabbed the coffee pot, and refilled their mugs. "My parents live outside Denver in a small community with like-minded people. It's a Fox News self-righteous feedback loop repeating the same views over and over. I'm surprised I managed to survive in that environment growing up." He hated the person he'd been back then, terrified that someone would find out his secret. "Who the hell knows what crap Mendeltom has been feeding them, or what they think they know?"

"That may be," Russell said. "But even I know that breaking a will is close to impossible. It requires a really high bar of proof. People can't just walk in spouting their crap and have it taken seriously. Those suits can go on for a long time."

"And as long as they do, the estate can't be settled," Rafe whined, hating himself for it. "It's not that I'm greedy, but I'd like to be able to start building the ranch up again the way Uncle Mack would have wanted me to. I can start doing that come spring, but not with all of this shit hanging over it."

"Let Luther do what he does best—he can be formidable when he wants to be. He knows how to handle money-grubbers." The venom in Russell's voice shocked Rafe a little. He figured there was a story there and waited a few ticks of the old clock on the wall before returning to his breakfast. Finally he asked, "Do you want to talk about it?"

Russell shrugged. "Do I want to? No. But I probably should." He drank some more of his coffee. "Jase actually threatened to sue me for part of my company because he said that he'd come up with the original idea. Of course he hadn't. Jase knew nothing about ranching or farming. He was a city boy, born and raised. But he tried to weasel his way back into my good graces a few months after he left. I was messed up and couldn't deal with him. So Dad called in Luther, who did his magic, and Jase disappeared. I don't know what Luther did, and frankly I wasn't sure I wanted to know. But it did the trick. I never heard from Jase again."

"Do you think he and your dad paid him off?" Rafe asked.

"If they did, I never found any paper trail. And I've since taken over the books for the ranch, so I'd know about it if they did. No. I think Luther has legal ways of making sure that if your parents want to contest the will, it will cost them dearly. For now, though, I'd try not to worry about it. I know that's probably impossible, but it's what I think you should try to do anyway. Have your folks actually filed suit?"

"No. They're still soliciting support. They consider this to be something of a religious crusade. You know, they gather all the like-minded people together, all spouting the same opinion, and then imagine that opinion alone will change a legal outcome." He shook his head. "I hate to admit that I'm related to them."

When Rafe finished his breakfast, he cleared the table, then simply watched the snow fall outside the kitchen window.

There were very few times in his life when he'd had nothing to do. The snow kept him cabin-bound. He'd made sure the small herd of cattle had food and shelter. The horses were snug in the barn, and he and the dogs had a warm house. There was really nothing he *could* do until the storm let up and he could start digging out. But he was starting to feel a little stir-crazy.

"Is there anything else you need to go through?" Russell asked.

"I don't know. There are things in the attic, but it's going to be cold as hell up there. We've pretty much cleared out the bedroom. And I had to go through Uncle Mack's office when I first got here so I could get up to date on the herd and the ranch records." He sighed and poured himself another cup of coffee. "I wish I had a line on who this Dale might have been. Those letters stick in my mind for some reason." Thank God his uncle seemed to hate email and computers in general.

"There was a return address."

"Yeah, but from sixteen years ago. There have to be a lot of Dales in Denver. Who knows if Luther will be able to track him down?" Rafe felt a little low. "It would be cool if he could find someone who knew Uncle Mack back then... who might have known Uncle Mack and Dale as a couple." But that was just wishful thinking. Rafe had known his uncle up until he was twelve, but after that, he had become largely a stranger.

Maybe this quest Rafe had set himself on, to get to know who his uncle truly was, was destined to fail anyway. He was probably just wasting everyone's time.

"Did you ever get through all those boxes in the closet?" Russell asked.

"Not yet." Maybe it would be a good idea—as well as something for them to do—to pull some of those boxes out and see what was inside. So he got up and went to the closet, pulled out a number of boxes, and set them on the table. "Some of them seem to be old family pictures."

"You go through those and see if there are any you might want to keep or even frame. This still feels like Mack's place. But it's your home and it should feel like it. Maybe we can replace some of Mack's horse pictures with ones that you like."

"Maybe. But I doubt that there are any in here that I'd want to put up." Still, he opened the box and flipped through the first group of pictures. He set them aside when he knew no one in them. Uncle Mack had placed them in envelopes, and they seemed to be grouped. There were some of him as a kid, him on a horse, playing with the dogs, even a few with Uncle Mack. Those he set aside to look at later.

The next few envelopes contained old pictures of the family, often featuring his parents. Those he growled at and set in a pile to be put back in the box.

"What are these?" Russell asked, pulling out a few flat boxes.

"I'm not sure," Rafe said. He opened the first one and pulled out a buckle. "I'll be danged." He turned it over and handed it to Russell. "Uncle Mack's buckles. This one is for a win before I was born." He brought the box over and pulled out six more buckles, all of them silver and shining as brightly as the day they were presented. Uncle Mack had kept them in a special kind of cloth that kept them from becoming tarnished.

"Wow," Russell said.

"Yeah. I never knew he rode rodeo." Rafe smiled as he looked over the buckles and then placed them back into the protective sleeves before returning them to the boxes. "This is pretty cool. I guess I get my ability from him."

Russell reached for the next box and then slid it over to Rafe after looking inside. "There are more." He poked into additional boxes and set another one on top. "It looks like three boxes total. It seems Mack was quite the rider."

"Yeah, it looks that way. Though he rode broncs instead of bulls, he must have been really something." It had never occurred to Rafe to wonder if his uncle had ever ridden rodeo. "Maybe we can find out something about Uncle Mack from the Professional Rodeo Cowboys Association. A lot of these buckles are for professional events. Maybe they'll know something."

"It's worth a shot," Russell agreed.

"Could you check for inscriptions on the buckles? Year, event, etc. Let's make a list and see if there are any records we can search." He was excited as he went back to the pictures and started pulling out more envelopes.

Most of the pictures contained images of people Rafe didn't know, but one envelope held pictures of Uncle Mack. "Check this out."

Russell came around the table as Rafe laid out pictures on the surface. "These are all of Uncle Mack, but look at these three—they're him with the same man."

Russell picked one up, turned the picture over, and then handed it back. "Look…." He turned it over again, showing Rafe the inscription on the back. "That's Mack and Dale. At least now we know what he looked like, even though we still don't have a last name."

"And given what they're both wearing, I'd guess that Dale might have ridden in the rodeo too." Rafe was getting excited. Finally he had something to go on. "I think the first thing we need to do is find out about Mack. If we're lucky, he'll lead us to Dale."

Russell gathered the pictures and set them aside. Then he went through the remaining boxes, but they were just papers and receipts.

By the time he had gone through all the boxes, Russell had made a list of the events and the years. Rafe put the boxes back in the closet, then went back in the kitchen and sat down, once again looking out the window at the windblown snow. "Thank you for your help with that."

"You're welcome," Russell said. Then, apparently seeing a box they'd missed, he went over and brought it into the kitchen. He opened it and quietly pulled out more pictures. "Whoa," he whispered.

"What is it?" Rafe leaned forward.

Russell continued looking through the pictures, his skin paling. "This may be some of what you've been looking for." Russell's voice grew rough, and he came around the table and sat next to Rafe. "I figured this was just another box of pictures." He began setting them out on the table, and Rafe looked them over.

"That's me at my high school graduation." Rafe picked up the image to look closer. "It is. Where in the hell…?" Then he studied some of the others. "That one is me at one of my earliest rodeos. God, I remember that. It was in Texas. I was so new and green. But I made the eight, and I was so proud of my ride in the second round." He smiled to himself as Russell handed him another picture. "That's the buckle presentation at that same event. It was my first one. I still have it in my things." He swallowed hard. "Uncle Mack was there?"

Russell laid out other pictures, and Rafe was in all of them, at various rodeos and events throughout his life. "That one was taken at last year's finals where I finished third. Hell, he was in Las Vegas too." Rafe could barely speak. "Why didn't he come over and say something to me? He had gotten my cards and letters by then. He had to know…."

"Everything he wrote was returned. Maybe he didn't know how you'd react to seeing him. I don't know." Russell held his hand. "But I think the important thing is that he was there. After all that time, even facing hatred from your parents, he still came." Russell seemed choked up.

Rafe wiped his eyes and blinked, because cowboys didn't fucking cry, though he felt like he was seconds away from it. "Fucking hell. I spent the last fourteen years out there alone. I made my own fucking way, and yet I had family so damned close and I didn't even know about it. He was in the audience. Hell, he was at my graduation, and that was just days before everything changed for me. I remember Mom and Dad fighting when they got home that night. They sent me to my room and went at each other. Then, a few days later… well… everything went to shit." God, he tried not to think about that time, but it seemed impossible not to. Every time he thought of the past, two dates jumped out at him—the first when he was twelve, and the other when he was eighteen. And the worst part about it was that both of those dates intersected with major changes in his life—and, it seemed, in Uncle's Mack's as well.

"Do you think your parents saw Mack in the audience? Could that have been why they were fighting?" Russell asked, squeezing his fingers. Rafe turned his hand over, and Russell slid his fingers between his.

Rafe didn't know. He remembered his father being absolutely livid, and angry at his mother because she seemed less so. It had been weird at the time, but Rafe couldn't remember the details. All he could recall were the feelings he'd had that day, especially his disappointment that his parents' fighting had ruined what should have been a celebration. But had that been all there was to it? Hell, there were many things in his past that weren't what they seemed. "I wish he'd come to see me."

"I bet you do. But this answers one of my questions, and it should answer one for you too. No matter what happened, it seems your uncle never stopped loving you. And that squares with the man I knew your uncle to have been." Russell smiled. "He was a lot like you—hard and tough on the outside, but with a big heart."

Rafe liked to think so. He leaned against Russell as he looked at the pictures of Mack and Dale.

"Is there any way to know where or when these were taken?" Russell asked.

Rafe thought for a moment, then went back to his uncle's bedroom and returned with the box of buckles. "Yeah, there might be. See the buckle Uncle Mack is holding? I bet he'd just won it." Rafe checked through each of the boxes until he found two that looked like the one in the photo. "What do you think?"

"It's that one," Russell said, pointing to a buckle with a rider embossed on it. "They both have an outline of Texas." The warmth in Russell's eyes was almost overwhelming. "I knew Mack for a lot of years. Looking back, I sometimes think that he was using me as a substitute for you."

"Do you really think that Uncle Mack would do that?" Rafe asked.

Russell thought for a moment, then shook his head. "Maybe not. But I always got the sense that he was missing someone—likely you." He sighed softly. "The thing is, I thought I knew him, and yet I didn't... not really." Russell looked at the buckle and the picture of Mack and Dale. "Do you think Dale was a cowboy like Mack? If he rode in the rodeo, there should be records of participation. And he *is* dressed as a cowboy."

"That he is. Maybe they started off as competitors and became friends. That happens a lot. I competed against a lot of guys, and some of them were my friends."

"Like Duane?" Russell teased.

Rafe shook his head. "Duane isn't capable of leaving it in the arena. Sure, there were guys I hoped to beat... and I did. But afterwards we'd have a drink together and talk about who would win next time. As for Duane, I considered him just another competitor, someone I measured myself against. But once the rodeo was over, that was it. But not for him. To him it was personal, as if being beaten by a gay man diminished who he was as a person. And he only got angrier and meaner over time."

It was a damned shame, but after meeting Grant, Rafe had no doubt where Duane's attitude had come from. But there was little he could do about it.

"Can I ask you something? Is your dad serious about leasing the land?" Rafe asked, changing the subject. This was getting way too heavy, and he needed to take an emotional breather.

"Yeah. He really is. Like I said, I've made some deals that will allow us to expand, but we can't do that if we don't get access to more grazing land. Dad is looking at purchasing some on the other side of the ranch, and we could get additional land in another valley, but it makes sense to try to get property adjacent to what we already have. Leasing your place would gain us a year or so until you decide what you want to do. It would also bring in some money for the ranch." Russell scratched his head. "There might be another alternative, though. Maybe you could raise cattle for us."

Rafe gaped. "Excuse me?"

"Hear me out. I'm just thinking out loud. Part of the expense of raising cattle is buying the calves, protecting them until they're big enough, and then grazing them until it's time to take them to market. I'm not quite sure how it would work, but maybe we could provide the herd, you would graze and care for the animals, and we'd pay you to do it... somehow. It would help us both get what we need."

"Are you serious?" Rafe asked. "Where do you come from? I only met you a few weeks ago, and now it's like... I don't know.... First you and your men help with repairs, and now you're offering a way to make the ranch financially viable?" He was speechless. "Do you try to help everyone this way?"

Russell stood behind him and slipped his hands down Rafe's chest. "No, I don't. But we need space to produce more cattle, and you have that space. So we should be able to come up with something that will help us both. We're a pretty large operation, but we can sell more than we can produce at the moment. So if you produce for us and the herd is up to the standards we need, then we can bring you under our umbrella and you'll get a better price. If you're interested, you and Dad can get together and work things out between you." He sat back, looking satisfied with himself.

"Damn, you're like my cowboy guardian angel or something." Rafe couldn't help smiling. This was something he could move forward with, as long as Luther agreed. And once everything was settled, he'd be that much further ahead.

"I've been called many things over the years, but that's a first." Russell leaned closer, and Rafe kissed him. Then he got up and added some more wood to the fire, and they both hunkered down on the sofa.

"So what do you cowboys do when the weather is too bad to go out in?" Rafe asked as the wind rattled the windows. The sound was enough to make him shiver.

Russell suddenly got up and left the room, heading down the hall.

"Hey, what are you doing?"

"Just a second," Russell called. "Yeah, it's still here." Then he returned with a beat-up guitar case.

"Where was that?" Rafe asked, not recognizing it.

"In the back of the spare room closet." Russell sat down and took out an old guitar that had seen better days. "Your uncle used to play, and he taught me."

Rafe inhaled sharply. "I remember that." He smiled as Russell strummed a few notes and tuned the guitar. Then he slowly ran his fingers over the strings, playing a few chords. The dogs lifted their heads as though they were listening and maybe wondering where Uncle Mack was.

"I'm not much of a singer," Russell whispered and then began playing again, his eyes shining as he glanced at Rafe. In a few minutes, the gentle sounds filled the room, and Rafe pressed closer to Russell, just soaking in the melody, happy all the way down to his heart. When the sound faded, Russell handed Rafe the guitar.

"I don't know how to play," he said gently.

"Hold it like this and put your fingers right here. Put that finger here, and this one here. That's a D." Russell positioned Rafe's hands. "Now gently strum the strings."

He was so close, Rafe could barely concentrate on anything except Russell's scent wafting through the air. "That's it. Now move your fingers like this. That's a G." Rafe copied him, and the strings sang a little higher. Rafe continued playing, alternating between the chords as Russell smiled. The fire popped, adding percussion to what Rafe was playing.

"There's something soothing about this," Rafe said softly. He stopped and handed the instrument back to Russell.

Russell returned to playing, and Rafe settled back, soaking in the music and the joy that floated on the notes. He didn't move until Russell finished.

Russell set the guitar aside, then turned toward him with a soft smile and put his arm around him. "You are an incredible person, you know that?" Russell asked, his voice rough.

But Rafe just leaned against Russell's shoulder, holding his hand and wishing they could stay like this for hours.

"I hate to say it, but it looks like the snow is letting up," Russell said. The amount of light coming in the windows increased, as if to accentuate Russell's words.

Rafe groaned and sat back. "I guess that means we should both get to work."

"Or we could pretend it's still snowing like hell," Russell offered, tugging him to his feet. "The day is pretty much shot anyway...."

Rafe really wanted to take Russell up on his offer, but there were chores to do. "How about we get some work done? I have steaks in the freezer—we can have dinner together. But the drive has to be cleared, and your truck is still stuck out there. But once we're done...."

Russell nodded. "You're right, of course. Work has to come first. And I need to get my truck off the side of the road and back home before Dad starts to worry. But I'll see you tonight." With a burst of sudden energy, Russell got himself bundled up and strode down the drive toward his truck.

It might still be cold outside, but the heat from Russell's kiss was enough to keep Rafe warm for hours.

Chapter 8

"I WAS wondering where you were," Russell's dad said. It had taken longer than Russell had thought it would to retrieve his truck and get back to the ranch.

"I need to make some calls and arrange to travel tomorrow." He was already on the way to this office.

Dad followed him. "If you're going to get out, you need to do it now. The break in the weather is only going to last three or four hours. Apparently there's another line of snow building to the west, and you know how it is most of the time. The snow settles over us and doesn't move. Get to Denver and you'll be able to get out. But that means you'll need to leave now."

"I'm supposed to have dinner with Rafe."

He got a smile in return. "And you'd rather go have dinner than finish the deal that could put both businesses on the map permanently." Russell flashed his dad a "don't go there, old man" look, but all he got in return was laughter. "It's about fucking time."

"Excuse me?" Russell snapped. "I told you not to play matchmaker."

"Don't be snippy… and I'm not. But I am allowed to be happy. It's about time that you found something more important than business. I was beginning to wonder if it was ever going to happen again." He smirked. "But that doesn't change anything. You need to get to the helipad in the next hour if you're going to be able to leave the valley. This needs to be done."

"Shit…." Russell swore under his breath. "My bags are still in the truck."

"Go. I'll call the helipad and make the arrangements. You can phone Rafe on your way and let him know what's going on."

"Okay. But while I'm gone, I need you to finalize an agreement with him. He's going to raise cattle for us as a partnership instead of us just leasing the land. And this way we aren't further extending our hands…."

"And it spreads our risk while giving Rafe an ownership stake. Good idea. I'll work out the details with him and then get with the foreman so we are sure we have the stock to place with him." Dad almost gave him the bum's rush. "Get going. You can work on the way, but the weather is going to turn against you."

Russell returned to his truck and took off, wishing he had been able to stay, but his father was right. He needed to get out and put this deal to bed. Once it was done, he'd be able to hunker down at the ranch for the rest of the winter. But Russell's anxiety built as he drove away and he realized just how much he hated that he was going to disappoint Rafe… and how much he was going to miss him while he was gone.

"No, THAT'S not part of the deal," Russell said for the fourth time in the same meeting. "We already have a framework for price and delivery for the software. I was crystal clear that the software contract and the beef delivery contract were separate and that they were not contingent on each other." He kept his rising frustration out of his voice.

"I don't see it that way," the thirtysomething wannabe in a suit said, as though anybody gave a damn what he thought. Russell had gone head-to-head with this guy for two days and gotten nowhere, except to the point where he was beginning to wonder if this guy actually wanted either deal.

Russell shrugged and pulled out a blank sheet of paper, then wrote down the original terms. "This is all you're going to get on both fronts. Take it or leave it." He passed the sheet over, and the dark-haired wannabe pushed it aside.

"You'll need to do better than that." He sat back and threaded his fingers together.

"Actually, I don't, and I won't." He picked up his phone, sent a message, and received an almost immediate response. He smiled and turned his phone around, then slid it over so the wannabe could see it. "I just went over your head. It seems your boss, the person I originally negotiated with, wants this deal done and sent you to work out the final details." He glared at the wannabe. "You tried to be a hero and failed, big-time."

He shook his head as an assistant entered the room. The wannabe paled and left. When he returned five minutes later, he acted much more reasonable. "Now let's talk delivery schedules," Russell said without gloating, even though he really wanted to.

The rest of the meeting went well. Russell confirmed with his father and the foreman once he was back in his hotel that the schedule would work, especially if they could add Rafe's potential production to the deal.

"I also have a line on some additional land to the west. I'd heard that one of the ranchers who's been leasing their land to Mendeltom isn't happy with the way Mendeltom's been treating it. So I talked to him and found him more than eager to do business with us. That would add another thousand acres or so that will be available in the spring. Mendeltom has already been given notice to vacate by Christmas."

"He's going to be steamed as hell—you know that." Still, Russell couldn't feel sorry for him.

"Yeah, but the lease is up and it isn't going to be renewed. I already have a letter of intent signed and ready to go." Dad was definitely pleased.

"Good. But you know that's going to have Duane and Grant putting more pressure on Rafe. They're going to get desperate, and God knows what Duane might do. Grant may bluster, but I'm more afraid of Duane's rashness. You know he'll go after Rafe."

"As soon as we hang up, I'll call him and invite him to dinner. We can let him know what's coming his way then," his dad said. "I hadn't thought of that angle. Poor Rafe. It seems that every bit of trouble in this valley intersects at Mack's place.

"It sure seems that way," Russell said, thinking of Rafe and how he'd felt that early morning, pressed against him, warm and hard, heat radiating from him. Russell inhaled and swore he could still smell him in the air. It was just his imagination, but damn, it was a powerful memory.

"I'm going to get both deals signed in the next few days, and then we can start getting our projects put together."

"Then what's the problem?" his dad asked.

"Nothing really. They're trying to stall a little in order to try to put me off my game and make a deal that's more to their advantage. But they aren't getting anywhere and they need this deal. I have my company attorneys on standby, and they're prepared to review the final documents right away so we can get this done as soon as possible. Then I'll head home."

"Good. Let me know."

"I will." Russell hung up and called Rafe. "Hey," he said with a sigh. "I'm sorry about the other day."

"I understand," Rafe said. "We got another dump of snow, but it's sunny right now and a lot of it is melting." Russell loved how Rafe's voice wrapped around him and eased some of his tension.

"That's really good. I should be home in a few days." He stifled a yawn and closed his eyes for a few seconds.

"You sound really tired," Rafe said. "Are you sleeping okay?"

"Not really." He tried not to yawn again and failed. "Dad is going to call you about the deal we talked about, and I'm afraid that Grant is going to be furious as hell because one of his leases isn't being renewed and we're optioning the land. So be careful and watch out for him—and Duane." He hated that Rafe was in the line of fire. "There isn't much he can do legally, but I suspect that won't stop him."

"I'm okay, and I have the dogs. My parents have filed with the probate court regarding the will. Luther says they have two weeks to submit their arguments. Apparently this type of thing isn't handled with a trial unless there's a reason for it. Luther says he's going to file a number of motions that they'll have to respond to, including one for outright dismissal."

"Good. Make them pay. There's no basis for contesting the will anyway… other than pure greed."

"Luther will let me know when a hearing is scheduled." He chuckled slightly. "The cattle are doing well, and I took the horses out for exercise today. Other than that, I'm just trying to get whatever repairs and chores done that I can."

"I see."

"I sent an email to the Professional Rodeo Cowboys Association about the attendance records of the events we thought Uncle Mack might have ridden in, but I haven't heard anything back. Who knows? I may never get a response, though I'd think I would." So did Russell, given that Rafe was the reigning bull-riding champion.

"Please let me know what you find out," Russell said.

After saying good night, Russell ended the call, then went to his computer and pulled up a browser window. He went to the website for the Professional Rodeo Cowboys Association and sent an email of his own. He also went to the individual sites for the rodeos they had identified and sent inquiries directly to them, just in case they might have the information Rafe needed.

Not that he expected an immediate answer, but he found himself checking his inbox often. It was stupid, and Russell forced his mind onto other things. He probably should be running through the contract details and getting ready for the final push, but all he could think about was Rafe—the feel of his skin on his. Those strong hands, with just the perfect amount of work roughness. Rafe was a man who'd worked hard all his life. Russell liked that, because he had done the same thing one way or another. Even though his hands were smooth now, he still knew what was required to clean stalls and care for the cattle. He had done all of it, up to and through part of college.

He turned back to his phone, tempted to call again just to hear Rafe's voice. Russell was so tired and worn out. Tired of it all—these people, and this city, with its heat, pavement, and constant sunlight that seemed to bake the color out of just about everything. At night the view from his window was a sea of lights, and during the day it was nothing but pale roofs and concrete.

He much preferred his view at the ranch—mountains and snow during the days, and the only brightness lighting up the nights was millions of stars. This place sapped away his energy, and he just wanted to go home. The funny thing was that somehow, whenever he thought of home now, the first thing that came to mind was a living room with worn, comfortable furniture, three dogs by the fire, and Rafe on the sofa, maybe taking a nap or just reading in that quiet way he had. Russell shook his head. He knew that was a stupid notion. But still, it persisted.

He and Rafe hadn't made any promises to each other. Hell, they had only known each other a matter of weeks. Russell needed to stop his mind from jumping ahead. He knew from experience that he should take things slower so he could be sure.

But Rafe wasn't anything like Jase. Rafe listened and was grateful, where Jase had expected to be given everything he wanted. Still, Russell knew he should slow things down.

Unfortunately, every time he closed his eyes, all he could see was Rafe, with those deep, warm eyes and the gentle manner that hid his strength, cloaked in the same kind of vulnerability that Russell carried himself. Maybe he was drawn to Rafe because he saw the same kind of hurt in him, as well as the same hope.

Russell picked up the hotel phone and contacted room service to place an order. He needed something sweet, and cheesecake seemed to fit the bill. While waiting for the knock on his door, he finished up some work and sent out emails to his staff to alert them to the pending contract and the list of customizations that the client was requesting. He stressed that this was simply a heads-up and that no work was to be done until he alerted them that the contract had been signed.

TWO FULL days later, he was on his way home. Russell had heard nothing on any of his inquiries regarding the rodeos, and Rafe had told him during their many calls that he hadn't either. Still, it was good to be going home in time for the holiday, and Russell figured once he was there, he could get in touch with some friends who might be able to help. After the flight to Denver, he took the helicopter to the pad in the valley before heading out into the night. He thought about going to Rafe's, but it was late, so he went home and started celebrating the holiday by sleeping late. When he got up, he found his father already watching football in the living room with a few of his buddies.

Russell said good morning and then left the men to their fun and headed out to Rafe's. He was still a little tired, but his truck seemed to have a mind of its own, and he soon found himself pulling into Rafe's driveway, where three vehicles and a police car sat in the drive. He pulled to a stop and went inside. There, he found Grant, Rafe, and Rafe's parents all glaring at each other, with Shelby Connors, the sheriff, looking on, totally bewildered.

What a way to start Thanksgiving Day. Then again, in many households, this holiday was the time for drama. But poor Rafe was getting a second helping of it.

Russell couldn't help chuckling when he saw the three dogs. They were sitting in front of Rafe like a line of soldiers, their stares just daring anyone to try and get through. "What's going on?" Russell asked, and the dogs hurried over to say hello.

"I'm suing him, that's what's going on…. And you! How dare you snatch my grazing land out from under me," Grant snarled, a line of spittle running down his chin, his eyes more than a little wild. For a second Russell wondered if he was completely rational. Jesus, he had always thought Grant was all talk and that Duane was the hothead, but he might have been wrong. Maybe Grant was more than bluster after all. The three dogs seemed to be tensing at Grant's tone and maybe the scent of desperation he was giving off. Dogs were amazing at picking up that sort of thing.

Rafe put the dogs out in the sunroom.

"Mendeltom has no basis in reality for whatever it is he's spouting," Russell said. Then he turned to the sheriff. "Mendeltom's lease is up. The owner of the land isn't happy with the way he's looked after it, so he's leasing it to us," Russell explained to bring the sheriff up to speed. Then he turned back to Grant. "As for suing Rafe, on what grounds?" he added.

"His uncle stole my water." Grant sounded like a petulant child. It was almost funny, except for how wide Grant's pupils were and the way he was breathing. He really was either stressed out… or totally losing it. Russell was afraid to find out.

Russell nodded. "Accusations against a dead man. I'm sure that's going to go over well in court." He chuckled. "That's going to really help you. Maybe I'll add that to the town Facebook group. See how that kind of idiocy goes over. Now, I suggest you leave. I'd like to celebrate Thanksgiving with my friend here. Right, Rafe?"

Rafe nodded. "Sheriff, please see that he leaves or I'll press charges. He is not to come back on my land for any reason. Please consider the next incursion as trespassing."

"Gladly." Shelby seemed more than happy to have something to do. He ushered a still-sputtering Grant out, and Russell stood behind Rafe so he'd know he had backup when dealing with his parents.

Russell was pissed off that he was coming back to this, and his patience was wearing thin. "Do you want to deal with them? Or can I?" Russell asked and got a smile in return.

"I got it," Rafe said. "They came here in a last-ditch effort to convince me to see things their way. They've obviously just figured out that they aren't getting anywhere. Now, if I'd had another family, you might rightly have presumed that they'd come because it was a holiday and they wanted to mend fences. But unfortunately, that's not the family I was born into." He didn't even look at them until he was done speaking. Then he turned to them, shaking his head in disgust. "What is it that you think you deserve?"

"Mack was your mother's brother, and he received money from their parents. That now belongs to her," his father said.

Rafe shook his head. "I remember that. Mom got her share, and Uncle Mack got his. Did you try to stop him from getting his fair share then too?" The way Rafe's mother bit her lower lip told Russell that he'd hit the nail on the head. "Well, you got all you're getting. So just go home and live out the rest of your miserable lonely lives. I've made a life here that doesn't include you. And I'm going to live it to the best of my ability, just like Uncle Mack did after you turned your backs on him. So, just because you seem to keep forgetting, let me spell it out for you. I will give you *nothing*. Not one red cent." He pulled out one of the kitchen chairs and sat down.

Russell stood next to him. He wasn't going to leave Rafe to do this alone.

"I used to wonder what I'd say to you if I ever had this chance. All of us in a room together. I used to imagine that I could somehow make you see just how badly you treated me after I was brave enough to tell you who I was. But that was a lost cause—then, and now." He sighed.

"What you told us was—" his mother started, but Rafe put his hand up.

"You get to say nothing. I made my own way after that, and I've done one hell of a good job of it. As for you two? You're nothing but my egg and sperm donors. You're definitely not parents. After all, you failed in your greatest duty—to love your child unconditionally.

"So now it's over. And whatever you think you're entitled to…. Well, dream on. Your failure has cost you everything important in life—you failed me, your son, and you failed Uncle Mack, your brother. So you will get nothing! I will fight you with every cent I have, if I have to. I will not pay you to go away, and I will make sure that your legal bills go through the roof. Everything you do will be countered multiple ways. If you file one motion, we'll counter with ten." He leaned forward. "Don't try to put this on me. It's your own fault. It's over."

"I…," his mother began again and wiped her eyes.

Rafe turned to her, his expression softening for a few seconds. Russell wondered if perhaps she wasn't as rigid about her beliefs as her husband. Maybe there was a chance for her and Rafe to have *some* kind of relationship. That would be a nice Thanksgiving present for Rafe.

"That's enough, Rachel," Rafe's father said, cutting off Russell's ruminations.

She turned to her husband, eyes as hard as granite, her crocodile tears drying up in seconds. "You're right. It is enough, Lyle. More than enough." Rachel left through the back door, leaving Lyle alone in the room.

"I mean it. You will get nothing from me, so you might as well drop it." Rafe seemed so strong that Russell almost believed he was calm and in control… until he noticed the way Rafe's fingers were twitching like crazy behind his back. "You should go too, or else I'll call the sheriff back to escort you."

He looked his father straight in the eye. "I made my way without you. I became a world champion with no help from you. And I'm going to build a home here. So I suggest you forget about me, because the next time I think about you, it will be when someone tells me that you're dead. Maybe then I'll have a drink to celebrate."

Damn, that sounded stone cold, but Rafe's telltale nerves let Russell know it was an act—one Russell had no intention of calling him on. In that instant, he understood just how hard this was for Rafe, but Russell suspected it was something he felt he had to do.

"You ungrateful little shit," Lyle growled between clenched teeth. "We did our best for you, but you insisted on pursuing this... lifestyle... rather than getting the help you needed. Your mother and I had no choice." His eyes burned with the heat of the devil himself. This was a sanctimonious man who thought he was right, and nothing was ever going to change his mind.

"And it never occurred to you that you could be wrong?" Rafe walked over to the door. "Of course it didn't. A good father would know better. Russell's did. But though you are a lot of things, a good parent isn't one of them. So, goodbye. And good riddance."

The sheriff met them at the door. "Please see that they leave the property," Rafe said to him. Then he closed the door, and his knees seemed to buckle under him. He leaned on the door, and Russell raced over to him. "Fuck, that was hard." He sighed and made his way to one of the chairs.

"I don't know what to say. It's shitty that you had to go through all that. But you were strong as hell." He took Rafe's hand, squeezing his fingers.

"I really used to hope that somehow they'd realize they were wrong. That maybe someday they would understand just what they threw away. I rode harder than anyone else, pushed myself to the limits. Maybe if I was champion, then they would be proud of me. But there was nothing I could do to change their minds. And it's taken me a lot of years to realize that it's their problem, not mine. Still, sometimes it hurts—though not as much as it used to. And hopefully, after today, I'll stop thinking about them altogether." Rafe lifted his gaze from his shoes.

"They don't deserve you. They never deserved you." Hell, Russell wished he knew exactly what to say to make Rafe feel better. For years Rafe had held out hope that his parents might come to love him and accept him for who he was. Today that hope had died—hard. The money-grubbing, self-righteous assholes had shown themselves for who they really were, and Rafe now had to deal with the truth. Russell knew how hard it was to cope with loss. His own mother had died a few years ago. But her loss had been final—there was no coming back from it. He wondered if it was harder when hope itself ceased to exist.

"I'm sorry about all this," Rafe said, forcing a smile. "How was your trip? Did you get done what you needed to?"

"Yes. The deals have been finalized, though I see that some of the implications of them ended up right back on you."

"Yeah, Mendeltom was really pissed. Not only is he *not* going to get his hands on my ranch, but he's now lost access to land he was counting on for his operation."

Russell shrugged. "Grant Mendeltom is not a good rancher, nor is he a good steward of the land. The reason he's losing access to those fields is because they're in danger of being overgrazed. As it is, we're paying less the first year because we will have to leave the land fallow to allow it recuperate before we place any cattle there. We'll just cut it for feed and let the area recover."

"I spoke to your father, and we agreed that in the spring, we'll put five hundred young head on my property," Rafe said. "You guys will provide the stock, and I'll provide water and grazing and care for them like they were my own. And we'll divide the proceeds once you take them to market. It should work out well for both of us. I'm thinking about hiring a couple of hands to help with the operation. And I want to start a bucking bull program."

"Dad is going to be so damn jealous," Russell said.

"I don't think so. Not really. I like your dad. He's straightforward and he knows what he wants. If the cattle agreement goes well, then he and I are going to work together on getting some bulls in stock. I was thinking of building some enclosures for them over by where our lands meet. It will be away from the rest of the herds, and maybe we can even look at breeding some good buckers."

It was good to see Rafe smiling, at least for a few seconds. "Never heard from any of the rodeo people, though. I'll give it a little time. Maybe send a follow-up. Sometimes things slip down in the email inbox and get lost."

Russell made a note to make a few calls himself to see if he could rattle a few cages. "Listen, you're going to want to be careful. Mendeltom is a mean son of a bitch. Now that he's lost a couple thousand acres, it's going to put a lot of stress on his operation… and him."

Rafe shook his head in disgust. "The man's a blowhard, just like his son. Duane always acted the big man, but when push came to shove, he always backed down, just like most bullies."

"Oh, Grant is a bully all right, but he isn't a blowhard. He's a pot stirrer, never happier than when he's getting people riled up. I'm afraid that he'll try to find some way to get even with me and Dad for the loss of those fields. And the easiest way for him to do that is through you somehow." And it would be all Russell's fault.

"Well, there's nothing we can do about it now. Let him try. Luther has things well in hand as far as the estate goes. My parents have been pretty well shut down, and Mendeltom won't have a leg to stand on. As far as the rest…." He shrugged. "I'm a rodeo champion. And we champions have to be made out of sterner stuff. He won't get the better of me." Rafe slid closer. "But I appreciate your support. It means a lot that you were here."

"I just wish I'd gotten here earlier."

"There was nothing you could have done. Mendeltom and my parents have been in league with each other for years. They kept tabs on Uncle Mack, probably out of spite and maybe to find out if he had something they wanted. I really wish I knew the reasons, but they don't really matter now."

Russell slipped his arms around Rafe's neck. "Do you think they'll be back?"

Rafe shrugged. "I don't know. My parents have lost, and now they know it. And since they don't want to have anything to do with me and my abhorrent lifestyle, they'll probably go back to Denver, stew over how unfair things are, and eventually go back to their miserable lives. At least, that's what I'd expect them to do." He shook his head. "All my life, I had their views of morality and religion rammed down my throat, but in the end, they set both those things aside just for money. Turns out their greed is more powerful than their faith." He hugged Russell, resting his head on his shoulder. "I'm so glad you're back. I really missed you." He tightened his hold, just standing there and breathing softly in Russell's ear.

"Are you okay? Really?" Russell asked, and felt Rafe shake his head.

"I didn't sleep well the past week," Rafe admitted in a whisper.

"Neither did I." Russell slowly rubbed Rafe's wide back. Rafe was a strong man—he'd had to be in order to survive everything he'd been through and come out the other side. But deep down, he could hurt, just like everyone else. What surprised Russell was that Rafe showed that vulnerability to him. And Russell wanted to help, to heal what had been wounded, but that was beyond his ability. He could be here for Rafe, but it was up to Rafe to find a way to get past that crap from his family.

"Sometimes people suck."

"Yeah, they do." And yet sometimes, the most amazing person showed up right in front of you. He'd been gone a week and had missed Rafe like a limb. Maybe it was time for him to open up and just say what he felt inside, what he'd come to realize lying alone in that damned hotel room night after night while the fucking client played his stupid games.

Russell took a small step back, gently cupping Rafe's cheeks in his hands. It was time for him to let go of his own crap. Jase had had a hold on him for too damned long. It was time for Russell to let him go and to allow himself to let someone else in. "I think...." He paused and lowered his gaze. Why in the fuck was this so damned hard?

"What?" Rafe asked, holding his gaze.

Russell moved his lips but couldn't make the words come out. *Damn.*

Chapter 9

Rafe held his breath, waiting for whatever Russell was going to say. He figured it was rare for Russell to be struck dumb. The man was usually very articulate and always had plenty to say. So this was something new. Rafe swallowed hard and blinked a few times, determined to wait for Russell to say whatever was on his mind.

"Sometimes things are…." Russell cleared his throat. "Why is it that the things a person feels are always the hardest to say?"

"I think that's a question for the poets," Rafe whispered.

"Or a cowboy." Russell smiled slightly. "Sometimes I think about the men who came before us. A cowboy's life was hard. They spent a lot of nights alone, out on the range sleeping under the stars, or in a wagon, maybe with little more than a bedroll and a tarp to keep out the rain. They had a lot of time to themselves, especially at night. So yeah, maybe cowboys were poets or musicians. It makes sense to me. But the thing is, I'm neither of those. Sometimes I wish I had the gift for words those men had."

"I don't know. I've never seen you as the strong, silent type," Rafe told him with a smirk. "And you usually don't beat around the bush." He held Russell's gaze. "Just say what it is you want."

Russell took a deep breath. "I don't want anything... other than to tell you that I love you." He paused a second. "I missed you the entire time I was away, but it's more than that. I feel like I can show you who I really am. I don't have to be the businessman, the son of the ranch owner, or anything else. I only have to be me. You see that... you see me."

"Of course I do," Rafe said. "What else am I supposed to see?"

"And that's why I love you. You don't even understand why it might be an issue. You accept me for who I am, flaws and all."

Rafe rolled his eyes. "Please. It was your flaws that I noticed first, after all." He pulled Russell closer. "Remember? You were kind of an ass that first day. Though I have to admit, you looked damned good on that horse, like a cowboy out of a Western movie, with eyes blazing at perceived injustice." He couldn't help a smile.

"Hey. I thought...."

"I know what you thought, because I thought the same thing at first. And now I think I understand why Uncle Mack left me the ranch, and I'm grateful to him... and to you, for everything."

Russell lowered his gaze. "I see," he said softly.

Rafe stroked Russell's cheek. "No, you don't. Sometimes I wonder what love really is. My parents were supposed to love me, and you saw how fucking well that turned out."

"Are you afraid I'm going to act the same way?" Russell asked.

That was the last thing that Rafe was worried about. "No. I'm afraid that I won't know how to love you back. I haven't had the best role models. You saw the kind of people I grew up with. Hell, I don't even know if my mom and dad ever loved each other. Their church doesn't condone divorce, so it's possible that they've stayed together just because of that. Who knows? My father only wants control." He shrugged. "Is that what love is?"

Rafe knew he probably sounded whiny and dumb, but his question was an honest one. The "love" he'd seen in his life had been toxic, controlling, and hurtful. That wasn't what he wanted with Russell.

"All you need to do is be yourself. Be the man who sent cards and letters to his uncle for years, even though you never heard anything back. Be the guy who inherited a ranch but spends his time trying to learn who his uncle is. Those are the things that show your heart. That's all you need to do." He smiled. "I was lucky. My dad would have done anything for my mother. He nursed her when the cancer got bad, barely leaving the house for six months, making sure she ate and helping her bathe and use the bathroom. They were devoted to each other. I thought he'd fall to pieces after she died. To me, that's love. It's caring when the other needs it, listening, putting the other person before yourself."

"You definitely do that," Rafe said, blown away by Russell's insight into Rafe's behavior, even when Rafe hadn't realized it himself. The truth was... he was afraid. "But what if I turn out like my parents?"

"You just sent them packing. You aren't going to turn into them. You're Rafe, plain and simple." Russell smiled again, and Rafe pulled him close and kissed him.

"I do love you. I know it seems fast."

"Me too, and I'm scared it's too fast. But when you know it...." Russell swallowed hard. "I have a history of jumping in too quickly."

He'd told Rafe that before. Rafe offered Russell a small smile. Weren't they a pair? Russell had had a tough time with love, and Rafe barely understood what it meant. Maybe they were meant to figure this out together. Maybe that was the lesson they both needed to learn. Who knew? But there was one thing Rafe was sure of—his heart felt lighter, and the sense of darkness he'd felt thanks to his parents' visit seemed to have dissipated like fog under the summer sun.

The thing was, Russell telling him that he loved him made Rafe happier than he could remember being in a very long time. Rafe guided Russell out of the kitchen and down the hall toward his bedroom, nearly tripping over one of the dogs on the way.

Russell paused and stepped away. "You need to take care of them."

"But...," Rafe was surprised.

"I'll be waiting in the bedroom for you," Russell said.

That was enough to spur Rafe into action. He called the dogs, filled their food and water bowls, and set them down before kicking off his shoes and heading down the hall.

He paused in the doorway of the bedroom, admiring the view. Russell was lying on the bed, arm resting over his eyes, beautifully naked, with all that perfectly golden skin against the white sheets. Rafe inhaled deeply, his throat going dry. He slowly stepped into the room, almost afraid to move in case this was a fantasy. He had spent the past week wishing Russell was here, and now he was back, in his bed. And fucking hell, Russell had actually told him that he loved him. That alone blew him away. Rafe had never been luckier than he was at this moment.

Slowly, he moved forward, meeting Russell's gaze as he unbuttoned his shirt and slipped it off. Then his socks followed, and finally his pants. His cock sprung free the moment his jeans slid off his hips. He closed the distance between them, then leaned over the bed and kissed Russell as he climbed onto the mattress. Russell wound his arms around his neck, pulling him closer. "Now what are we going to do?" Rafe whispered.

Russell chuckled. "If you don't know, I'd say we're in trouble."

He smiled. "I mean… this is different. This isn't just sex. It's something more, and what if…?"

Russell rolled his eyes. "Sweetheart, in case you haven't noticed, it was always something more between us. Because if what we've been doing was just sex… then God help us when we're making love. We both might die of heart attacks." He waggled his eyebrows and laughed until he snorted, then covered his mouth. "This has to be the least romantic conversation in the history of sex."

"I don't know about that," Rafe said. He sucked lightly at the base of Russell's neck, loving the way he tasted and the sounds he made. There was no doubt about how excited Russell was—his passion and pleasure came out in the sounds he made. That alone was sexy. And when they came from a man as gorgeous as Russell, it was nearly overwhelming. And yet Rafe did his best to control himself. He wanted to make this last.

"Oh yeah," Russell moaned.

"You know, I think words are overrated at a time like this." Rafe kissed Russell hard, sliding his hand over his smooth chest and belly, his fingers slipping through the nest of curls until they wrapped around Russell's thick cock, which elicited a whine of pleasure from Russell that grew louder with each and every movement. "That's more like it."

"But you're talking," Russell protested.

Rafe smiled. "Don't worry—I intend to have you almost incoherent in a few minutes." He kissed him again before proceeding to reduce Russell to groans and openmouthed cries that the air seemed to swallow up.

Neither one of them said anything. There was no need. Rafe reveled in every part of this moment, seeing Russell in the throes of complete passion. No words, just shaking limbs, pebbled nipples, skin seemingly on fire, and eyes as wide as saucers. This, *this* was what he wanted. And when Russell gripped the bedding, wrapping his legs around Rafe's waist as he slid his wrapped cock deep inside him, all Rafe could do was hang on for one hell of a ride. Rafe let Russell take charge for as long as he was able. Then, when Rafe took over, Russell rocked against him, each and every movement countered at the exact right time to send Rafe closer to the edge.

He was determined to hold out for Russell, wrapping his fingers around his length, stroking in time to their movements until Russell's breathing grew shallow and urgent. Then he doubled his speed, and Russell filled the room with his cries of passion as both of them careened over the precipice, flying together for precious seconds, holding one another as they soared in their release, before slowly returning to lie in each other's arms.

"Don't you have Thanksgiving dinner to go home to or something?" Rafe asked. It had been quite some time since he'd actually celebrated any holiday, and certainly not in the way he and Russell just had.

Russell checked the time and climbed out of the bed. "Violet will have dinner ready in a few hours." He slipped on his pants and tossed Rafe's clothes toward him. "Come on. We should make sure everything is secured, then head over for dinner."

Rafe shook his head. "I don't want to intrude…."

Russell laughed hard. "We're having a cowboy Thanksgiving. Dad invites all the single hands, as well as his cronies. They show up and Violet puts out a spread of epic proportions, and then everyone sits around Dad's big-screen television eating and watching football for most of the day. The holiday was different when Mom was alive, but Dad started this tradition after she passed. I think it's easier for him to get through the day if he spends it doing completely different things than what he and Mom used to do." Russell leaned over the bed. "So come and join us. We can watch a little football, drink some beer, and eat all we want."

Rafe nodded, trying not to think too much about the implications of going home with Russell for the holiday.

"Think of it this way. It may not be the kind of Thanksgiving you grew up with, but it will be fun. Uncle Mack used to come by too, the last few years. He was part of our family, and now, you are too." Russell's eyes shone as he kissed Rafe gently.

Rafe was more than a little overwhelmed as he got out of bed and went to his dresser. "If I'm having Thanksgiving dinner with your dad and his friends, I'm not going to look like a schlub." He found fresh clothes and pulled out his good boots. Maybe this was what he needed—a chance to put the family he was born into out of his mind. Tonight, he'd be celebrating Thanksgiving with the family he was hoping to join.

"WHAT THE hell is that?" Russell asked later that night, jumping out of Rafe's bed. They'd nearly eaten themselves into a food coma and yelled at the television for hours before returning to Rafe's place for the night.

The dogs were barking like crazy. Rafe got out of bed, pulled on his pants, and headed to the living room. He peered out the window as the dogs propped their paws on the sill, still growling. "Do you see anything?" Rafe called out to Russell, who was already dressed and pulling on his coat. As he headed to the door, Rafe called out, "Don't go out there."

Rafe hurried back to the bedroom and threw on the rest of his clothes on and then his outdoor gear before joining Russell at the front door. "I can't see anything, but the dogs definitely hear something." They pranced around the room, growling and then jumping to look out the window.

Rafe kept the dogs inside as Russell went out. He followed, making sure the dogs stayed in the house. Then Rafe heard a sharp whinny. "The horses!" he yelled as he ran across the yard. He slipped into the barn, where the horses were lunging in their stalls.

"It's okay. Everything is fine," he crooned, trying to calm them. Out of the corner of his eye, he saw the flicker of a flame in one corner of the barn. "Shit." As he watched, the flames grew, and before he knew it, fire was licking at the corner of the building. He turned, hearing the back barn door bang closed. Rafe raced to the corner of the barn, connected the hose, and doused the flames before they could really take hold.

"Someone was running toward the road," Russell said. "Shit." He grabbed the fire extinguisher from inside the tack room and sprayed the area. He finally put out the fire. "That was close. What the hell happened?"

"I'm not sure. I think I may have startled some-one. Whoever it was seemed intent on starting a fire, but I think I scared him off." Rafe pulled air into his lungs. "Can you calm the horses while I try to clean up this mess?" He made sure the walls and floor were good and wet before turning off the hose. Then he grabbed a shovel and a wheelbarrow, scooped up the bedding, and got it outside. The barn walls, though old, had only been scorched.

"You got lucky. A fire in here would spread fast," Russell said as the horses started to calm.

The scent of smoke hung in the air, so Rafe flung the barn doors open to air the place out, even though it was bitterly cold. After a few minutes, the breeze had pushed a lot of the smoke, and most of the smell, from the barn, so Rafe closed the doors again. Then he turned on the heaters and gave the horses some extra oats and warm water.

"Did you see who did this?" Rafe asked.

"Not really. I'd guess it was a man, but I couldn't swear to that. It was hard to see. Mostly I just noticed movement against the snow." Russell shrugged. "I'll call the sheriff to come take a look. Maybe he'll come across something that will tell us who's behind this."

While Russell made the call, Rafe finished making sure the horses had what they needed, then went back to the house to wait. It was going to be a long night.

IT TOOK the sheriff a while to arrive. He looked things over in the barn and scolded them for cleaning up, before checking out the trail left in the snow. "I

need to do some looking around," he said levelly.
"There's been plenty of activity here today." Rafe
wondered what he meant by that.

"Shelby, you know as well as I do that someone
tried to set fire to Rafe's barn. Getting angry with
him isn't going to help you figure out who did it."

"No. But it's been one hell of a day. It took me
half an hour to calm down your neighbor," the sheriff
groused.

"That has nothing to do with Rafe. Grant sees
slights everywhere… doesn't matter if they're real
or not." Russell drew closer. "What sort of trouble
has Rafe caused? Beating out Duane for the championship? Inheriting the property from his uncle? I
know—maybe he's the one responsible for the avalanche that changed the direction of the stream?"
Russell was bordering on the ridiculous, but Rafe
loved him for it. "Come on. Nothing is ever Grant's
fault. The land he's complaining about losing… he
overgrazed it, and the owner isn't happy. Grant Mendeltom's issues are his own making, and if he's behind this…." Russell's eyes blazed with anger.

"Let the sheriff do his job," Rafe said gently.
"What can we do to help?"

"Nothing at the moment. I need to follow some
things up and see where they lead." He tipped his hat.
"I'll be in touch." Then he left, while Russell muttered
under his breath as he watched from the barn door.

"What?"

"The sheriff didn't turn back toward town. He
went the other way," Russell reported. "To Mendeltom's. Maybe he thinks one of them is involved."

"Do you really think Grant would do something like that?" Rafe asked.

"I have no idea. Before yesterday, I would have suspected Duane. But who the hell knows? Duane isn't the most stable of people, and there's definitely no love lost between you two. But after Grant came unglued this morning, I'd say anything is possible." He met Rafe's gaze. "If the Mendeltom ranch is in trouble…."

"Then Duane loses out too."

"Yeah. He's always lorded his position over people. Grant bought Duane a brand-new car when he turned sixteen, and then another one when he graduated. They've always seemed to have money, but I bet they've been living above their means. And now, with the ranch not doing so well and Grant's chickens have come home to roost, he's got to be stretched pretty thin."

Rafe slipped an arm around Russell's waist. "How do you know this?"

Russell paused. "I'm a businessman, and there are certain signs that tell you when a business is healthy. The first one is that bills are paid on time. The second is that when they sell to you, they don't beg for payment as soon as possible. Mendeltom always needs to be paid right away, yet he holds his bills until the people he owes threaten to turn him in for collection. This is a small town, and a guy can hear plenty of things if he knows what to listen for."

"I suppose." Sometimes it was difficult being the new person, the outsider. "Do you think whoever did this will try again?" Rafe wondered if he should sleep in the barn, but then what if someone decided to light up the house?

"I doubt it. What I think is that someone had way too much to drink and is now on their way home, scared out of their wits because they nearly got caught. Either that, or they are already sleeping it off." Russell guided him out of the barn and made sure the door was closed. "Come on. Let's go back inside."

Rafe was still rattled, so he let Russell comfort him. The dogs all gathered around him and Russell when they came inside, and after giving them treats, he let them outside to take care of business. A few minutes later, all three trooped back inside and dropped onto their blanket in front of the fireplace. They had done their duty. The dogs had warned him, and now it was time for them to rest.

Rafe was tired as hell but afraid to go to sleep in case their firebug came back. This was his home—or at least he was trying to make it a home—and now it felt like it was under attack.

"I'm not sure what to do. I want to get a gun and stand guard all damned night." He remembered feeling the same way back when he'd lost everything thanks to his parents' rejection. He actually wondered for a moment if they were behind it. Then he realized that setting a fire wasn't his parents' style. They were more likely to get another lawyer, or forget he existed, than physically attack.

"Unfortunately, we have to wait and let the sheriff do his job."

Rafe growled. He wasn't angry at Russell, just the entire situation. "I'm not particularly good at things like that. I mean, what is the sheriff going to do? Whoever did this is long gone." He rolled his eyes and tried to resist hitting something.

"Just relax." Russell picked up his phone to make a call. "Hey, Dad. We need a little help. Someone broke into Rafe's barn and started a fire. We put it out, but it's just the two of us over here…." Russell nodded. "Okay. Thank you. We'll watch for them." He put his phone on the table. "A couple of the guys are on their way over. They'll be here in the next half hour, so we should put on a pot of coffee. One of them will stay out in the barn, and another will keep watch here." Russell lightly patted Rafe's leg.

"You didn't need to do that." Still, Rafe was grateful for the help.

Russell shook his head. "What part about helping your neighbors don't you understand?"

"But what about your place?" Rafe asked.

Russell offered him a wicked grin. "Have you met our foreman? If anyone tried to pull something like this at our place, Jessup would find them and rip their throats out. He's been with my father for thirty years, and no one in the valley messes with him. You remember when we came over to help you? Jessup wasn't with us, and yet he was the one who made sure the men had what they needed. They listen to him more than they listen to me."

"Okay…." He wasn't sure where Russell was going.

"Half the valley is afraid of Jessup, and the other half is in awe of him. Sometimes I swear Jessup has eyes in the back of his head. Violet taught me how to cook, and Jessup was the man who taught me all about horses. And I got my business instincts from my father."

"So in other words, you're not worried at all."

"Nope. And you don't need to be either." Russell's gaze met his. "We look out for the people we care for. If anyone hurts you, it's the same as hurting us. Period. My dad really likes you, and he hated Jase on sight. I should have known the guy was bad news if Dad didn't like him." Russell smiled and then sighed. "Let's get the coffee on before the guys get here."

Rafe nodded, still worried. It wasn't like he could keep Russell's men here forever. Hopefully the sheriff would get to the bottom of this soon.

Chapter 10

RUSSELL WOKE after a fitful night. Rafe hadn't slept much and kept waking up. The dogs refused to settle, even after they'd greeted Brad and Dustin again. Finally, after almost an hour, everyone in the house had managed to get to sleep.

Russell slipped out of bed and grabbed his clothes, then headed across to the bedroom to dress. Rafe needed to sleep, and he left him to it.

"Anything?" he asked Brad when he found him in the kitchen getting some coffee.

"No. It was quiet. Dustin was in here a little while ago, but he went out to check the barn again." He sat down with his mug, and Russell poured himself some coffee as well. "Where's Rafe?"

"Still sleeping. He was up half the night, and the dogs prowled around until we brought them in the room with us." He stifled a yawn.

"This really sucks." Brad downed his coffee like he was desperate. "If it's okay, Dustin and I will take off soon. But I'll tell the guys to keep their eyes and ears open. Whoever did this is probably just dumb enough to actually talk about it." Then Brad got up and quietly left the house.

Russell sat at the table, drinking his coffee, thinking about the situation. It all centered around Rafe and the ranch.

He and his father had made business decisions, and the ripple effects had affected Rafe's place. Russell had known that this piece of land was a keystone of sorts to the health of the valley, but never before had so much focus been put on it. Or maybe it had, and he just hadn't known.

Mendeltom wanted the land for its water so he could grow his business and push as many cattle through his operation as possible. Rafe's parents wanted the land, or at least the money it represented, so they could further their own agenda. Even Russell's father wanted use of this piece of land, but he was willing to work with Rafe rather than pull it out from under him.

Still, even in the past, this particular spot had seen a lot of action—the avalanche that changed the flow of the river, and Mack's escape to this place to build his own life. Russell kept thinking there had to be something that connected it all, a key of sorts. But what if there wasn't? What if it was simply that everyone just had their own miserable objectives?

He finished his coffee and moved into the living room. The dogs ambled in to get petted, then went right to the kitchen. Russell let them settle while he checked his email on his phone. When he saw a response from one of the rodeo organizing committees, he immediately called the number provided.

"Yes, is this Jessica? I'm Russell Banion."

"Yes, hello, Mr. Banion. I wanted to let you know that we have the records from the rodeo for the years you asked about. They are paper records, so it took me a while to locate them, but I have the participation logs you requested. I can take pictures of them and send them to you if you like."

He grinned. "You're wonderful. A friend of mine is related to one of the buckle winners. We found the buckle and a picture of him after he passed away, and we have been trying to determine who else was in the picture. All we have is the name Dale."

"I see." His phone chimed as pictures began coming through as texts. "Hopefully what we have will help you," Jessica said.

"From his outfit, we figured he was one of the participants." A thought occurred to him as he spoke. "But he might have been one of the pickup men. We'd really like to know who this man is. He seemed like a good friend, and if he's still alive, maybe he would like some of the old pictures and things." It sounded like a good enough reason, and he figured he didn't need to go into anything deeper.

"I'll send you those lists as well. Give me a few minutes."

"Thank you very much."

"It's no problem. We're a small rodeo, but we have a longstanding tradition that goes back almost a century." She indeed sounded very proud.

"Well, I appreciate all the help you've given me. I'll let you know if we have any luck." He thanked her again and ended the call. A few minutes later, more images came through. He forwarded the images to Rafe's email so they could look at them once he got up.

The dogs all sat next to him, waiting, tongues out. "You hungry, guys?" He got them some water and food, which fortunately was still where Mack had kept it. That alone brought home just how much of this place was still Mack's. Some of the pictures on the walls had been replaced. The one on the kitchen wall grabbed his attention. Someone had captured Rafe midaction, the bull in the air, Rafe's hand over his head, the hat flying away, but it was the eyes and the set of Rafe's jaw that pulled Russell into this image. It truly was like he was there with Rafe. He could almost feel the tension and excitement of that moment.

"You like that one?" Rafe asked, scratching his head.

"Yeah, but why is it in the kitchen?" Russell asked as Rafe poured himself some coffee.

"I guess because this was the room where I spent the most time with Uncle Mack. He sat me down at this table and told me that I could do anything I wanted. That it didn't matter what anyone else thought—as long as I worked hard and put everything I had into what I wanted, I'd succeed. And that photo? That's the moment. One of the networks sent me a print of my last ride—my world championship ride." He took a sip of his coffee. "I didn't know it at the time, but maybe Uncle Mack was there with me in spirit."

"But what are you going to do about the rest of the house?" Russell asked.

"I don't know. For now, though, this photo makes me feel close to Uncle Mack, and that's what I want. I reworked his bedroom and made that my own, but I'm okay with changing the rest of the house a little at a time." He sat down, and Russell took the seat across from him.

"I messaged the directors of the rodeo we thought was in those pictures, and I just heard back from them. The organizer, Jessica, sent me the rosters for the events, and I passed them to your email. We could take a look at them when you're ready."

"I'm ready." Rafe hurried away and returned with a laptop, which he placed on the table. He opened it and brought up the email, then sifted through the images. "Here's Uncle Mack." He pointed to his uncle's name in the registration, as well as on the list of winners. "Awesome!" He looked through the rest of that list and then went on to the next.

"No Dale?"

"Not yet. I checked the other bronc and bull riders." He went through the rest of the lists and then shook his head. "I don't see…." He sighed. "No. It's not one of the pickup men or…." He turned away with a shrug. "I guess this was a dead end."

"Check one more time before we move on," Russell asked. So they went through them again, but this time Rafe stopped on the bull-riding entries.

"What?"

"Look here." He enlarged the print, zeroing in on the bottom of the sheet. Russell leaned forward, peering over Rafe's shoulder. "It's handwritten. I thought I saw something the first time but wasn't sure."

The name *Dale Westmoreland* was written in what looked like pencil that had faded.

"Do you really think that's him?" Russell asked.

"I don't know. But we have a last name now."

"Google him and see if anything comes up."

Rafe searched on the name and a few pictures came up. Then he tried adding the word "rodeo" and got a few more hits, but nothing really useful. "What else do we know?"

"Dad said that he thought Mack was going to Denver. Maybe add that and see if we get anything." Rafe gave it a try, but the images and information that appeared were for close names and younger people. "That sucks."

"Yeah, it does. But it's a start. I'll let Luther know what we've found. Maybe he'll be able to take it further." Rafe sounded discouraged, and Russell put his hands on his shoulders.

"We'll figure this out." He was just as curious about Mack as Rafe was. Russell had known the man for years, yet at times his close friend now seemed like a stranger. "Maybe search for his name on some of the other rodeo sites. There could be some older records."

Rafe gave it a try but found nothing. "Can you think of anything else?"

Russell slowly sat down and met Rafe's gaze. "Try the Denver obituaries." He was running out of ideas.

"I'm not getting anything," Rafe groaned. "I thought that once we had a last name, we'd be able to find out more."

Russell gently massaged his shoulders. "I'm sorry. I know this is important to you. When you have a chance, contact Luther and tell him what we've found. Maybe he can put the pieces together."

"But how?"

"I wish we had more than a name, maybe even an address. But Luther should be able to figure it out. That's part of what he does—find people. Or he knows people who can find people." He sighed and let his hands slide down Rafe's strong chest. "I just wish we could do more."

"Maybe I can," Rafe said, grabbing his phone. "His name on that roster tells us that he rode bulls. And that means he would have gotten points with the PBR. Let's see what they have." Rafe made a call, and in a few minutes he was speaking to one of the officials.

"Harvey, I need a small favor. I'm looking for a rider, someone who rode bulls some years ago. All we have is a name—Dale Westmoreland. I was hoping that maybe you guys might have something on him." Rafe smiled, and Russell wandered out of the room while he talked. There was no need to listen in.

He looked around the living room, which had become a strange combination of Mack and Rafe. Mack's pictures still hung on the walls, and it was still his furniture, but Rafe's book sat on the coffee table, and a few other little things, like Rafe's socks on the floor, made the room his as well. Russell realized that Rafe hadn't accumulated very much, living on the road all those years, so there wasn't all that much for him to put out.

It seemed strange to Russell that a person's whole life could fit in a few bags behind the seat of a truck. But that was how Rafe had lived for a long time now. Russell wasn't sure he could have done it.

Footsteps behind him pulled his attention. "We got something," Rafe said. "Another old address. I already called it in to Luther. Now we can see what he comes up with." He wound his arms around Russell's waist. "It finally seems like I'm getting closer to understanding Uncle Mack. I know it sounds kind of dumb, but Dale was an important part of his life. Maybe he's still alive and could tell us about Uncle Mack when he was younger." He swallowed hard, pain filling his eyes. "I know I'm being stupid, but I wasted all that time. Uncle Mack was right here, and I thought he didn't care."

"Hey, he did care, and whether you knew it or not, Mack knew you cared. Maybe that's the most important thing. He knew that you were out there, and he made it a point to see you—at your graduation, at all those rodeos—even though you didn't know it at the time."

"I just wish he'd let me know," Rafe said, blinking. "Maybe things could have been different for both of us."

"Maybe." Russell gently cupped Rafe's cheeks in his hands. "But things work out the way they're supposed to sometimes. Think about it. You lost track of your uncle, and your family treated you badly. There's no denying that. But if things had been different, maybe you wouldn't be here right now. Maybe all that bad stuff brought about something good. It brought you here... to me." Russell gathered Rafe into his arms and held him as tightly as he could. "Then again, maybe we could have gotten to know each other sooner...."

"Yeah. But would you and I have connected earlier?" Rafe asked.

"Maybe. Then again, maybe not. I've been told I can be arrogant as hell." He smirked, and Rafe rolled his eyes.

"You still can be, just so you know." Russell loved that Rafe could joke at a time like this.

"I suppose what's really important is that we enjoy what we have now," Russell said. "Sometimes just thinking about those what-ifs can really mess with you."

"Tell me about it," Rafe groaned softly. "I spent years wondering if I should have just kept my mouth shut, dated a few friends, and never mentioned my sexuality. But I thought that if my folks really loved me, they should know who I was. But if I hadn't said anything...."

Russell pulled him close again. "You wouldn't be a world champion bull rider, and you certainly wouldn't be here. You might still be in Denver, under your parents' thumb. Hell, you might even be married, living a lie, with no way out. You don't know what might have happened. None of us does."

Russell swallowed hard. "Look," he said, resting his head on Rafe's shoulder, "when I was trying to figure out how I was going to get out of the mess I'd made with Jase... I thought of taking drastic measures. I really did. I couldn't see a way out, and he was trying to take everything from me, including part of who I was." He swallowed and clamped his eyes closed. "I never told anyone that, not even Dad." He sniffed, not afraid to show his pain to Rafe. "I would never want you to feel like that."

Rafe's arms closed around him. "What am I going to do? Because I don't want to feel this way. Yeah, I sent my mom and dad packing, but I shouldn't have had to."

"No, probably not. But there are things beyond our control. So the best we can do is understand that, and just let it go." Russell chuckled. "I know that sounds really simplistic, but it's all we can do." He pulled back and guided Rafe's lips to his for a quick kiss.

"And maybe find something or someone who makes us feel whole again?" Rafe said.

"There is that too." Lord knows that Russell had held back because of what Jase had done to him. Now he felt like he could really love someone else again. Hell, he'd fallen for Rafe even before he was really ready to. It had just happened.

Rafe cleared his throat. "As much as I'd love to stand here with you... someone let me sleep in, and I need to get my chores done."

"And I should get some work done myself. I have meetings all afternoon to get the ball rolling on this new contract." Russell didn't want to leave, but they both had things to do. "Why don't you come over to the house this evening? Dad will be home, and Violet is cooking. You and Dad can talk business, and then we can have a little alone time."

"I'd like that," Rafe said quietly.

"Is something wrong?" Russell asked, hating that Rafe seemed down. "I know you're disappointed that we didn't find Dale yet, but we will. One way or another, we'll figure out this little mystery." He smiled, and Rafe nodded. Russell took his hands, loving the feel of Rafe's skin against his. The simple touch sent a zing of pleasure through him that dissolved into warmth.

"I know. That's the pretty amazing part. I never really understood the power of *we*. Up until now, it was always just me." He flashed a smile.

"Look at you, getting all literary," Russell teased.

Rafe shrugged. "What else am I going to do? It's winter on a ranch. We do what we can and then hole up until spring brings everything back to life. And the nights are damned long when I don't have you here to help light some of the darkness." He smiled and actually blushed. "Dammit, I need to be reading something other than Mack's copy of *Pride and Prejudice*, if it's going to have me talking like that." He released Russell's hand and placed one on his chest, then fanned himself. "I must be careful or I'm going to give myself a fit of the vapors."

Russell snorted and then put his hand over his mouth. "I think we need to get you some cowboy books."

"Nah. Surprisingly, Uncle Mack had a thing for romance novels." He leaned closer. "I found a really good book about two cowboys falling in love. I really liked it. And not one of them got the vapors." He winked. "Okay, now I better get to work before the horses start to think they've been forgotten, and you need to get to your meetings." Rafe kissed him hard, with plenty of promise for later. Russell figured he needed to leave… and soon… or else they were going to end up back in bed, and the horses would have to go even longer without fresh hay.

"I WAS on the phone with Luther, and he said that he had something to talk to you and Rafe about. I asked him to dinner and figured he could talk to you afterwards."

Russell looked up from where he'd been making notes on the meeting he'd just finished. "Sounds good, Dad. And could you please tell Violet to set six places for dinner? Tell her that Rafe was asking about Coreen. He's going to need a good financial person in his corner too." Violet's niece was wonderful. "Besides, it's probably the only way to get Violet to stop eating in the kitchen."

His dad seemed skeptical. "I'll give it a try." He left, and Russell finished up his notes before sending some final emails. Then he closed his computer and sat back to clear his head. A few minutes later, he checked the time, then hurried out of the office and up to his room to get ready for dinner.

Once he was back in the great room, Russell pulled the cork on a fine bottle of wine and set it on the cart to breathe.

"What's this?" his father asked as he strode in.

"Something different. Rafe and Luther will be here soon, and I figured the two of you could talk a little business if you wanted."

His father sat as Russell poured him some wine. "What are you up to?" his dad asked.

"Nothing." Okay, he was a little nervous and wanted things to go well. "I figured once we have the details with Rafe narrowed down, we could get it in writing and finish this up."

"Writing?" His dad was ordinarily someone who did things with a handshake. He lived by his word and expected others to do the same. "Why would you want that? I thought you liked him."

Russell poured himself a glass of the pinot and sat across from him, loving the comfortable chocolate leather chairs. They still reminded him of his mother in a way. If this room had been for her, she would have decorated it very differently, but she had wanted Rafe and his father to be comfortable, so she'd gone with large, comfortable, and leather. "I do," Russell said. "That's why it needs to be in writing. I don't want there to be misunderstandings. Make your agreement and then put it down on paper. That way everything is clear and the business part of things won't get in the way." He sipped from his glass, smiling at the fineness of the vintage. "And Dad, I punted this to you for a reason. If things with Rafe and me don't work out, I want you to treat him just the same. It isn't to affect his business or ours." He met his dad's gaze. "I know I can count on you to do that should things change."

His dad nodded. "Son." He leaned forward, clapping Russell on the knee. "I would anyway. I like him, and I think we can do good things together. But I'm glad to hear you say it." Pride rang through his voice.

The doorbell sounded, and Russell set his glass on the coaster and went to answer it. Rafe stood on the step, and Russell ushered him inside, took his coat, and hung it up. Luther arrived right behind him, and Russell led them into the great room and poured a glass of wine for both of them.

"What's going on?" Rafe asked Elliott.

"I ran into Luther, and he told me he needed to speak to you and Russell, so I invited him to dinner. After we eat, you three can talk all you want. But I wanted to discuss some business with Rafe before dinner, and Luther here can help us draw up the arrangements." He took a sip from his glass, then went into detail about how they could work together.

It was fascinating, but Russell really didn't need to pay much attention—his dad had this handled—so instead he found himself watching Rafe, who threw himself into the discussion, sharing ideas on how he wanted to use the land and adding to their plans to maintain quality. Dad was happy, and so, it seemed, was Rafe. But what was amazing was the light that shone in Rafe's eyes when he and Dad shifted to their plan to breed bucking bulls.

"Do you want this to be part of the cattle agreement?" Luther asked.

"No," his dad said. "The bull operation is a separate agreement. Rafe and I are going to start a new business together. I've always wanted to do this, and Rafe has the expertise. We're both going to chip in some land for the operation and resources." Dad was as revved up as a teenager. "It will take some time, but I have no doubt we can put together a top-notch program. I understand that Whistler is for sale. He isn't bucking any longer, but he was a highly ranked bull. We could use him to sire us some buckers." He leaned a little nearer to Rafe. "What do you think?"

"I rode him three times and he threw me twice. I say we go for it, as long as he's got the drive left in him."

"Good." They went through details of how things would work, and Elliott said he'd arrange to purchase Whistler. Then they talked financing and breeding. It was pretty amazing how much they accomplished before dinner was ready.

"I'll get the agreements drafted, and you can review them," Luther said. Then they followed their noses to the dining room, where Violet had an amazing meal set out for them.

VIOLET AND her niece Coreen had joined them for dinner, but now it was just him, Rafe, and Luther at the table. "I understand you have something to tell us," Rafe said as he set his now empty glass on the table. "Did you find something?"

"Well… it's a mixed bag, but I'll lay out what I can. I'm afraid Dale Westmoreland passed away fourteen years ago."

"Two years after my family found out about Uncle Mack and turned their backs on him," Rafe said.

"Yes." He opened a notebook. "I was able to find a few relatives and a nephew, Austin, who was willing to speak to me. He said that his uncle Dale died of cancer and that his uncle had had a regular visitor." Luther looked right at Rafe. "It was your uncle. He apparently came to see him every few weeks, spending weekends at Dale's home. Austin said that his uncle was happiest when Mack was there, but that Dale's family wasn't. Apparently Austin's aunt, his mother's sister, was livid about the whole thing and tried to make it so that Mack couldn't visit. But Dale banned her instead and apparently left word in writing to that effect." Luther folded his hands on the table.

"Could he confirm anything more?" Rafe asked.

Luther nodded and handed Rafe a stack of letters. "You found the ones your uncle kept—these were the ones Mack sent to Dale. I haven't read them, but Austin described what was in them. He said they couldn't be anything but love letters."

"Why weren't they living together?" Rafe asked.

"Apparently it was because of what Mack's family had done to him. And it was about the same time that Dale was diagnosed. He stayed in Denver to be close to the doctors, and Mack had his ranch."

Russell nodded. "So they lived apart but were joined by the heart." Damn it all, Russell was tearing up, and it looked like Rafe was as well.

"Austin said that Mack's letters were beautiful. He read them after Dale died. Judging by what Austin said, and from the letters you told me you found at Mack's, it sounds like Dale was a man who kept his feelings to himself. Austin said that his uncle Dale was a kind man, a man of action, but one of few words. He called your uncle Mack a cowboy poet, going by his letters, and he had no doubt that they were devoted to one another." Luther cleared his throat, and Russell got up and poured glasses of water for each of them. Hell, maybe he should have grabbed a bottle of whiskey, but he had a feeling that there was more to this story.

"Did Austin know how long they were together?" Rafe asked.

"In one form or another, since they'd met at the rodeo. Maybe fifteen or twenty years." Luther drank his water. "Times were different then, and they had to be extra careful." Rafe nodded in understanding. "I want to say that there will always be things that we'll never know. But I was able to follow a legal paper trail. Dale's will was registered, and I was able to find a copy of it. He left almost everything to Mack. And I believe that's where the items in the safe-deposit box came from. Keeping on that subject a minute, all of the stocks are registered to your uncle. Once the estate is finalized, I'll get them transferred to you." Luther cleared his throat as the clock on the sideboard ticked. "Rafe, the stocks alone are worth millions... many millions now. The bonds, with decades of accumulated interest, are worth nearly as much."

Rafe's jaw hung open. "You're kidding."

Luther shook his head. "Dale also had a house, which he left to Austin's mother, and he set up a college fund for Austin. So they weren't left out. But Dale left almost everything to the man he loved."

"And Uncle Mack held on to all of it and kept it in that box."

Luther sighed. "It looks to me like that was Mack's way of holding on to Dale." He paused. "Once I'm able to, I'll make sure everything is transferred to you."

"I'd appreciate it," Rafe said. He paused with his glass partway to his lips. "I found some pictures of Mack and Dale at the house when we were clearing out some things. Do you know someone who could duplicate them, maybe make some enlargements? We could give copies to Austin, if he'd like them."

"I know a place," Russell said, "and yes, they can definitely do that for you." Russell felt more than a little worn out, and he figured Rafe had to be in the same shape.

"There's more, if you'd like to go over it," Luther said, biting his lower lip. "I spent quite a while on the phone with Austin. The name Westmoreland seemed familiar, but I didn't know why. But I know now. Austin said that he had an aunt who did everything she could to keep Mack away from Dale. That aunt was Melva Westmoreland."

Just then, Russell's dad poked his head in the doorway. "Excuse me, I thought you were done," he said. "What is this about Melva? What the hell has that family done now?"

Rafe motioned his dad over to the table. "What are you talking about?" he asked.

"Grant Mendeltom's wife, who passed away six years ago. Melva. Everyone called her Milly because she hated her name, but it was really Melva. And her maiden name was Westmoreland."

Chapter 11

RAFE COULD barely breathe. "Jesus Christ," he swore. "I knew that Grant spied on Uncle Mack and shared things with my parents. But damn it all to hell."

"The leap you made is probably true," Luther admitted. "Austin told me that it was Melva who found out about Mack and Dale. He and his mother were with her when she barged into Dale's, looking for something, apparently thinking she could take whatever she wanted."

"Sounds like Melva," Elliott groused. "She was always holier-than-thou and thought her shit didn't stink."

"Anyway, she found the two of them together having coffee first thing in the morning. As soon as she figured out what was going on, she left in a huff. Then she found out who Mack was and told his family. From there, I think you can figure out the rest of the story."

"Yeah, I can. She and Grant kept tabs on Uncle Mack and then reported it to my parents. But I suspect after Dale died, there was nothing to report until

I inherited the property, and then the old connections started buzzing again. Even though Melva was gone, my guess is that Grant picked up where she'd left off. That was why my parents showed up wanting money, then agreed to sell the ranch to Grant."

"But Mack was smarter than all of them. He specifically stated that they should get nothing. Mack was a smart cookie when he wanted to be," Luther said. "It was a privilege to know him. I'm just sorry that there are people who can't leave well enough alone. If they had, maybe he and Dale could have had a life together. They could have been happy."

Rafe clutched his wineglass in his hands so tight, he was lucky it didn't break. "I knew Grant Mendeltom was an ass on sight, but for him and his wife to do something like this…." He wanted to beat the shit out of him… and her. "What did Uncle Mack ever do to deserve this?" He looked around the room.

"I found your uncle to be a cowboy among cowboys," Elliott said. "He always did what he said he'd do, he was quiet, a good steward of his land, and his word was his bond. Period. Yes, he could be standoffish and even arrogant sometimes, but that goes with the breed. When you live close to the land, you have to be strong or the land and the elements will get the better of you."

"Mack rode broncs. I found the pictures and the buckles to prove it. So yeah, he could be an ass, but then again, so can we all." Rafe smiled at Russell. "It takes a bit of assholeness to last on the rodeo circuit."

Luther cleared his throat. "I was not supposed to reveal this, but I think it's okay now that Mack is gone. Do any of you remember a few years back when the town wanted to rebuild the park on Birch?"

Both Russell and Elliott nodded. "I used to play there as a kid, but after a while, Mom wouldn't let me go," Russell said.

"Yes. It fell into disrepair and needed a lot of work. Mack paid for all of it. He had me present the money to the town, and the park was regraded. The new grass and all those trees, the paths, the playground equipment, even the pool…. Mack gave all of it to the town, and he never said a word about it."

Rafe swallowed hard. "That's what he used some of Dale's money for?"

Luther shrugged. "I don't know where the money came from. All I know is that he handed me a check and told me to turn it over anonymously. I suppose if you looked at his taxes, you'd find the deductions, but that would be the only record. So if you want to remember Mack for the man he was, think of that. I will."

He drank his water and stood. "Now I think I need to go. I'll put together those contracts and get them over as soon as I can." Luther shook hands around the table, then left the room. He might have wiped his eyes when he thought no one could see. But Rafe did didn't mention it. He reckoned it said a lot about a man when just the memory of the things he'd done could bring another grown man to tears.

"WHAT ARE we going to do about Mendeltom? I bet he was behind the fire in the barn," Elliott said once they'd settled in the great room again.

"Dad, the sheriff is looking into it. The days of riding someone out of town on a rail are over."

"Pity." Elliott looked as ready to kill as Rafe felt. "Still, we now know that he isn't going to get his hands on any of Rafe's land, and his ranch has lost access to a large amount of other acreage. That is going to put a great deal of stress on his ability to move forward. And maybe one of them decided to burn Rafe out to try to relieve some of that pressure."

Rafe leaned forward. "What are you saying?"

Elliott shook his head. "Nothing. Nothing at all." He still had that "fox in a henhouse" expression on his face. "I was just thinking about doing some digging into the real state of his finances... then making sure his access to money is cut off. After that, it will be just a matter of time before he's done. I'll arrange to buy the ranch through a subsidiary we set up, and that will be that." He made it sound easy, but his voice was cold.

"Dad, I don't think that's what we need right now."

"Bullshit. Getting that asshole out of here is exactly what we all need." He turned to Rafe, and a chill went up Rafe's spine. "Do you want Mendeltom spying on you?"

Rafe just shrugged.

"We have enough money that we could force him out with very little effort," Russell added.

Rafe put his hand on Russell's. "Please don't, both of you. I appreciate what you're trying to do, but I doubt that is something Mack would have wanted." He sat back, still touching Russell. "If you do anything, the Mendeltoms will target you too. It will be Grant, Duane, and his friends against you and your friends, and things will get ugly. There's already been enough of that. You have your business, and we'll have ours together. Let that be the end of it. We'll grow and do our best to prosper. If Grant and Duane fail, then it will be on their own heads."

"Are you sure?" Elliott asked.

Russell shifted over next to him. "You're just like Mack—strong and tough on the outside, but with a heart of gold." Russell leaned close enough that only Rafe could hear him. "And I guess that's why I love you. And maybe once Dad goes to bed, we can go back to your place and I can show you just how much."

Rafe shivered and felt himself blushing again. Elliott turned away, but Rafe figured he was trying not to laugh. "Russell," he whispered but couldn't help smiling. "You shouldn't say things like that."

"Come on, boys," Elliott said. "You young people think you invented sex and passion. I'll have you know that Russell's mother and I were quite the couple when we were young." He snickered as Russell groaned and sat back. Elliott stood. "I'm going to go to bed." He headed out of the room. "Don't set fire to the sheets."

RUSSELL STRETCHED as Rafe turned out the light across the hall. He turned his head just in time to watch Rafe glide into the room. Damn, he would never tire of looking at this stunning man. Clothes on or off, Rafe was a work of art... and all his.

That was the strangest thing. Russell expected to feel jittery now that he'd opened himself up to Rafe. But he didn't. His heart raced at the sight of him.

"What are you smiling about?" Rafe asked as he slipped under the covers.

"You," Russell said. It was freeing to just be able to say what he felt rather than keeping it bottled up inside. Or worse, wondering if showing tenderness was going to backfire on him.

"Your father told us not to set fire to the sheets." Rafe grinned, tugging Russell close. "It was touch-and-go there for a while." Rafe kissed him tenderly, but with enough heat to rekindle their spent passion for a few seconds. Then Russell settled next to Rafe and closed his eyes, letting the contentment of after-glow wash over him.

"What's bothering you?" Rafe asked after Russell shifted for the third time in as many minutes.

"I can't stop thinking about Mack," he answered softly. "I know it's a strange thing to say at a time like this, but I keep wondering about him and Dale. They could have been happy together."

"Who says they weren't?" Rafe said. "You met my parents. Maybe being disowned by them is a badge of honor. I'm starting to think I got lucky when they rejected me." He shifted. "Mom and Dad would never accept me—I know that now. They have no tolerance for anyone who's not like them. Hell, they cross the street if a Black person approaches. I've seen it." He shook his head. "It's disgusting. So maybe Uncle Mack being disowned was a blessing of sorts too." Rafe's hurt tone told Russell he didn't really believe that.

"Come on. They cost you a relationship with your uncle, and I can tell that that's the real loss here. Mack was a great man. And to think what Mendeltom and his wife did all those years…." Russell clenched his fists and then relaxed his hands again. "Are you sure you won't let me and Dad run him out of town? I'd do it for you and for Mack. The guy deserves it."

"Maybe he does," Rafe said. "But that doesn't mean you should do it. Mendeltom will end up hanging himself, just like my parents did. And it won't be on our conscience." He rolled over. "Please. If we sink to his level, then we'll be just like him. And that is something I don't want."

Russell nodded and settled closer, trying to understand. He loved Rafe for his kind heart, but that was only going to take them so far. Kindness was often stomped on.

"At first I hated my parents for what they did to me," Rafe continued. "But now I think I pity them more than anything. Uncle Mack left me a lot of money, and I could use it to make their lives miserable. But why bother? The same goes for Mendeltom. Why expend energy and resources to make him pay when he's going slit his own throat eventually anyway?" Rafe held Russell closer. "Besides, we have things that we have to do, like plan for the spring and get our bull venture off the ground. That's where we should put our energy."

Rafe sounded so reasonable that Russell relented. He would do whatever Rafe wanted. He only hoped that Mendeltom would play the game the same way.

THE NEXT few weeks brought no more incidents… and a lot more snow, just in time for the holidays. Dad hadn't really bothered to celebrate Christmas since Mom passed, but this year he seemed more like his old self. He even had the men cut down a tree. Then he pulled out Russell's mom's ornaments and decorated the huge conifer that measured more than twenty feet.

"Don't you think it's a little much?" Russell asked. He stood in the great room, looking at the tree. It filled the front windows, and the thousands of twinkling white lights made everything seem okay.

"Your mother wouldn't think so," his dad answered quietly.

Russell chuckled. "Nope, Mom would have picked an even bigger tree." It was good to see his dad in the festive spirit again. It had been too long. "By the way, Rafe is joining us for dinner tomorrow."

"He'd better. I invited him weeks ago. He already sent over some gifts," his dad said, pointing to the pile under the tree. Then he turned to Russell with the same expression he'd worn when Russell had been a kid. "No peeking, now, or Santa will skip by the place."

"Is that why you did all this?" Russell asked him.

His dad nodded. "In part. When I invited him, he told me he hadn't celebrated Christmas in years. He said he'd spent most of them in hotels or something. So I decided that we all should celebrate this year. Your mother would be happy you've found someone, just as I am." Damn, sometimes his dad was an old softie. "Now, Violet is making us a huge feast for tomorrow, and we have some of the men joining us with their families. I suspect there will be twenty people for dinner, and I'm giving you the job of making sure Violet knows that she isn't to be eating in the kitchen."

"Good. And later I'll add the gifts I have for everyone." Russell had decided a while ago that all the people who worked on the ranch or for his software company were going to get a bonus. He had the cards already made up. "Then I can help you bring down the gifts you've bought. I took a quick look in one of the rooms upstairs—it's damn near filled to the brim."

Dad snorted softly, and Russell knew he'd hit that nail on the head. "Then come on and help me. We can bring them all down now." He headed upstairs, with Russell following.

THE NEXT morning Russell was up early and was just putting the coffee on when Rafe arrived. He had asked him to stay the night, but Rafe had had to make sure his animals were taken care of. "Is everything good at your place?" he asked.

"Yes. The dogs already opened their gifts, and they're happy." They shared a kiss that threatened to grow heated.

"Get your coffee and get in here, you two. These presents aren't going to open themselves." Russell's dad was already dressed and settled on the sofa, ready to go. He was worse than a kid. And Russell loved every minute of it.

Russell grabbed mugs and handed one to Rafe, then carried his and his dad's coffee in before they all sat down.

"You all know that I didn't have much of a family before Uncle Mack died. But now I realize that not only did he leave me his ranch, but also the people who'd treated him like family." Rafe reached behind the tree and pulled out a package, which he handed to Russell's dad. "I'm not one for shopping…." He didn't say anything more as Russell's dad took the small box, ripped off the paper, and lifted the lid. "I thought this would be something you might like."

His dad was speechless, his mouth hanging open as he lifted out a silver buckle.

"That's one of the earliest ones Mack earned. I won the same buckle at the same rodeo three years ago."

Dad honestly looked like he was going to cry. Of course, the old cowboy would never do that, so he took a drink of coffee. "Thank you, Rafe. It's perfect." The last word barely made it past his lips, and Rafe pretended he didn't notice, as did Russell.

Rafe then handed Russell a much larger package in a huge gift bag. Russell opened it and pulled out Mack's battered guitar case, then lifted the lid on the same instrument Mack had used to teach him to play. "I thought you'd like it."

Russell tried to swallow around the lump in his throat. He lifted the instrument and lightly strummed the strings. "Jesus. And all I could come up with to give you was a watch." He had always been crap at giving gifts.

Rafe chuckled and sat next to him. "You've already given me more than I could ever hope for." He leaned down, and Russell blinked before sharing a kiss with the man who had stolen his heart.

Chapter 12

THE PEACE and quiet that followed the holiday were something Rafe could get used to. No parents showing up unannounced. No neighbors threatening legal action or physical violence. For the next few weeks, Rafe got into a routine of tending the livestock and exercising the horses. The snow had been light during that time, with a lot of what had fallen already melting in the sun. Rafe was able to go out riding with Russell a few times, and they took the dogs, who'd romped and played until they were all a happy, muddy mess.

"You know, if you keep that up, you're going to need baths before you come in the house," Rafe told the three as they raced off across one of the fields on one of those rides. The sun shone, and it was one of those days when everything seemed beautiful. A light dusting of snow from overnight covered the brown of the grasslands, making everything seem fresh and new. The dogs romped and chased each other, heading toward the cattle as Rafe and Russell crested a slight rise on their horses.

"They're enjoying themselves," Russell said.

"After all those storms a few weeks back, I was beginning to think I'd end up inside for most of the winter," Rafe said as they continued forward.

"This is more typical. A little snow and then some sunshine, though it can be unpredictable at this elevation. Clouds can sock us in for weeks at a time. You just never know. The way I look at it, you get out when you can and enjoy the fresh air. Tomorrow we may be snowed in again." He smiled, and Rafe pulled his horse to a stop next to him.

"I never expected this... any of this," Rafe said, leaning over slightly to share a kiss. He turned back toward the house.

"What exactly?"

"All of it. A place of my own, a home." He took Russell's hand. "You. Even finding out about Uncle Mack. All of these were things I never figured I'd have." He shrugged. "Maybe I'm simply happy."

"Can I ask you how you got there?" Russell shifted in the saddle.

"Aren't you happy?" Rafe asked tentatively.

"Yes, I am. But that's when I usually start to worry," Russell said.

Rafe rolled his eyes and slapped him on the shoulder. "Please. We're both cowboys at heart. What we have is what every cowboy dreams of—and has for hundreds of years. Every book ever written describes the same dream: wide open spaces, a place to call your own, and someone to share it with. That's all we really want, isn't it?" He turned. "Unless...." He left the last part hanging on purpose.

"It isn't that. Because you're right; I know it. I keep thinking that the ghosts of my past will go away. That I could leave Jase behind."

"Maybe I had it easier in that regard. I got to stand up to my parents and tell them to take a fast ride off a tall cliff. That gave me closure. But you never got that. Jase is just gone, and yet you're still carrying him around." Rafe grinned and tilted his head. "Come on. I have an idea." Rafe took off, and Russell followed. Rafe grinned, and once he reached the edge of the stream, he tied up the horses and climbed off.

"What the heck are you doing?"

"Making a snowman. Come on, it's packing snow." He rolled the first ball as large as he could, right up to the edge of the water. By then Russell had a smaller one, and Rafe placed it on top. He got sticks for arms and found some large pods for eyes and a nose. Russell drew a mouth, and a cluster of small leaves made for a nose.

"That is one ugly thing," Russell said.

"I think we should call him Jase," Rafe added.

Smiling, Russell quickly made a snowball and tossed it at Rafe, hitting him square in the chest.

"Is that how you want to play it?" Rafe asked, laughing and tossing one back, then ducking behind the snowman for cover.

"Not fair." Russell picked up a bunch of snow and tossed it over the top of the snowman so that it rained down on Rafe.

"God, it's going down my back." Rafe shimmied to try to get the snow out, and Russell tackled him, rolling them both until they knocked over their snowman and ended up covered in snow. Rafe chuckled and leaned forward to steal a kiss before getting up and helping Russell to his feet.

"We're going to be soaked," Russell said.

"Then we should probably get back. Oh, and by the way…." He pointed at the destroyed snowman. "There's your closure." He was still smiling as he mounted his horse.

THEIR RIDE was good, and Rafe felt light. Russell seemed happier. The dogs raced ahead and into the barn, milling around while he and Russell took care of the horses. Rafe patted each dog. "Are you guys hungry? I'll have to feed you outside. You all need baths." They had rolled in something dead and smelled awful. Fortunately all three of them were water babies and didn't put up a fight. "How about some lunch?"

Rafe opened the door, keeping the dogs outside.

As soon as he stepped into the kitchen, he knew something was wrong. He couldn't put his finger on it, but he came face-to-face with the issue as soon as he went into the living room. "Sit down," Grant Mendeltom snapped from behind the gun.

"What the hell are you doing?" Rafe asked. "Get out of my house. You don't want to do anything you'll regret." He stood still, hoping like hell that Russell would stay outside. He didn't hear anyone else in the house.

"I already have. I should have gotten rid of your uncle years ago. Nothing good ever comes of your kind." He slowly got up from where he'd sat waiting in Mack's chair. "Do what I say, or else. I will gladly shoot you. I have no use for you or that damned Banion brat. I saw the two of you out riding."

"Russell went home," he said flatly. "So, what do you think you're going to do? Kill me? Go ahead. Then you'll just end up in prison. You aren't going to get away with it. I have friends, and my death won't go unnoticed." If it weren't for the gun in Grant's hands—and the crazed look in his eyes—this situation would be completely ridiculous. "Hurting me isn't going to help you."

"Sure, it will. If you die, your parents will inherit everything. They're your closest relatives. Then I'll get this ranch from them and go on as though nothing has happened. All I have to do is get you out of the way and I can have whatever I want. Your parents will sell the ranch at a good price, and everything else that was your uncle's will go to them." He had clearly thought this out. "See? It's simple. I just have to take care of you first."

"Is that why you set fire to my barn?" Rafe asked.

Grant shook his head, his hatred burning brighter.

"Was it Duane?" Rafe asked, taking a shot on the dark, and from the way Grant narrowed his gaze, Rafe knew he'd hit the bullseye. "Why would he do that? Was he drunk?" Shit, a notion slammed into him. Duane had probably come to the barn, stupid drunk, trying to impress his father. He could almost hear Grant going on about the injustices, and Duane wanting to make his father happy. "Did you put Duane up to it?"

Grant stood and motioned with the gun. "Move." Rage washed off him.

"Why?" Rafe refused to show any fear, even though the hatred and craziness in Grant's eyes was more than enough to let him know that the man was serious, if deranged.

"Go to the basement door," Grant said. "You're going to take one hell of a fall." He was almost gleeful. The changes in his mood were nearly as frightening as his actions.

Rafe walked slowly, trying to think of a way out of this and to give Russell a chance to help him. Frankly, he was surprised Russell hadn't rushed in already. "That's interesting. But there's one thing you didn't consider. When I inherited this place, I wrote and filed a will of my own. So my parents will get nothing." Rafe paused with a grin. "And neither will you." He had never been good at lying, so he hoped he could pull this one off. "I had Luther put it together a few weeks ago. He's already filed it with the county." Maybe he could instill some doubt.

Grant groaned but pushed him forward. "That's a crock and you know it. People like you never think they're going to die, so they don't have wills." A hint of cool air reached Rafe's skin as he pulled open the door. Darkness loomed from below, and he did his best not to swallow as he stared at his fate.

"Are you sure?" Rafe pressed, just as the sound of barking filled the house, followed by footsteps on the kitchen floor. The barks turned to growls when the dogs saw Grant.

"Get him," Rafe commanded. He had no idea how the dogs would react, but they grew more menacing, and Grant turned toward them as Russell burst in from the back. Rafe kicked the back of Grant's knee, sending him downward, then shoved him with all his might. A shot rang out, glass shattered, and Grant hit the floor, screaming as the dogs went after him. Russell got the gun, and they pulled back the dogs.

Grant had curled into a fetal position to try to protect himself.

"Sorry it took so long," Russell said. "I was trying to wipe the dogs off and didn't realize you were in trouble until I let them in...."

"Are you hurt?" Rafe asked Russell, and when he shook his head, Rafe checked each of the dogs. They were all fine too, thank goodness. Then he saw his oven door, broken into a million pieces.

"He didn't get you either?" Russell asked.

"No. It looks like we're all okay."

After that, Rafe called the sheriff while Russell subdued Grant, holding him on the floor until the sheriff and his men arrived. The next hour was filled with questions and getting Grant out of the house. They secured his gun and took plenty of photographs. "None of you were hurt?" the sheriff asked.

"No. He shot the oven, but that was all. He wanted to kill me and make it look like I'd fallen down the stairs. That way my family could inherit what I own and he could buy the ranch from them. It sounds ridiculous, but that's what he told me. I don't really think the guy is all there. He admitted that he saw me with Russell, but then he didn't even check where he was. He just sat in the living room waiting for me." Rafe almost felt sorry for Grant, in a way.

"And that was it?"

"Well, Russell got here before anything could happen." He squeezed Russell's hand. "I'm just glad he didn't come in with me. He and the dogs were the cavalry."

"Was there anyone else?"

Rafe shook his head. "I don't think so." He lifted his gaze. "Please make sure he gets the help he needs." He figured there was something really wrong with Grant—normal people didn't act the way he had. "We're both okay, and so are the dogs. That's what really matters." He was already trying to put this behind him.

"Okay, then. We'll take things from here."

Rafe stood and saw the sheriff to the door.

"What's going to happen to him?" Russell asked.

"He'll be arrested and then go before a judge. The prosecutor will charge him, and then from there, things will progress according to his actions." The sheriff then said good night and left the house.

Rafe closed and bolted the door. As he did, his knees gave out, and he slid down the back of the door as the reality of what had just happened slammed into him. Russell was there immediately. "Hey, you okay? Do I need to get them back here to help?" Fear rang in his voice.

"No," Rafe answered quietly. "I'm okay." He managed to get his legs to work and made his way over to the sofa. "Grant was really going to kill me." While it was happening, it felt like it was happening to someone else. But now…. Fuck, he could get on thousand-pound bulls, but….

Russell held him tightly. "It's over now."

"I know." He felt like he could catch his breath. "You came to the rescue."

Russell smiled as he drew closer. "Of course I did." He stilled, and Rafe felt a shiver run through Russell. He held his gaze and waited. "You blow me away sometimes."

Rafe grinned. "I could make a dirty joke right about now."

Russell lifted his gaze to the ceiling for a few seconds before lowering it again. "If you can make bad jokes, then I know you're okay."

"I'm going to be fine." He really was. Grant had been off his nut, but Russell had been there for him. Rafe had always thought he could go it alone. He'd had to. But it was nice that he didn't have to do that anymore. "Can I ask you something?"

"Now?" Russell asked.

"Yeah." He drew closer. "I know a lot has happened between us… but I want to come out and say that I don't want a repeat of what happened to Mack and Dale. I don't want to be apart and yet together."

"Where would you get that idea?"

"Well, you have your home with your father and the big house. I'm just figuring out a home here, and…." Rafe wasn't sure what Russell wanted or how things might look. Maybe it was just the aftermath of the shit with Grant, but he needed some things settled, though he was probably doing a crappy job of explaining it.

"How about we figure it out as we move forward?" Russell stroked his cheek. "We've only known each other a few months. I don't have an exact picture of how things will work for us, but I do know that when I look forward, you're with me, right there. I never thought I'd be able to see that sort of thing again."

"Me neither." Rafe leaned in and kissed him. "As long as we can figure it out."

"We definitely will. I'm not going to let you go. And when we settle down, it won't be in your home or mine, but ours." The dogs all ambled into the room and took their places around them. "And, of course, the cavalry's."

Epilogue

"WE SHOULD go," Russell told Rafe as Rafe left their bedroom and walked down the hall that now held all of Mack's pictures. Instead of putting them away, Rafe and Russell had covered the walls with them, including photos of Mack's horses and even an enlargement of the picture of Mack and Dale. The rest of the house, they had filled with their own things. While Mack's presence hadn't been eradicated, the house now reflected Rafe and Russell's life together, including a painting over the fireplace of a lone cowboy and horse that was probably worth as much as the house. It had been a gift from Elliott for their home. Another addition, probably the most important, was the cabinet in the corner, the light always on, shining on his and Uncle Mack's rodeo buckles. One, embossed with the outline of Texas, sat front and center on the top shelf.

"I know. I'm coming." He sat in one of the leather chairs that now filled the room. Mack's chair was still there, but it had been re-covered. Rafe pulled on one of his boots, then took a second to think.

"Sweetheart," Russell said gently, his hands working Rafe's shoulders. "Everything is going to be great. The hard part is done. Now it's time for the victory lap." They shared a smile and a warm glance before Rafe pulled on his other boot and stood.

"I want to take the dogs," he said.

Russell sighed. "I figured as much after you gave them baths last night. I already have them in the truck, so you need to move that tight cowboy butt of yours."

Rafe followed Russell outside, locked the doors, and headed for the truck.

"Everything under control?" he asked Clyde as they passed in the yard. He and Dustin had come over with Elliott's blessing. Dustin was now Rafe's foreman and doing an amazing job. He waved as he headed out, and Rafe got in the truck, the three dogs in the back seat all looking out the windows. Russell started the engine, put the truck in gear, and headed for town, music on the radio and windows down. He was happy… just happy.

May had always been Rafe's favorite time of year, and this particular day was stunning. It couldn't have been any better if he had placed an order with the weather gods personally. The sun shone, there was a slight breeze, the trees in the park had fully leafed out, and the grass had just been mowed, so the air smelled fresh and clean. Rafe sat next to Russell on one of the park benches, closed his eyes, and listened to the laughter of children as they played. "Is this what you wanted?" Russell asked.

"It's perfect," Rafe said. Flowers filled the gardens around the pool building in one corner of the park, and new planters occupied the formerly open spaces, adding color to the surroundings. He held the leashes for the dogs, who sat, tongues out, wanting more than anything to be let loose to play with the kids. "We should go."

They both stood and headed over to the main park entrance, where a sign was draped in white fabric. "Hey, Luther," Russell said as they approached. They exchanged hugs with both him and Stacey. "We're glad you could come."

Luther grinned. "I wouldn't have missed this for the world."

"Me neither," Stacey said, holding Luther's arm. They shared a quick look that made Rafe smile. It was nice to see the two of them together. Luther was a good man who deserved someone special.

Rafe and Russell, along with the dogs, made their way to where people were gathering around the sign.

"We'll be starting in about five minutes," someone informed the crowd.

Rafe stood off to the side. "I'll be back in a minute," he told Russell. He handed him the leashes before striding down the sidewalk to where Duane was walking away. He thought of calling out but doubted it would do any good. With his father on his way to prison and the ranch gone, Rafe was sure he was the last person Duane wanted to see.

Elliott had helped Rafe arrange the purchase, and he'd added the land to his ranch. The plan was to let it heal from Grant's overgrazing, and then he and Elliott would increase the beef herd. Rafe sighed as he watched Duane's retreat—shuffling along, shoulders bent—and felt no joy in what had happened. But it hadn't been Rafe's fault, no matter what Duane might think. Grant and Duane—who Grant had fingered for nearly setting Rafe's barn on fire— had paid a high price for their actions… and would for a long time.

With a sigh, Rafe turned away and went back to the gathering.

"Thank you for being here today," Mayor Jane Wilkins said, smiling at the audience. "I spend most of my time dealing with problems of one kind or another, but today I get to enjoy the best part of my job. We're here to celebrate someone who gave a great deal to this town and the people in it. He never asked for anything in return… not even recognition. I've always thought it's a shame that we don't find out what we have until it's gone, so today, we're going to rectify that." Mayor Jane, as she was known, stepped aside, and Rafe took a deep breath as he stepped forward.

Rafe swallowed hard before looking out at expectant, friendly faces. "I'm Rafe Carrera, and I'm a cowboy. I have the kicks, weird tan lines, and scars to prove it, just like all of you. And I wouldn't have it any other way. A cowboy's life is richer than most people would believe. It's filled with the land, our herds, the ones we care for and love. I'm not exactly good with words, so I'll rely on someone else's." He unfolded one of the letters Uncle Mack had written to Dale, and his eye went right to the appropriate passage. Rafe had decided to read part of one of his uncle's letters because his uncle's words said what he was feeling better than he could himself.

"A cowboy is strong and rides the range, as I do every day. He tends his herd and watches over his charges with the protective fervor of the bulls I once tried to tame. Day in and day out, cowboys and nature do battle just to see the herd safely home. But a cowboy's heart has wings, and the distances don't matter. My heart flies to you, the one I love, holds on, and stays with you always. Time and miles mean nothing, because my heart is always with you, no matter where I am."

Rafe managed to get through the letter without his voice breaking, and then Mayor Jane returned and he stepped aside again.

"Thank you," she said with what might have been a slight sniff. "Up until today, this park was always just referred to as Birch Park because of the street it was on." She motioned, and servers approached the crowd with trays of sparkling wine for the adults and glasses of cider for the kids. "But from this day forward, I'm pleased to say that it will be officially named the Greene-Westmoreland Community Park." She pulled away the covering on a huge piece of white granite with the name deeply carved into the stone. When she raised her glass, everyone did the same, the dogs woofing as though they too knew that something important had happened. Rafe lingered, looking at the names of his cowboy uncle and the man he'd loved. Then he made his way through the crowd as people asked to speak to him. Most asked about riding bulls or just wanted to say hello. A few of the kids asked for his autograph or wanted to pet the dogs. Rafe obliged, and so did Riker, May, and Lola, shamelessly soaking up the attention.

AS PEOPLE eventually faded away, Rafe stood in front of the naming stone. No one in the town needed to know who the two men were beyond the fact that they were the ones who had made sure that the park existed for everyone. For them, that was the point. But for Rafe, it was so much more. This was where his uncle had lived and where he had given Rafe a home. It was time that his uncle's love was celebrated, even if most people didn't know that was what it had been.

"Are you ready?" Russell asked.

Rafe nodded, then paused and took a picture of the stone.

"Yeah." He smiled as he brought the image into a message and pressed Send.

Russell narrowed his gaze. "Did you just do what I think you did?"

Rafe grinned. "Sorry, I couldn't help it. A cowboy is many things, and today, I think I deserve to be a little bit of an ass." He put his phone in his pocket, not caring if his parents responded to the message. "Let's go home."

Keep reading for an excerpt from
Hard Road Back
by Andrew Grey

I KNEW some of his secrets, but by no means all of them. Lord knows there's no man alive, other than Scarborough himself, who knows all of those. He keeps shit to himself better than any man I've ever met, and that's saying a hell of a lot, being a cowboy—well, of sorts.... All in all, you meet a whole hell of a lot of guys with chips on their shoulders, and even more keeping stuff to themselves. I have been friends of a sort with him for fifteen years now, and sometimes he still seems like a stranger. And yet, I think I can see a little boy behind the bluest, biggest, most perfect eyes God ever put on a man. But I know I shouldn't go there because that is a road I should not go down. It's laced with more potholes than Scarborough's driveway... and that's saying something.

Normally I would try not to think about Scarborough Croughton, at least as much as I can, but his ranch borders my small piece of property, so I get to see him more than just about anyone. This morning, either by luck or by a visit from the devil, the damned phone rang just as I was getting out of bed... and I'm not going to say I was dreaming about that cantankerous pain in the ass.

"Yeah, Scarborough, what do you need?" I checked the clock, and it was just after five in the morning. I should be getting up anyway, but it would have been nice to get another few minutes of sleep.

"I got a problem and I need yer help," he said. No indication of what the problem was, just those few words. Sometimes I wondered if Scarborough figured he only got to say so many words in his entire life, and being as he was determined to live until doomsday, he had to use as few as possible.

"I'm supposed to be at Sandy Reynold's place today. I can come over for about an hour, but then I got to go see her."

Scarborough humphed. "'Kay."

I could tell he was about to hang up, and I groaned silently in my head. "Let me get dressed and I'll be over. You got coffee on?" I hoped to the ever-loving gods. "I'll be there as soon as I can."

"Thanks." The line went dead.

I shuffled off to the bathroom and scoured my face with a razor, thankful I didn't cut myself all to hell, used the toilet, and finished my morning routine before dressing and heading right to the door.

Beau met me there, tail wagging, eyes bright, looking up at me as though he knew I was heading out. I checked that he had food in his dish and water in the bowl. He was a good dog and pretty much ate when he was hungry. As soon as I opened the door, Beau took off to make his morning rounds. That dog had a sixth sense, I was pretty sure. He ran to the small barn to check on the horses, waiting for me. I let my babies out into their paddocks and made sure they had plenty of water for the day, scratching noses and saying hello. Each of those beauties was a horse I had rescued and rehabilitated in one way or another, and each had a story. But I was in too much of a hurry to think about that right now.

I headed to the truck, and Beau jumped in and went right to his spot, with his front legs on the arm of the passenger's side door, his tongue hanging out as I started the engine. As soon as the cool air started blowing out of the vents, he got down, his nose in the stream, his mouth open.

The trip to Scarborough's took all of five minutes, but walking would've been a real pain and taken much longer. I pulled into the drive and noticed that I didn't get shook all to hell. He must have graded the thing at some point. He came out of the house as I slowed, and by the time I was out of the truck, he'd caught up to me with mismatched mugs in each hand.

"Oh thank God," I said as I took the mug and sipped what I knew was the strongest damned coffee in the state of Wyoming.

"Over here," Scarborough said, and I let him lead. I was going to have to find out for myself what was happening. But that didn't mean I couldn't enjoy the view, at least for a few minutes.

Scarborough had grown up on this land. That much everyone in town knew. His mom had passed in a bad way, and as far as I knew, his father was distant. I'd met him fifteen years ago when he'd moved in down the road. Losing his mom to a drunken truck driver was not a prescription for good emotional health, as far as I was concerned.

"Did you pick up a new horse?" I asked as we got closer to the paddocks. Beau stopped, plopping his butt on a small patch of scraggly grass, watching, his tongue lolling, but coming no closer. We turned the corner of the low barn, and I stopped dead in my tracks. A horse as black as midnight looked back at me with some of the wildest eyes I had ever seen.

I motioned to Scarborough to stay where he was as I took small steps forward. "That's a good boy," I said, letting the breeze carry the words to him, making him strain to hear. "My gosh, you are stunning." He stayed still, but the wildness and fear in those huge brown eyes pulled at my heart. What the fuck had happened to this magnificent horse to make him that way? "I'm not going to hurt you. I just want to see you." I didn't reach for him and just spoke a string of nonsense words.

There was intelligence behind those eyes and the way they held my gaze. The horse began breathing more heavily, a front leg shaking, and Scarborough took a step back and then another. Finally the horse turned, raced to the far side of the paddock, stopped, and turned again to watch.

"Where did you find him?" I asked.

"Auction," Scarborough answered.

I sipped from my mug, completely surprised. That made no sense at all. Not that Scarborough didn't go to auctions—he did. The man had a good sense about horses, and an even better one about anything profitable. Scarborough could make money, and, well, he didn't spend it unless he thought he could get more. It was just that simple. I've known penny-pinchers in my life, but Scarborough made Abe Lincoln scream bloody murder before he spent anything at all. "Why did you buy him? You know there's the possibility that he will never be of any use to anyone." But damn, he was stunning as all hell, nonetheless. "What's his name?" I turned to Scarborough just in time to see him roll his eyes.

"Whoever had him before actually named him Black Beauty." Scarborough made a face. "I hate it." He usually didn't do that sort of thing, and I liked seeing Scarborough's playful side. "I'm going to re-name him, but I don't know what yet."

"Maybe he'll suggest a name," I offered, and Scarborough nodded but grew quiet once again. That was his usual way, and I was more than used to it. With Scarborough, you had to read between the lines quite a bit. And sometimes there weren't even lines—you simply had to guess.

He lifted the mug slowly to his lips. "I thought you could fix him, and then I would use him for stud. His bloodlines are amazing, and… look at him."

Was that softness I saw around Scarborough's eyes, even for a second? I wasn't sure, and any tenderness that was there didn't last too long.

"I'll pay you."

I nearly took a step back. Those words never crossed Scarborough's lips. I wanted to put my hand over my chest to check that I wasn't going to have a heart attack, or run to town to see the doc because I wanted to make sure I wasn't hearing shit. "You sure?" There was so much fear and pain there that I wasn't sure anyone could ever get through it, but for Scarborough I was willing to try. And if it was important enough for him to offer to pay me, then I would definitely do my best.

Scarborough nodded and mumbled an assent.

"Okay, I'll do what I can. I'll text you over an agreement that states my terms and rates, like with anyone else. If you agree, you sign and return it, and I'll get started as soon as I can. Don't let anyone near him for now, and feed and water him yourself. Let him associate both things with you. It will help. And for God's sake, don't stomp or make any sharp noises around him."

"Huh?"

I rolled my eyes. "Just be nice to him, okay? I know you can do that." I smiled.

Scarborough humphed but then nodded, and a ghost of a smile formed on his lips. "I will. I'm better with horses than people." He turned to look at the horse once again. "Just make him better and stop the cycle of pain that's going through his head right now."

I blinked because I honestly wasn't sure if he was truly talking about the horse or himself.

Beau ambled over, and I patted his head. Nodding, I checked my watch and headed toward the truck. "I'll send over the agreement, and I can start in a few days. I'll probably work with him in the mornings before my other jobs. So have the coffee on." I waved and pulled open the door. Beau jumped in, and I climbed into the truck and headed back down the drive.

I wondered about Scarborough for the next half hour as I drove to Sandy's place. I pulled in and parked in my usual spot in front of the house. Her pack of dogs came over, barking and wagging their tails. I let Beau out, and he greeted his old friends with happy barks, and soon he was off with the pack.

"Martin, you're late," Sandy said as she stepped out on the porch. "I got coffee and some breakfast for you. Come on inside and eat, and then we can get to work." She motioned, and I wiped off my boots before stepping inside.

"Sorry. Scarborough called this morning and said he needed my help."

She scoffed. "Looking for free work?" She, like a lot of the people in town, was not particularly a fan of my neighbor. They had all, at one time or other, been on the cheap end of his ways, and that made them skeptical, so they tended to avoid him if possible. Not that I could exactly blame them.

"No. He bought a horse at auction that he needs me to work with." I sat down at the kitchen table, which had seen at least three generations of her family, the scuffs and marks a history of family meals.

"For free?" She brought over a plate and set it in front of me, along with a glass of juice and some more coffee. Only hers was danged good. No one made coffee like Sandy.

"Nope. He said he'd pay me." I took a bite as she fumbled with her chair.

"Well, I'll be damned." She sat down and sipped her coffee. "I know it was hard when his mom died, but something changed him. Not that I blame him for being hurt after she was gone, but he never seemed to spring back all the way. He did for a while… and then… he didn't."

"Everyone thinks it was the accident."

She nodded and seemed thoughtful. "It could have been, though I think it was more than that. There's something else that happened. But I don't know what it is. I think only Scarborough does, and he isn't going to talk about it to anyone." She sighed. "Every time I have to deal with him, I try to remember the way he was and not the skinflint he is now, but it's damned hard."

"Mom, bad word," her five-year-old daughter said as she toddled up.

Sandy lifted her onto her lap. Megan was Sandy's surprise baby, and no child was loved more. Sandy and Joe had never thought they could have kids and had long before given up. Then surprise, along came Megan—about the time that Joe took up and then off with June Mather, the former mayor's wife. What a mess that was for all of them. Thankfully Joe had had the sense to get the hell out of town before he got run out of it.

"I'm sorry," she said gently, and Megan cuddled close. She was dressed but seemed a little clingy.

"Did you sleep good?" I asked, and she shook her head.

"She has a case of the sniffles. The doctor says she'll be fine in a day or so, but right now she just wants her mom as much as possible." Sandy sat back and let Megan rest against her while I ate the feast she had made for me. "Why would Scarborough buy a horse at auction with a lot of problems?" Sandy asked. "That seems like a lot more trouble than it's worth for him." There was a lot left unsaid in that statement.

"I wondered the same thing. He wants me to calm him down enough that he can be used for stud." I savored the eggs, which were perfect sunny-side up, and picked up a piece of bacon. Megan turned toward me, and I offered her a piece. She smiled and took it. "The thing is, he's stunning beyond belief. The coloring and his gait. Just seeing him move was a thing of beauty, but he's filled with soul-deep fear. I have no idea how anyone got him into a trailer for transport. They must have drugged him, which can lead to a whole set of problems." I finished the last of the food, drank the juice, and wanted to sit back and close my eyes, but there was work to do. And Sandy, while she always gave me breakfast, wasn't paying me to sit around and jaw.

"That's a real shame. Things like that are only going to make it worse for him… and you in the end." She put Megan down and took care of the dishes. "Do you think you can help?"

"I'll try." I thanked her for breakfast and went out to spend the rest of the morning working with one of her new horses that had picked up some bad habits. But for some reason, Scarborough and his horse stayed in my mind. Yes, what Scarborough had said might have made sense, but it was so unlike him. Scarborough bought horses when he thought he could make money. He didn't buy horses that needed rehab, because of the additional cost and the uncertainty. That kept me thinking about what Scarborough was actually up to.

AFTER THE morning at Sandy's, I spent the afternoon at a few other clients' before stopping at the house to check on things. Beau ran around like he had been gone for days, checking out his spots and making sure all the animals that might come roaming knew this was his. The silly dog did it every single time we went away, even if it was for a few hours.

"Hey, Dad," I said when my father came out of the barn. "What are you doing?"

"Just looking," he answered. My dad was the quintessential cowboy, in his jeans, boots, hat, and one of the buckles he'd won when he rode broncs. That was how he met my mother. Dad always said that she was a buckle bunny and that he'd had to fight off dozens of guys to win her attention. Every time he said it, Mom would wink, which meant she was letting Dad have his fantasy. The truth, from Mom, was that she saw him and wasn't going to make it too easy to be caught. I believed her. "Ted had a horse that he needs to sell, and I want to buy it. I have a buyer out near Casper for it, but they aren't ready for him until next month. My barn is full, but...."

"I got space," I told him. "Go ahead and make the deal. I got your back." I loved that I could help my dad out every once in a while. I'd bought the place because it was next door to my folks. That way I could be close if they needed me, and yet have a place of my own. The plan was that I would eventually inherit the entire ranch, and my idea was to put everything together.

"It's too good a deal to pass up. This horse is a beaut, and Ted needs the cash bad, so I made him a fair offer, and he took it. This guy from Casper is looking to pay top dollar." Dad grinned. He was literally a horse trader from way back. Dad raised some horses on the ranch, as well as running some cattle, but he really made his money trading. It was in his blood, just like horses and what they needed was in mine. "You coming for dinner? Your mom wanted me to ask."

I was about to answer when Scarborough's truck turned into the drive. He pulled to a stop and lowered the window. "The new horse is going crazy. Can you come now? I don't know what to do."

"Go on. I'll do the evening feed while I'm here." Dad was already heading back toward the barn, so I hopped into Scarborough's truck. Beau instantly barked his head off, and I opened the door to let him jump in.

"What is he doing?" I asked as we rode.

"Stamping and rearing and braying constantly. I tried to see if anything was in the paddock, but I can't get close enough." The concern in his voice rang like a bell. "I don't want him to hurt himself, and if it goes on for much longer, he's going to." As soon as he hit the road, Scarborough floored it, whipping down the street and only slowing when he approached his drive, and we skidded a little nonetheless.

As soon as I opened the door, a wave of fear washed over me. The air was palpable with it. As much as I wanted to run, I forced myself to walk to the paddock, where Black Beauty had nearly exhausted himself in his panicked frenzy. His coat shimmered with sweat and his mouth foamed a little. "Scarborough, go around the back and open the gate. Give him an out and let's see if he'll take it. That area is bigger, but fenced, right?"

"Yeah. But there are other horses in there."

"Get them out, now," I said, and Scarborough hurried away. I started talking softly, trying to calm the horse, but he wasn't having it. Black Beauty was too worked up to allow for that. I still attempted to distract him and at one point had him still and breathing deeply, but his eyes were wild. I tried to keep him calm, but then he reared again and nearly clocked the fence on his way down. "Open the gate," I called, and Scarborough swung the large gate open with a loud squeak.

The sound drew the horse's attention, and he turned and raced through to the roomier paddock, then stopped in the center. From where I stood, I saw him still breathing heavily, but at least the frantic stomping and jumping had ended.

Scarborough closed the paddock gate and locked it. "What the fuck was all that about?" he asked as he came over.

"Go get him some hay, and make sure there is plenty of water for him. I want to check out this enclosure." There was something strange going on, and I was determined to get to the bottom of it. "Keep plenty of distance." I knew we were damned lucky the horse hadn't keeled over from a heart attack. Horses are strangely fragile creatures, powerful and beautiful, but also delicate. I wondered how many times during his tirade Black Beauty had come close to breaking a leg.

I climbed the fence, dropped into the paddock, and walked the area. It was clear to me that Scarborough hadn't used the paddock in a while. Not that it was in bad repair, but the grass inside was longer and hadn't been eaten down. Anyway, I knew I had to be careful.

"Find anything?" Scarborough asked.

I shook my head, then paused. A snake lay in the grass. I stilled instantly and backed away, watching it, but the snake didn't move. I went back, grabbed a shovel, and approached once again. The snake was in the same position. I slammed it with the shovel, expecting a pile of guts. Scooping it up, I carried what should have been a carcass to Scarborough and tossed it at him. He jumped back, shrieking as the rubber snake bounced off the fencing.

"What the hell?"

"Exactly. Someone put this in the paddock." I continued around and thought I'd found another. I was about to scoop it up when the familiar rattle sent a zing up my spine. I pulled back and the sound stopped. "Good God."

"What?" Scarborough hurried over, and I put up my hand to stop him.

"There's a live one in here too," I called out.

Scarborough had had more than enough experience with snakes, and he wrangled the little slitherer into a bag and got rid of it. The situation was beyond crazy as far as I was concerned.

"What the hell did you do to someone that they would put a snake in one of your paddocks?" Yeah, I knew Scarborough was cheap, but as far as I knew, he didn't cheat anyone and paid his bills. It wasn't like he was cruel or mean, just skinflinty.

"You really think someone put that in here?" he asked.

"Well," I said, pointing, "someone put the rubber one in here. Think about it. They got a live snake, put it in here, and then added the rubber one, so the horse thought they were all around him and went out of his mind." Everyone knew that horses didn't like snakes. The reaction was pretty common. But to have an already wild horse and to add a snake to its paddock was a recipe for disaster. Thank God it had been diverted.

Scarborough bent down and lifted the remains of yet another rubber snake that had been trounced to pieces. "I think you're right." He tossed the remains to the side of the paddock. I tried to read what he was thinking, but like so much of the time, Scarborough was stoic as hell. Still, his posture seemed more rigid than usual, and he kept looking around.

"Who might want to get even with you or cause trouble?" I knew Scarborough didn't have disgruntled employees, because it was just him here on the ranch. He did whatever he needed himself because help would require him to pay them.

He stood still, and I took a few seconds just to watch him and wait for some sort of response. Scarborough had spent his entire life outside, working hard, and it showed in every muscle in his body. I had been to the city and seen guys whose bodies came from gyms, with their perfect bubble butts and chests that seemed to sprout plates. But Scarborough wasn't like that. His was a body of a life of hard work, with corded muscle and a compact strength from lifting bales of hay and splitting enough wood to heat the house for the winter.

His jeans were old and maybe a little threadbare in places, hugging his legs and backside like a second skin. I knew it was a bad idea to be looking at my neighbor that way, but what the hell? He seemed lost in his own thoughts for a few minutes, and I sure as hell could let my own mind wander. It didn't hurt anything, and I didn't have any illusions that Scarborough was going to suddenly wake up and realize that I was his dream guy. He wasn't going to open his arms and change his ways at the drop of a hat—or because of a single longing look across a paddock. That sort of thing was not Scarborough Croughton in the least.

"I don't know," he finally answered, then turned away, going about cleaning up the rubber snakes and checking the last of the paddock.

Not that it was likely that he was going to be able to put Black Beauty in this paddock. He was going to remember, and it would only make him nervous again. At least he seemed to be eating now and drinking some, which meant that the panic in him was over. But this afternoon's incident had made my job a little harder, and I was going to need all the patience I could muster to try to help that horse—and Scarborough, for that matter.

"Keep an eye on him, and I'll get the paperwork sent over right away. I should have some time in a few days."

He nodded. "I'll do my best to try to keep him calm and see if maybe he'll forget some of this incident."

That was our only hope to get him past whatever trauma had left the horse so full of fear that he'd spook like that. I also wondered what could have happened to Scarborough to make him withdraw from everyone the way he had too. I wondered which of the two would be easier to understand in the end.

ANDREW GREY is the author of more than one hundred works of Contemporary Gay Romantic fiction. After twenty-seven years in corporate America, he has now settled down in Central Pennsylvania with his husband of more than twenty-five years, Dominic, and his laptop. An interesting ménage. Andrew grew up in western Michigan with a father who loved to tell stories and a mother who loved to read them. Since then he has lived throughout the country and traveled throughout the world. He is a recipient of the RWA Centennial Award, has a master's degree from the University of Wisconsin–Milwaukee, and now writes full-time. Andrew's hobbies include collecting antiques, gardening, and leaving his dirty dishes anywhere but in the sink (particularly when writing). He considers himself blessed with an accepting family, fantastic friends, and the world's most supportive and loving partner. Andrew currently lives in beautiful, historic Carlisle, Pennsylvania.

Email: andrewgrey@comcast.net
Website: www.andrewgreybooks.com

FIRE AND SAND

ANDREW GREY

CARLISLE
TROOPERS

1

Carlisle Troopers: Book One

Can a single dad with a criminal past find love with the cop who pulled him over?

When single dad Quinton Jackson gets stopped for speeding, he thinks he's lost both his freedom and his infant son, who's in the car he's been chasing down the highway. Amazingly, State Trooper Wyatt Nelson not only believes him, he radios for help and reunites Quinton with baby Callum.

Wyatt should ticket Quinton, but something makes him look past Quinton's record. Watching him with his child proves he made the right decision. Quinton is a loving, devoted father—and he's handsome. Wyatt can't help but take a personal interest.

For Quinton, getting temporary custody is a dream come true… or it would be, if working full-time and caring for an infant left time to sleep. As if that weren't enough, Callum's mother will do anything to get him back, including ruining Quinton's life. Fortunately, Quinton has Wyatt for help, support, and as much romance as a single parent can schedule.

But when Wyatt's duties as a cop conflict with Quinton's quest for permanent custody, their situation becomes precarious. Can they trust each other, and the courts, to deliver justice and a happy ever after?

www.dreamspinnerpress.com

ANDREW GREY

Two cowboys.
Twenty years together.
One chance to save their love.

SECOND
GO-ROUND

Former world champion bronco rider Dustin and rancher Marshall have been life partners for more than twenty years, and time has taken its toll. Their sex life is as dusty as the rodeo ring. Somehow their marriage hasn't turned out how they planned.

But when a new family moves in up the road with two young boys, one very sick, Dustin and Marshall realize how deep their ruts are and that there might be hope to break them. After all, where they're from, the most important part of being a man is helping those who need it.

A new common purpose helps break down the deep routines they've fallen into and makes them realize the life they've been living has left them both cold and hollow. Spending time with the kids— teaching them how to be cowboys—reignites something they thought lost long ago. But twenty years is a lot of time to make up for. Can they find their way back to each other, or are the ruts they've created worn too deep?

www.dreamspinnerpress.com

PAST HIS DEFENSES

ANDREW GREY

When a case reopens old wounds from the kidnapping of his younger sister, police officer Robert Fenner is told in no uncertain terms that he needs a break. And maybe his superiors are right. He books a flight to visit an old friend, who happens to be the one who got away, and hopes for the best.

Electronic security consultant Dixie Halewood works from his home in Paris, where he lives with his adopted son, Henri. Dixie doesn't expect a message from an old flame asking for a place to stay, but he agrees. Their past is just that—the past.

Things between them aren't as settled as they thought—Henri, Paris, and proximity work their magic. The two men are drawn closer and old flames burst back to life, but Dixie's work brings a new threat to their safety and the budding family they missed out on the first time around.

www.dreamspinnerpress.com